The Girl with Two Left Breasts

The Girl with Two Left Breasts

Stories by

D. V. Glenn

Red Hen Press | *Los Angeles, CA*

Book layout by Sydney Nichols

ISBN: 978-1-59709-139-8
Library of Congress Cataloging-in-Publication Data

Glenn, Daryl.
The girl with two left breasts : stories / by Daryl Glenn.—1st ed.
p. cm.
ISBN 978-1-59709-139-8
I. Title.
PS3607.L45G57 2009
813'.6—dc22
2009043884

The Annenberg Foundation, the Los Angeles County Arts Commission, and the National Endowment for the Arts partially support Red Hen Press.

First Edition

Published by Red Hen Press
Los Angeles, CA
www.redhen.org

Acknowledgements and Thanks

A tribe of people helped me to get this book written.

Thanks to Forzan Vaziri-Glenn, who supported and inspired me, and who gave me her ideas outright so that I didn't have to steal them.

Thanks to my mother, Barbara E. Glenn, who sweetened my early ears with song and exposed me to the power of language—spoken, written, sung or staged.

Thanks to Don Davis, the composer (*The Matrix*, *Rio de Sangre*) who told me in so many words never to doubt that I was an artist.

I'd like to thank the novelist, Josh Pryor, for editing some of these stories.

Thanks to Bruce Herrier, generator of concepts par excellence.

Thanks to Barbara Pitts (a.k.a. "Suzy") for being a great sister.

Thanks to Kate Gale and the Red Hen staff for their patience, their patience, and their patience.

Some of the stories in this collection appeared in the following publications, which the author would like to acknowledge: "The Hypothetical Nigger" appeared in *HEArt*, May 2001; "The English Teacher's Pupil" appeared in *HEArt*, Winter 2002 and in *Apostrophe: USCB Journal of the Arts*, 2002; "Reverse Gender" appeared in *Thin Air Magazine*, 2003 and in *Phoebe: A Journal of Literature and Art*, Fall 2003; "Footage" appeared in the *Sulphur River Literary Review*, 2005; "The Serial Killer Museum" appeared in the *Journal of Experimental Fiction 34: Foremost Fiction*; "My Father's Penis" appeared in the *Journal of Experimental Fiction 24: A-Way with it!*; "That Will Be Then and This Is Now" appeared in the *West Wind Review 20th Anthology*.

Contents

The Hypothetical Nigger

His mother named him Wave because she had never seen the ocean. After he was born, she looked into his eyes and was startled by how the pupils, black as keyholes and wreathed in gray, seemed to draw her down to the floor of his being. She imagined that the ocean she had never seen was the misty color of his eyes and for that reason she named him Wave.

Wave's wife, Alexis, wants him to talk about his childhood. They are in bed and the headlights of passing cars slide and tilt across the bedroom ceiling like children who lose their footing when the ice suddenly breaks on a frozen lake.

They are in bed. Sometimes a siren wails in the distance from the north, only to be answered minutes later by another shrill siren spinning like a tornado across distances from the south, as though a slow chess game is in progress and the advance of a black pawn is mirrored in a countermove by a white pawn, resulting in an impasse.

They should be sleeping. Tomorrow will be a long day for both of them. Tomorrow will be the kind of day where, as heavy bricks of hours are stacked one upon the next, shoulders round woefully under invisible weight. They should be sleeping but Alexis wants Wave to tell her a story about his childhood.

They are married and she would like to know everything there is to know about him.

Wave will tell her a story about himself. It might turn out to be one that she is glad to hear but after, she might be sorry, too.

He is seven years old and his parents are taking him to visit his grandparents in Rockwell City, Iowa. His parents have made a pallet for him in the back seat of their black Buick and they have driven for days across three states in stern August heat. They are pursued by thunderstorms dragging their black robes across the sky. From the back seat Wave sees rain and his father's eyes reflected in the rearview mirror. As always his eyes are pieces of floating driftwood, lost and powerless as though tossed by tides.

In Rockwell City the days go by pleasantly, his experiences a porridge of rural sights, sounds, smells stirred lazily together by the sun's sweltering ladle. One day his father drives Wave to the public swimming pool downtown, mysteriously called a "natatorium." His father then leaves, promising to return in approximately two hours. Dressed in bright red swimming trunks, Wave stands self-consciously at the lip of the pool, blinking into the spectral blue water at a group of children of varying ages, splashing and yelling. Chlorine drifts through the air like tissues yanked from a Kleenex box. A group of about five children climb out of the pool and stand around Wave, whispering in low tones among themselves at first, then becoming alarmingly bolder. Finally a freckle-faced boy points at him and exclaims loudly, "Look, a nigger!" Wave has a sudden full awareness of something that had previously danced, in an ill-coordinated fashion, as though on an icy floor, across the surface of his mind: that the entire town, with its meager population of eight hundred, was filled with people who in some fundamental way looked nothing like his grandparents, or his father or mother, or him. "Nigger" hung above his head like a guillotine blade in the afternoon's heat and sudden stillness. He shivers in the heat, his flesh contracting toward invisibility. Hornets of eyes swarm about him, stinging the parts of his body that have not been absorbed into invisibility.

Wave's father picks him up in two hours as promised, and on the way home Wave asks, "Dad, what's a nigger?" His father stares unblinkingly out the windshield while driving and after a long deliberation answers, "I don't know what you're talking about. Don't ask me ridiculous questions."

"Imagine this child," Wave now says to Alexis, "the resentment he feels for this man who not only didn't explain the way things were so that the kid wouldn't go stumbling out in the world unprepared for what he'd find, but then totally denied the validity of the kid's experience." Alexis says, "Maybe what he meant to say was that he refused to invest the whole concept with any validity and that it was ridiculous to act as though it had any reality." Wave wants to explain how, at the age of seven, in Rockwell City, Iowa, that was the beginning. That was his day of commencement, somber as any ritual of sacrifice. That was the day when the curtains parted and the storm of confetti fell on the hypothetical nigger. From then on he begins to see with nigger eyes and taste with a nigger tongue and hold objects of both animus and affection in nigger hands. He spends nigger money and cries nigger tears, does nigger math and swims nigger laps, eats nigger food and walks through nigger cities, talks on nigger cell phones and pays nigger taxes, operates nigger computers and signs nigger checks, bleeds nigger blood and breaths nigger air, prays nigger prayers and feels his heart expand when he sees the fullness of a nigger moon.

Wave listens to the sirens rising and falling in the distance. He watches the shadows sliding and tilting across the bedroom ceiling like children who lose their footing when the ice suddenly breaks on a frozen lake. He remembers his father's eyes held captive in the Buick's rearview mirror. He had not known at the time that they were the eyes of a hypothetical nigger.

What he had known was that they were like driftwood, lost and powerless. He tries to recall how the rest of his face looked, but the only other thing reflected in the glass that day was rain.

Metal Dogs

The golden knitting needles are gripped in Crystal's fists, the points up-tilted like slender musketry angled from brows of trenches. Both fists are wedged into the flesh below her stomach where thighs socket into pelvis,[1] fixed there, braced, immovable; the effort, her body's tension, brings a roseate bloom to the surface of her tawny skin. Her elbows flare slightly,

1 Where thighs socket into pelvis: This felicitous fit, this instance of the connectedness of disparate things, is but one example of many such marriages, marriages between dichotomies great and small. All around there are holes and vacuums and an abundance of people, places, and things to fill them. Laughter or screams may be used to fill the black open hole of the mouth; energetic comings and goings may be used to fill fissures of boredom and fear; in the absence of sexual partners, masturbation may be employed to flood feelings left by an aridity of non-masturbation—and the examples could go on and on. All these examples are as a palm placed in the middle of the back, friendly, urging you forward with a little push, as though you were a child reluctant to get on the bus that will convey you to a first day of school. Just a little push, a nudge of encouragement, and you see that the bus isn't so bad, that there is room for you there, that the bullies of chaos and meaninglessness and unhappiness shrink back if there is willingness to step forward, open the eyes, observe what appears to be evidence of a grand design, such as where thighs socket into pelvis. This is a willingness Binder is constitutionally unable to muster. These are Binder's feelings, not his thoughts.

her whole body, as she sits, is clenched in anticipation of the impalement. Binder is kneeling, his palms flat on her thighs for support, as he aligns his eyes with the needle points, then tosses his head back like a restive stallion.

"You don't need to do this, Binder. You don't want to be blind like the rest of the world," Crystal says.

ooooo

Binder Trogg was accustomed to the reaction his name provoked among people inclined to comment on it at all. Invariably they reached a fork in some remote, secluded road of free association and traveled down one of two paths: Some told him that they would never suspect the owner of such a name to be black, that the name suggested no particular ethnicity. Others insisted that the name had a rustic languor about it, evoking towns with names like Tubalo, Mississippi, sleepy dust above dreaming dirt roads, dead heat pouring its molasses out of a spilled bucket of August sun, bluesy lean-to shacks where a black youth might be glimpsed standing in the doorway wearing faded bib overalls as someone called from far away, across a lifetime of fields, "Binder . . . Binder, don't just stand there, come on out and prove what you can do." Binder inclined favorably toward people in the first category.

ooooo

Crystal told him constantly that he must not do it. Not allow himself to be consumed by hatred, like the time he was standing in the elevator of the Warner Building in Woodland Hills, California, the fall from the twentieth floor to the lobby floating his stomach in sudden linear, zero-G nausea as the only other passenger in the elevator, a middle-aged white woman, pressed herself with prim apprehension into the corner to be farther away from him. Did he look like a derelict, in his eight-hundred-dollar Italian loafers, his expensive Robe di Firenze leather briefcase dangling from his dark hand, his gray Kiton suit priced at $2,457 with its gossamer-thin fourteen-micron wool caressing his six-foot frame, the jacket's lining luxuriously woven of seaweed and horsehair? Did she imagine the air to be darkened by ghetto fetor?

Before the elevator could reach the lobby he had disrobed, to show her that no weaponry or devices of torture were secreted beneath his wardrobe, to let her see that he stood as naked and vulnerable in his mortality as the next man.

"But what's in the briefcase," the woman said, pressing herself backward into a crouch.

ooooo

Once, when he was leaving the Grand Hyatt in New York, at Park and Central, a taxi driver with a complexion so pink it appeared to deliquesce into orange, coasted to a stop at the curbside where Binder stood, attired in a tailoring of sleek priceless silk befitting a sultan, and said to him, I don't drive certain neighborhoods in Harlem.

ooooo

The gated Southern California community Binder lives in is an incubator for great wealth. His home is tucked snugly into the crotch-like V made by a backdrop of abutting San Fernando foothills. Visitors must pass through an iron gate that opens with electronic stealth between two tall pillars. These pillars are stately as the legs of the Vegas showgirl named Crystal, who now lives with Binder but who, prior to moving in some months ago, had worried obsessively that once the lines and curves of her twenty-two-year-old figure ceased to assert a voluptuous symmetry in a few years, she would lose her job, though the Manager of Entertainment at the MGM Grand Hotel would most certainly be shrewd enough to contrive her termination without adducing weight as the cause of her dismissal and entangling the MGM in a discrimination lawsuit. Crystal lives with Binder in this exclusive gated community and no longer works; but she nevertheless frequently imagines in lurid detail the consequences of joblessness as if still employed at the MGM—hunger, eviction, and homelessness—a tendency based on vivid recollections of her early childhood experiences of poverty in a small Midwestern town.

ooooo

Binder, after doubling down on a providential hand at blackjack and retrieving a cashier's check in the amount of $120,000 for his chips, had met Crystal in Las Vegas where she worked in the MGM Grand Hotel. She was a dancer—one of the few black showgirls to prance on the requisite sculpturesque legs across the MGM stage—who had finished her shift and seen Binder saunter away with his winnings and silently followed him and entered the elevator he rode to his comped penthouse suite. She watched him stride down the maroon-carpeted, sensuously hued hallway and enter his suite. Then she waited a while and knocked on the door he had just entered and when Binder had opened it she said, "Room service!"

ooooo

The iron gate opens and the road which is wryly known by the inhabitants of this community as the Yellow Brick Road winds through what is indeed an Oz-like enclave that seems the product of wizardry, as though a wand had been waved, transforming the landscape into a haven where men and women lived enchanted lives.

Binder lives in a smallish mansion purchased with money made pyramiding or rather leapfrogging futures contracts and options on futures contracts established in short and long positions, an audacious array of calls and puts, combinations of exotic hedges and straddles executed in accordance with certain abstruse tools of technical analysis, utilizing Gann and Elliot Waves and the somewhat recondite principles of Fibonnacci numbers. There had been December heating oil, March gold, January sugar, September rice, April lumber, and of course soybeans—all successful trades, resulting in his current extravagant lifestyle. When Binder left Mississippi years ago, he did not know what a futures contract was, had never seen a double top formation on a chart, did not know what a strike price was or how algorithms could be used to determine one, and knew only that Wall Street had something to do with money.

Binder was an unlikely candidate for stardom in the world of commodities, but there is no predicting the fruits of a determined will. While other children in his neighborhood challenged gravity's supremacy on scrofulous playground basketball courts, Binder dreamed of leaving Mississippi and acquiring great wealth and changing the manner in which he was perceived by the white people of the world whom he was certain must surely be an extension of the whites in Tubalo, those tobacco-chewing, eternally old men who had not thought twice of referring to him as "You there, nigger boy" when they could not recall his name. And thus, armed with splenetic determination, Binder went on to achieve two out of the three components of his dream.

ooooo

Binder had placed an ad in the *Los Angeles Times* business section that read, "Wanted: Silicone Valleyesque Computer Genius to Program Metal Dog for Millionaire."

ooooo

Crystal tried to convince him that self-inflicted blindness would settle nothing, resolve nothing, accomplish even less. Binder strode through the mansion's high-ceilinged, lush-carpeted hallways with their idiosyncratic architectural arabesques and the sweeping glass planes that conveyed to the eye a sense of convexo-concave acceleration, his cell phone pouring the usual obsequious lackey nectar into his ears, oblivious to Crystal as she trailed behind him, striving to dissuade. In desperation she phoned his octogenarian grandmother, Bertha, back in Tubalo, but the old woman, reluctant to bite the hand that lavishly fed her with the astronomical checks Binder tossed her way almost as an afterthought each month, would not listen to reason.

"He knows what he's doin', even if he don't know," she scolded Crystal.

ooooo

For a child wallowing in the quicksand of backwoods poverty, a three-legged mongrel dog may be quickly elevated to the status of Boy's Best Friend. Ten-year-old Binder christened the stray dog Chase, a name that was the reflection of young Binder's own sense of running nowhere fast, objectified. Boy and dog clung to one another in pitiful symbiosis, and when Chase bayed and howled at the bloated Mississippi moon, yellow as the pages in a moldy book, Binder was right there beside him, howling and baying in soprano harmony, until pickup-truck-enthroned and intoxicated white men pelted them with beer cans as they drove past, boy and dog plunging back through the lavender and white pandemonium of jimson weeds choking the shoulder of the road to huddle together in a conspiracy of invisibility. When the trucks passed, they ascended to the shoulder of the road to continue their duet of hunger, their dissonant propitiation.

ooooo

By the time Binder had reached the age of ten, mostly but not always gone were the days when blacks could be pursued through woods with virtual impunity by white men propelled by bloodthirsty exhilaration, captured and strung up in the mournful scaffolding of long-limbed trees. The drama of those times had since descended into acts of petty terrorism, the acts of vandals so imbecilic that they had been unable to parlay belonging to a racial majority into an advantage in a country where the color of their skin should have tilted the odds for attaining prosperity overwhelmingly in their favor. At any rate that was the consensus among the predominantly poverty-hammered black citizenry of Tubaloo: "White man can't make it in a white man's world, waaall . . . there's a fella must be dumb as a dog."[2] One afternoon when Binder returned home from school, the demonic eye of the sun staring down and draping everything in dead eyelashes of heat, he saw that Chase had been bound with a rope to the diseased oak tree in the grid of dirt that was his front yard. The dog had been shaved and resembled an emaciated pig. Painted on its side were the words "nigger dog." The eyes had been gouged out, but with an attention to precision that was almost surgical and appeared to bode well for the animal's speedy recovery. The dog bore no other wounds and after Binder's grandmother examined Chase with a diagnostic acumen derived from her mysterious congress with supernatural forces, she declared he had not been poisoned and stood an excellent chance of propelling himself through the rest of his hapless life with his

---

2 Most of the black townspeople had little better than fourth-grade educations and could not have been expected to grasp the fact that race was the great smokescreen for the deeply buried elitist apparatus governing the acquisition and distribution of wealth. Modern global-economic realities tend to validate this theory, which is unfortunately further smokescreened by unsavory suggestions of socialism or communism—at least, this would become Binder's autodidactic conviction later, when he would come to invent the aphorism, "It's not the skin you're in, but the green you can glean" after seeing a movie called *Deep Cover* in which a white actor, Jeff Goldblum, explains to a black actor, Laurence Fishburne, without any condescension that Binder could detect, "there's no more black and white . . . there's only rich and poor . . ."—a line of dialogue that for Binder triggered a small but crystalline moment of epiphany.

signature three-legged shamble, although blindness would now augment his lurching gait and the gaping holes in his head enhance the beast's already repellent appearance. Yet poor Chase expired later that night—his death attributed by Binder to nothing more than humiliation.

ooooo

Many years later Binder wrote a letter to the actor Laurence Fishburne explaining the beneficial impact that the movie *Deep Cover* had had on the course of his life. He agreed with the assessment that there is only rich and poor but went on to write that racial smokescreens seemed to constitute an almost insuperable obstacle. He did not receive the personal reply he had hoped for, but did receive an 8 x 10 glossy publicity photo of Laurence Fishburne with an expression of brooding intensity masking his face, the corner of the photograph bearing an ink-stamp signature that read "Thank You for Being a Fan, Cinematically Yours, L. Fishburne."

ooooo

Rayner "Mother Board" Richards was a source of fecund anxiety for his parents, Jayne and Randy. His parents had combined their names to produce the son's own in a flashbulb pop of giddy creativity triggered by slight intoxication the night they discovered that Jayne was pregnant and the two uncorked a seven-thousand-dollar bottle of Domaine de la Romanee-Conti to celebrate.[3]

3 They had discovered Domaine de la Romanee-Conti (DRC) while attending a formal, high-powered wine tasting event in the cinematically beautiful coastal town of Carmel in central California, where they actually lived. This town had goldenly basked in the celebrity of its mayor, Clint Eastwood, for his two-year term in 1986 and still radiated something of a golden afterglow. The wine, largely responsible for spawning the term "cult wine" which enlarges the vocabulary of criteria and definition for connoisseurs, boasts a mushroom-like, pleasantly fungal flavor with muted

Rayner was highly intelligent but a classic underachiever with innate narcissistic tendencies greatly exaggerated by the desert-like stretches of self-absorption that typify the onset of adolescence. Rayner's psychiatrists explained all this to his parents, but the explanation did not make his behavior any easier for them to bear. Even among his like-minded peers, Rayner was seen as something of a proto-maverick, setting standards of delinquency they could only lamely aspire to.

Rayner was indefinitely grounded for destroying the marriage of his high school math teacher, Mr. Berser, who had given Rayner an F in algebra.

Rayner had long suspected that Mr. Berser was a "pervert"—a word that shimmered with undefined promise for the sixteen-year-old—and determined to establish his suspicion through incontrovertible evidence. To accomplish this, one Saturday afternoon in his bedroom he connected his laptop to his cellular phone, brooding on the screen as a map was drawn of each cellular phone call that was currently being

---

overtones of strawberry and red currant. Samantha Ringwold, a real estate mogul of legendary prowess in that part of California, a thirty-something woman with striking aquiline features who would eventually be instrumental in increasing Binder's real estate holdings farther up the coast, and who was having an affair with Randy, also attended the wine tasting event. Alcohol she had consumed prior to the event—she was a pathologically lonely woman despite her success—prompted her to approach Randy's wife and hand her an envelope filled with photos depicting fetishistic sex scenarios with a pervasive black leather motif between Randy and Samantha. After a tempestuous six-month period during which Jayne and Randy struggled to resurrect their marriage from its shambles, the couple reconciled with the aid of counseling and conceived Rayner. Oddly, Randy sees Rayner as Samantha's offspring, almost as if Samantha had been the man in their relationship and he had been the woman impregnated; then, during sex with his wife, it seemed to him as if Jayne had somehow been transformed into his old self, Randy, while he became the impregnated Samantha; finally, in the end, it was as if he had somehow transferred his Samantha-self to his Randy-wife, who gave birth to the seven-pound Rayner, perfectly healthy, the boy's face bearing, in a perverse example of synchronicity, pencil-sharp aquiline features.

placed in a "cell."[4] And bingo—Mr. Berser, obliviously driving to his destination, was caught like a fly in Rayner's digital spider net. Rayner then faxed the address of Madame Tootsie's and the time of Mr. Berser's regularly scheduled weekly sexual rendezvous with her to Mrs. Berser, who confirmed the information for herself. Of course, it would have been so much easier had Rayner possessed a driver's license and been able to simply shadow him by car, but not as much fun as the tracking scheme Rayner was able to employ with a common laptop and cell phone. His only mistake was to tell others of his exploits. Soon his friends ignited a wildfire of rumors, and those rumors somehow burned a swift trail of disclosure back to his parents.

Rayner saw the ad in the *Los Angeles Times* that read "Wanted: Silicone Valleyesque Computer Genius to Program Metal Dog for Millionaire," and decided that his period of exile from the world had gone on long enough.

---

4 A cell may be defined as the area circumscribed by a single broadcast unit in the cellular phone network labyrinth. Rayner knew that when phones traverse one cell to the next, as they typically do in moving vehicles, information in the form of hidden code was married to the phone transmission. It was therefore relatively easy for Rayner to coerce the network to query cell phone transmissions to current real-time locations. Knowing the location of each cell allowed Rayner to see displayed on the laptop's screen the geographic location of active phones, as long as the user was engaged in chatter. It was in this way, more or less, after extending the software on his laptop, that Rayner discovered Mr. Berser's addiction to prostitutes, the location of the massage parlor—Madame Tootsie's—the teacher frequented three times a week in the evenings (all the while the teacher was en route to Madame Tootsie's, he made a habit of engaging in "nasty talk" to his masseuse, Dala, which heightened his sense of anticipation and inflamed fantasies that were to be shortly realized). While he was grounded, he amused himself by thinking through an even more formidable monitoring task: that of pirating the data from the cellular network's paging channel (a special frequency that cellular networks use to communicate administrative information to cell phones) to trace car phones through the networks. Each time a relay occurred from one cell to the next, that data could be recorded on the laptop's screen—enabling Rayner to track users whether or not they were engaged on the phone.

ooooo

Rayner traversed mainly by skateboard the 350 miles between Carmel and Encino, where Binder lived, and when the smooth stretches of pavement and asphalt that were necessary to facilitate his journey succumbed to boils and pockmarks on the uneven face of the terrain, he hitchhiked. He contrived a ruse to ensure his progress: Male motorists saw a young white girl standing by the side of the road dressed in black fishnet stockings and a black leather miniskirt, a zippered black vinyl halter vest, black, straight, shoulder-length hair hanging in a glossy promiscuous curtain. Rayner had found these items in a box hidden in the back of the garage, the props and playthings of his father's and Samantha's affair that had passed into sexual antiquity. On his journey to Encino he would, when hitchhiking was required, enter service station bathrooms wearing his everyday surfer togs and emerge in full sluttish regalia, three inches added to his five-foot-nine-inch height by black stiletto heels. On one occasion two cars pulled over at the same time and the men battered each other with fists in debased competition for the privilege of accommodating the illusion Rayner had so easily manufactured.

ooooo

Lately Binder was held captive by a peculiar feeling that time was running out, that he stood at a dark crossroads. He had not been close to his grandmother growing up, but for a short time had he not been close to Chase? The moth-eaten dog was taken from him before he could learn all the beautiful lessons that would surely have blossomed as their relationship deepened. They both felt a sort of terror in the face of life. The boy would peer into Chase's flinching eyes, holding the dog's loose jowls, lathered in a beard of saliva, to prevent him from scrambling out of his grasp, while the dog whimpered and moaned piteously, his hunger-flattened haunches tensed in a quiver of attempted retreat, and Binder would glimpse himself. Binder had been deprived of the chance to deepen his relationship with Chase, and he believed that as a result he was not equipped with the tools needed to master the mysterious carpentry of relationships.

ooooo

Binder and Crystal visited a number of pet shops and animal shelters. He watched the fluffy romp and tumble of puppies in their cages, looping about one another like clothes circling in the spinning drum of a dryer, but could not find a dog that would restore to him the memory of Chase.

ooooo

The next day Binder's near-infallible sixth sense that extended itself, antennae-like, and routinely ascertained the rising and falling, tick by tick, of the volatile futures market betrayed him in a bad position where his vision of the big picture was accurate but his timing was off. The commodity did break out of the narrow channel on the charts where it had been non-trending laterally for the past month and rocket swiftly up as Binder had predicted it would, but not before plunging fifty ticks on the down side. He would have been fine had he not neglected to specify the placement of predetermined stops to his broker, who at Binder's request had executed a trade establishing a huge number of long positions for September cocoa.[5]

5 Binder's broker, Ted Leebron, might have casually quizzed any other noninstitutional mega-client to determine whether there was a reason for not placing a stop-loss order below the entry point of sixty-four (per pound) at which the open order was activated, but Binder's strategic repertoire exceeded Ted's—more than once, Binder had embarrassed the broker by pointing out an oversight or flaw in Ted's proposed strategy, so that he was not predisposed to question Binder's maneuvers. Ted also believed—though he considered himself to be otherwise muticulturally enlightened—that blacks were intellectually inferior (but not by all that much,

For the first time in his acrobatic career as a futures trader, Binder received a margin call from broker Ted Leebron, who managed to conceal a that's-what-you-get tone of righteous self-justification beneath those of sepulchral consolations. Binder's account was wiped out in forty-five minutes. Cocoa rebounded from its free fall and ricocheted upside to scratch ninety-six one hour later.

ooooo

When Crystal discovered that Binder had lost millions of dollars in the space of a single afternoon, she locked herself in one of the mansion's four bathrooms that was more spacious than her apartment in Las Vegas had been, and looked at herself in the mirror. She was accustomed to looking at herself with assessing eyes that placed her at a distance from herself, as though she were one of the many men who all her life had gazed at her as though she were a cog in the mechanism of their lust. She whispered, "Hey girl, what would you do if you were Crystal?"

ooooo

---

he would freely admit) to whites, and so was reluctant to place himself in a position that would undermine this belief. Where opportunities for his own edification arose in observing certain of Binder's more complex stratagems, he dismissed them, preferring to think that the black client's acumen was due to some unfathomable combination of luck and gambler's instinct which favored him with wild, improbable successes. Deeper down, where his thoughts resembled those aquatic monstrosities bred by the sea to lurk in the blackness at its bottom, Ted was aware that even the most propitious combination of luck and gambler's instinct would crumble in the face of Binder's consistent record of accomplishment, but he was the sort of person who, in general, was averse to introspection. This trait had drawn him to the adrenaline-flushed world of commodities trading as a career in the first place, so that for him the preservation of dimly lit levels of awareness was inextricably linked to states of high-voltage gratification, a gratification that had all the self-reinforcing potency of an addiction to be maintained at all costs.

Rayner stood before Binder and Crystal in a dimly lit room where the walls were hives for embedded television monitors and tables were stacked with computer hardware buzzing in the frequencies of low-hovering bees. For his interview he was asked to expatiate at length on any topic pertaining to technology that interested him. He spoke of the latest developments in artificial intelligence with neurotically inflected bursts of passion, pausing only to sweep thrashes of wig from his face.

Binder interrupted Rayner to ask, "Are you a boy or a girl?"

Before Rayner answered Binder's question, he concluded his elaboration of his own modest attempts to design electronic replicas of neural networks in order to demonstrate how electronic networks might be made to generate logical thought processes, then asked, "Discounting biology, what is the difference between a male and a female?"

ooooo

Binder took Rayner to a room commanding a breathtaking view of the coastline embracing an ocean freckled with sunlight and surging sedately from horizon to shore in dissolves of texture like honey. The seascape was not real; it was a virtual ocean shimmering in a space carved holographically out of the northern quadrant of the room—in this way Binder could enjoy the visual glory of the Pacific while avoiding what he called "the stench of eternity in decay," which he found to be a repugnant olfactory drawback. The beauty of the holographic ocean contrasted boldly with the ugliness of the walls, white walls covered by furiously scribbled ink sketches of robotic mongrels with viciously contorted faces. He led Rayner to a pedestal in the corner of the room covered with a drop cloth. Grabbing one end of the cloth, he signaled to Crystal, who was standing by the door and pressed a button on a panel built into the wall as the cloth was pulled away. Music spilled into the room like acid from a beaker, a concoction that filled the air with corrosively loud strains alternating between Wagner's "Flight of the Valkyries" and N.W.A.'s "Fuck tha Police."[6]

The metal dog stood on the pedestal: cylindrical stove-pipe legs flared down, widening in the manner of bell-bottomed pants, from a barrel-shaped torso studded with bulky rivets that were cosmetic rather than functional. The muzzle was elongated and snout-like, terminating in an O-shaped mouth with hinged jaw gaping open upon a ragged ring of stalactite teeth. Shaggy patches of fur sprouted as if haphazardly glued to the metal dog's frame with no attempt to completely cover the chassis, giving the whole apparatus a mangy, diseased appearance, and the beady coal-red eyes were asymmetrically positioned in the head, which sprouted the inordinately large ears of a bat, crudely stitched from overlapping patches of leather. From the squared drums of its disproportionately large and jutting hindquarters, a rodent-like tail of hirsute leather dangled thinly.

"Time for you to mine some coin," Binder shouted to Rayner above the soaring walls of music.

ooooo

When Rayner was not working on one of a variety of computers, he and Crystal watched from an upper-story window a platoon of bulldozers razing the splendidly landscaped property. Gone were the Edenic sweeps and verdant slopes, the

---

6 N.W.A. (Niggaz Wit' Attitude): Long-defunct band from LA's Compton district, seminal in its influence, initiating hip-hop's gangsta epoch. The original lineup showcased future rap megastars Dr. Dre and Ice Cube, and was bankrolled by the group's frontman, ex-narcotics-dealer-turned-rapper Eric "Easy-E" Wright, who would die of AIDS in 1995. Despite minimal air support, the 1989 album *Straight Outta Compton* soared to platinum heights. Mainstream cynosure was gained as a result of the track "Fuck tha Police," which was denounced by both the F.B.I. and the 200,000-member Fraternal Order of Police. Binder here was attempting to achieve an ironic synthesis of warring aesthetic perspectives that he believed reflected a larger, irreconcilable cultural schism.

sculpted hedges and marbled fountains and flowering gardens, the trestled pathways and the Olympic-size swimming pool. The small continent of opulence had been plowed under, the earth ripped open like a gunshot wound; there was nothing now but an expanse of dirt. Workmen built an outhouse, dug a well, scattered rotted wooden planks and junkyard debris and rusted car parts, planted a diseased oak from which a patched inner tube hung from a rope fastened to one of the gnarled branches. Binder, wearing bib overalls, choreographed the placement of debris and garbage, waving his arms in frustration or nodding in satisfaction.

"What's he doing?" Rayner asked.

"Making it look like Tubalo, Mississippi," Crystal said.

"Why?"

"That's where his family is from," Crystal said. She was biting her nails.

"Families sure can fuck an individual up," Rayner said, running his fingers through the raven-black strands of the wig.

"I wouldn't know. I never had one."

"I have one," Rayner said.

"How are they?"

He thought for a moment, then said, "Nice little slices of Wonder Bread."

"How old are you?"

"Sixteen."

"I wonder how'd you look without all the chick gear?" Crystal asked.

ooooo

Once Binder was a first-class passenger on a 747 flying over the sun-polished mirror of the Ionian Sea, bound for Athens, Greece. He had decided to visit after reading statistics which listed the division of ethnic groups as 98 percent Greek, 2 percent other, followed by a single footnote, the content of which was sufficient to pique his curiosity with its contradictory assertion that "the Greek government states there are no ethnic divisions in Greece" and was the sole impetus for his visit to that country. He wanted to ladle his presence like an ingredient in a recipe into the two percent other bowl and compare this experience to the invisibility he experienced as unwanted admixture in the nonexistent United States melting pot (save for those instances in which he was momentarily lifted by racial epithet to malignant visibility). The man sitting next to him engaged Binder from time to time in chatter that seemed to borrow its effervescence from the flute of Perrier-Jouët Fleur de Champagne he regally tilted to tomato-red lips. This fellow traveler, a vice president of corporate communications for AT&T, summarized an article he had recently read, and concluded by asking what Binder thought of the idea of the United States government making monetary reparation to African Americans for slavery, which the man felt was absurd.

Binder said, "In 1990, the United States paid 1.5 billion to Japanese Americans for what happened during World War II. In '85 they paid $105 million to the Sioux of South Dakota."

"It's not the same thing," the man replied, and did not speak to Binder for the remainder of the flight.[7]

---

7 The issue of the $105 million paid to the Sioux of South Dakota aside, the man—had he known the facts, and had his thoughts not been afloat in a voluptuous muddle enhanced by the thin atmosphere of heightened altitudes—would have heatedly proposed for discussion the case of James King, a former U.S. Marine, who had been among the troops and civilians taken prisoner after a small American garrison on Wake Island in the South Pacific mounted a brave but ultimately futile resistance against the overwhelming foe of Imperial Japanese forces on December 23, 1941. King, along with other captives, was shipped to Kyushu, Japan, where for the remainder of the war he toiled as a slave laborer in a steel factory and was subjected to maltreatment in a prison camp by night. King was twenty years old when captured and weighed 167 pounds; he weighed ninety-seven pounds at the conclusion of the war. King was one of the plaintiffs (King vs. Nippon Steel Corp) seeking judicial redress through monetary reparations from Japanese corporations for forced labor and injustices suffered in WWII. At that point Binder would have similarly retorted, It's the not same thing, whereupon—best case scenario—the two may have toasted

ooooo

To the best of his recollection, Binder had been called a nigger (or equivalent) 4,578 times when he lived in Tubalo. The dog, Chase, only once.

ooooo

Rayner, during the two weeks that he was working on the metal dog, did not know that his father had hired a private detective to track him. His father did not bother calling the police; Rayner had run away from home on five previous occasions when being punished for his resistance to the disciplinary actions his parents regularly and ineffectually meted out. Rayner would typically disappear for days at a time; his parents had cried wolf too often now and did not need the grief, the embarrassment that police intervention had always brought in its wake.

ooooo

Binder held the diamond-studded leash and walked in the razed front yard bordered by the mansion's circular driveway, the metal dog moving smoothly and swiftly with him over intestinal ruffles of terrain. The legs rose and fell in a general approximation of walking, but movement was actually accomplished by means of the four small wheels attached to shock-absorbing rods enclosed by the legs' cylindrical casing with their lank spangles of fur which swept the ground around hoof-shaped paws. The marching of the legs resembled the frictionless rising and falling of carousel horses on their poles as they circled to the accompaniment of bubbly calliope music.

---

one another in acknowledgment of a bond grudgingly forged from the gray viscid stuff of irresolvable ethical complexities.

"Sit," Binder commanded abruptly. The dog sat obediently, its tail swishing eagerly in the dirt like a windshield wiper.

The metal dog had already retrieved a ball, vaulted into the air to catch a Frisbee in snapping jaws, and on Binder's command to pee, lifted its leg to release a stream of pseudo-urine (Gatorade) on the side of the outhouse. Before executing each command, the dog had answered in a voice that seemed to expand and contract in a loose gargle of mechanical beeps, "Yes, Binder, I will do that." Binder squatted and looked fixedly into the dog's beady, coal-red eyes.

"The eyes, they lack terror," Binder said to Rayner, who was swinging in the inner tube while Crystal pushed him.

ooooo

Binder was well satisfied with the modifications that were made to the metal dog's eyes. Now they were glassy pools in which Rayner had somehow managed to drop jagged pebbles of terror, with resulting ripples of loneliness spreading across the eyes' crimson surfaces to the edges, sometimes spilling over in a non-saline rust-retardant solution and dripping down the pockmarked muzzle in a mockery of tears.

"The subsidiary effect of loneliness, I thought you'd like that," Rayner said tentatively.

Binder nodded in deep appreciation.

ooooo

Then the wandering began through the rooms and hallways of the mansion, at all hours of the day and night, the blindfold an ebony petal wrapping Binder's eyes in a blackness as unequivocal as that of soil exhumed from deep in the earth. Sensors built into the dog, whom Binder named Chase Again, detected and measured objects and obstructions, distances and depths, spidering the environment in a circumambient web of lasers that bounced information back into the metal dog's computerized radar receptors. Binder clutched Chase Again's harnessed leash, but found that it was his feet, enveloped in the bulky ill-fitting shoes of his distrust, that caused him to repeatedly stumble and fall, not the dog's inability to successfully maneuver the pitfalls of blindness. When Rayner or Crystal rushed forward to help Binder to his feet, a vicious snarl like clacking marbles rolled out of Chase Again's throat, teeth flashing a serrated warning.

ooooo

Binder began to trust Chase Again. He allowed himself to become a passive beneficiary of the surety with which the metal dog moved around the shallow ditches and hillocks of junk in the rustic desuetude of the grounds outside, grounds once maintained by a small army of environmental engineers and devoid now of the sculpted and cultivated landscape that had been like an exteriorization of the sweetly effortless affective states generated by Prozac. Binder had been betrayed by a world of appearances that readily shifted on the vector of his whims in proportion to the amount of money he spent; he could dictate the actions of people, purchase their responses, but sight flowed from their eyes freely and he was caught in the tightly woven net of their perceptions.

It was only because he could see that Binder knew he could be seen by others.

ooooo

At around this time, Crystal embarked on a buying spree, as if in preparation for something inevitable. In a dungeon of hours she watched the QVC channel on an enormous screen in the viewing room. Rayner sat beside her in his wig and accompanying trashy garments, keeping a record of her purchases. Her consciousness lay dissolving in the viscera of glittering images as if bathed in will-corroding digestive juices of innumerable trinkets and allurements: body-sculpting and toning devices, workout machines and paraphernalia, age-retarding creams and lotions, teeth whiteners, volume-maximizing shampoos and conditioners, a rainbow selection of colored contact lenses.

"Why's he wearing the blindfold?" Rayner asked. They shared an obscenely large sack of Lay's potato chips. A ghost town of empty cellophane bags at their feet had provided them with the metabolic fuel required for unbroken stretches of television viewing. With that dull hollow energy derived from high-sodium-content food that crunches, they watched the screen.

"He's practicing to see how it'll be when he's blind."

"Binder's going blind?"

"No."

Rayner's silence was feline, like a cat coiled in sleep. "Are you his wife?"

"No. I'm somebody money makes a big impression on."

"Money should be a means to an end."

"Easy for you to say. You got paid one hundred K for tweaking a mutt that looks like it belongs to the Tin Man. So what's the end your hundred is a means to?"

He shrugged. "Coming down from Carmel, I found out I can make people do what I want if I can convince them that what they see is real." Rayner's shrug slid into his tone of voice like a baseball player sliding into home plate and he concluded, "And I did it without money."

"Been doing that all my life, but it doesn't seem like it's enough," Crystal said.

"Maybe it is enough, but not if you think you need money to pull it off," Rayner offered.

"My zenji gender bender," she said, leaning over and pecking him lightly on the cheek.

Then he asked, "Do you love Binder Trogg?"

"That's a funny question to ask a girl when she's busy spending money," Crystal answered.

ooooo

Binder and Chase Again howling hoarse poetry into the rapt, astonished microphone of the moon.

ooooo

Binder wore the blindfold and it was not the prison that sight had been. Chase Again responded when Binder touched him, sniffing the air with affection under the pheromone of his master's touch. And Binder, in a Technicolor of recall made ferocious by memories of what his eyes could no longer feed on, visualized every detail of Chase Again's grotesque appearance, his mangy asymmetrical beauty, so like the original Chase's repugnant beauty. At night, Chase Again lay growling protectively on the floor at the side of his master's bed, his eyes fervid and crystalline, as though he could see his sleeping master's dreams. "No, Binder, I will not do that," the metal dog murmured.

ooooo

Arms akimbo, Crystal modeled her handcrafted Las Vegas showgirl costume for Rayner, at his request. She strutted with stately serenity about the bedroom in a cranberry-red rhinestone bra and matching French-cut briefs sequined with crystal, a fantail cinching her narrow waist and displaying six chandelle tails, a turban-style headpiece sprouting two-foot-long ostrich feather plumes. Gloves, neckpiece and nude fishnets completed the ensemble.

Rayner licked his finger, touched an ostrich feather, and made a sizzling sound.

"Why do you wear girl's clothing?" Crystal asked.

"Well," Rayner said, "this was the first time, but I like it."

"Because you want to be a girl?"

"No, because people think they know who you are based on what they see."

"I thought you wanted to be a girl, or you were maybe a transvestite," she said.

"And as a result of that, what?"

"That you didn't like girls."

"Wrong. See what I mean? You were effectively psyched."

"Or that you didn't like me."

"Wrong," he said, in a softer voice.

"But you are sixteen, you know."

"And as a result of that, what?"

She thought about that, then smiled. "I see."

ooooo

The golden knitting needles are gripped in Crystal's fists, the points up-tilted like slender musketry angled from brows of trenches. Both fists are wedged into the flesh below her stomach where thighs socket into pelvis, fixed there, braced, immovable; the effort, her body's tension, brings a roseate bloom to the surface of her tawny skin. Her elbows flare slightly, her whole body, as she sits, is clenched in anticipation of the impalement. Binder is kneeling, his palms flat on her thighs for support, as he aligns his eyes with the needle points, then tosses his head back like a restive stallion.[8]

"You don't need to do this, Binder. You don't want to be blind like the rest of the world," Crystal says.

Chase Again and Rayner stand off to the side watching Binder and Crystal on the pedestal in the room flooded with Wagner, N.W.A., and the leonine roar of the holographic ocean.

---

8 It appears that his logic has completed itself in a syllogism of darkness, in the black womb where his world waits to be born again, in the prairie of midnight where he is convinced tumbleweed eyes will roll and ricochet off him harmlessly, in the placeless present tense where his life now unfolds in a syntax of ambient ebony. It only requires the perfection of a gesture, a leap of faith cemented into irreversibility. He has removed his blindfold for the first time in the seamless day-night fabric he had stitched himself into; he has removed his blindfold just long enough for a final orientation, eyes tracking on the points of the knitting needles.

Rayner snaps his fingers, as if in time to a single unifying beat lurking below the pulses of music clashing violently against one another.

Binder plunges forward, plunges down.

ooooo

At that moment Binder's grandmother, Bertha, calls from Tubalo, Mississippi. For days she has been thinking about what Crystal told her, Binder's plan to hurl himself into perpetual darkness. She has burned St. John the Conqueror root with mugwort, the fumes rising in an oracle of dense pungent plumes, the smoky rungs of a divinatory ladder descending beneath her feet as she climbs to an a eminence of clarity where she is able to see through the clouds of a thirty-five-year-long hesitancy. It is time to tell the truth: that it was she who had gouged out the dog Chase's eyes to reinforce and add dramatic weight to the lesson she had hoped the boy Binder would learn when the white men had bound Chase to the tree and painted the words "nigger dog" across the hairless body. The lesson she hoped the boy would absorb was that a similar fate awaited him, crucifixion as a powerless and humiliated thing, if he did not discover a way to open his eyes to the searing light of the world's machinations.

The ringing of the telephone is muffled by the music that quilts the mansion. They would later hear Bertha's message played back on the answering machine, her voice like something thrown into a blender set to the highest speed, choppy and jittered by the years, a mixture of apology and self-justification sieved through the phone's mouthpiece.

"I might have lied to you, Binder, but you got to admit that damn mangy dog stank to high heaven."

ooooo

Chase Again responds to the snapping of Rayner's fingers, front and hind legs extending in flight, the metal dog slicing air in a flattened trajectory, eyes married to the needles pointed at Binder's eyes, neural-imitative circuitry flashing a code-red simulacrum of thought: No.

ooooo

Rayner has anticipated Binder's anger at being thwarted. In the two weeks he has spent in the mansion, he has come to know the grooves, the tracery of Binder's pattern of thought, both through observation and sympathetic resonance, having detected the same anger building to a storm behind his own eyes at seeing himself perceived in a certain reductive manner. He had taped what happened, guessing that if Binder could have witnessed the metal dog in its graceful airborne lunge, he would be chastened by the sight of a thing so ugly temporarily transformed by flight into a thing of improbable beauty.

Rayner is right. Again and again Binder replays the tape where Chase Again soars, hurling himself into Crystal, jarring the knitting needles from her hands, and in the process dislocating her right arm, which now hangs in a sling.

ooooo

Crystal and Rayner sit on the bed in the palatial master bedroom, waiting for Binder to enter the room.

"What's taking you so long," Rayner shouts. They can hear Binder shuffling about in the hallway.

"I don't like it," they hear Binder say from beyond the hallway door.

"You don't have to like it," Rayner says. "It's just to show you how easy it is."

"Oh, come on," Binder, Crystal urges. "We won't tell anybody."

The door opens reluctantly. Binder enters the room, wobbling on high heels, his head tilted at a precarious angle as he attempts to balance the turban-style headpiece with his gloved hands. He stands awkwardly in the cranberry-red rhinestone bra and matching French-cut briefs sequined with crystal, the fantail sprouting ostrich feathers.

"Now strut," Crystals commands.

"Hell, no," Binder says, and immediately begins to remove the outfit.

"That's just one way to do it," Rayner says. "Trick is, you to come up with variations on a theme."[9]

"Out of the mouths of babes," Crystal confirms.

ooooo

"So what will you do now for money?" Crystal asks.

"Oh," Binder says, "I'm not worried. I still have some property up north I can dump. I can always make money."

"No doubt," Rayner says, fingering the strands of the wig.

They stand in the mansion's doorway.

"Maybe re-do the prototype for Chase Again," Binder says. "Pretty him up a little. Scout some venture capital and manufacture the next generation of Seeing Eye dogs. Metal Dogs, Inc. What about you?"

"I thought I'd give Rayner here a little taste of Vegas."

"They think they're smart," Rayner says knowingly, "with their zillion-deck shoes at the blackjack tables in the casinos. They're not so smart."

Binder and the metal dog watch Crystal and Rayner walk across the annihilated grounds, skirting the stacks of merchandise ordered from the QVC channel and delivered in boxes by a UPS delivery truck a few hours ago. They disappear down the winding footpath to the yawning gate.

---

9 Rayner here alludes to the perfection of a gesture, a leap of faith cemented into irreversibility.

ooooo

A silver Jaguar pulls up to the curb across the immaculate, tree-canopied street. After two weeks spent accumulating and following leads, the private detective has finally managed to trace Rayner to Binder's address. Rayner's father opens the door and slides out of the driver's seat; the detective gets out on the passenger side, walks around the front of the car, and stands next to Mr. Richards. Both men lean against the car and look at the open gate to Binder's mansion, speaking to each other in discreet tones.

What they see is a young black woman, arm in a sling, striding on statuesque legs, heels biting smartly into an apple of crisp echo, holding hands with a raven-haired teenage white girl wearing a black miniskirt, black halter top, sunglasses, and stiletto heels narrow as the stems of champagne glasses. The men openly stare as the pair exit the gate, cross the street diagonally, and walk directly past them. The teenaged girl taps her sunglasses down an inch with her index finger and winks solemnly at Mr. Richards.

Mr. Richards, shaking his head in disgust, watches his son vanish into distances zebra-striped by sun and shadow, but fails to recognize him.

There Are Signs Everywhere

1. What is not detailed by the myriad sources of information about Kalil Franklin is easy enough to deduce, extrapolate, or imagine. The information is in part a matter of public record and includes data culled from testimonies, interviews, psychiatric evaluations, tabloid articles, internet bulletin boards and news groups, special reports, anecdotal urban legend, the official declarations of law enforcement spokespersons, and documentaries casting light on the tormented inner lives of psychosexual killers. On the other hand, the drab pedestrian garment of my sister's life has been hung out to dry on the clothesline of public scrutiny and flaps pitifully as though in some breeze created by the sweep of rudely curious and assessing eyes. She is reduced rather than aggrandized by a swarm of mundane facts, and the significance of her life must be mined from biographical minutiae scattered throughout columns of newspaper print in articles devoted to someone else.

2. Kalil is standing in line at McDonald's, thinking that his father did not even have the banal decency to be a man cut down in his prime by the scythe of gratuitous tragedy, or one who had fled the suffocating responsibilities of domestic life to perhaps discover his potential—an act of male dereliction

likely to be characterized by just such a forgiving or at least neutral catch phrase, except where the father in question is black, as presumably Kalil's was, and the whole business in the end is made to support some sociologist's shrewd puppetry with statistics regarding the disproportionately high number of African-American families deserted by black fathers. His father had at no time been a flesh and blood presence, his identity unknown to Kalil, a fact that left unanswered the most fundamental speculations regarding who, what, when, where, why. A man not even the simulacrum of a father, on whom Kalil could not even contrive to hang some threadbare and tattered garment of lurid biography: the debased life of a crack addict, perhaps, or the life of a high-ranking member in a street gang, slain in one of those pyrotechnical shoot-outs involving the Los Angeles County Sheriff's Department, or any number of convenient fictions with which to fill the vacuum of fatherlessness.

Because vacuum it was, or had been, for a time, with all the attendant problems. For the longest time he had been the snot-nosed, butter-hued kid bullied by marauding boys on the block who had formed a loose coterie they called, with an oil-and-water mixture of pride and self-denigration, Club Negro, a fraternity where the requirement for membership was a complexion at least as dark as the inky skins of blackberries. Even at the age of seven or eight, inundated by a sea of televised white faces that washed over his own darker world, Kalil understood that Club Negro was a defensive gesture, the stacking of psychological sandbags in an attempt to build a barrier against which the waves of a color-obsessed society could hurl themselves, dissipating into harmless foam. And he did not blame those boys, who took the blackness they had been told was tainted, the mark of savagery, and burnished it to a militant gleam, made it a symbol of legitimacy and inclusion.

No, as they drove their knees into his stomach and scraped his face in ghetto dirt to darken it, he didn't blame them, knowing what he and they would be up against. But he did long for the strong arms of a father to lift him from the folds of his pain, some man who would straighten him out and set him on his feet and teach him to become a shield before stones, a coat of armor against blows, a thesaurus deflecting their insults and returning them in refined form, a superior fictionist in the face of lies crudely fashioned and executed. Because there was no father to explain the peculiar ways of the world or to apply the bandage of wisdom to his wounds, Kalil was left to his own devices and that, he is now sure, has been the source of his inability to see clearly all the signs by which others so effortlessly seem to navigate their course through life.

"You want to know about your father? I'll tell you this much. He wasn't a husband. He was simply a sperm delivery system—a way for *me* to get to *you*. A means to an end. The two of us had an agreement. Nothing more, nothing less. You'll understand later. Or maybe you won't. At any rate, it's just you and me, kiddo," was his mother's answer when Kalil, at four or five, asked who and where his father was.

The glaring mistake of his boyhood—which he now calls Major Fuck-Up #1—had been the black fingerpaint he smeared all over his face as he stood before the bathroom mirror, massaging the cool smooth pigment deep into his pores, covering every inch of his skin, including ears, lips, neck, hands, until it seemed as though the night itself had invaded his body, taken on human features and form and propelled him against his will to the playground where the boys of Club Negro gathered to play basketball. Wearing this minstrel-mask of seamless and ancient black he approached them, spreading his arms wide as if to embrace them all, offering himself as a candidate for membership, saying "Check this out, am I black enough now?" and rotating a flamboyant 360 degrees to display himself with the same air of casual triumph projected by models who glide down the catwalk, reach the end, then twirl. He was nine. His desire to be a member of their club had driven him to delirious extremities of poor judgement. They looked at him with mouths agape for a few moments and then swept down on him like an avalanche. “Daddy, daddy,” he cried out, but, of course, there was no answer.

When Kalil reaches for his bag containing his Big Mac and fries, the cashier stares at his arm. “Cool tattoos,” observes the youth who had taken his order with a sullen reluctance that Kalil at first had thought inexplicable and then, reflecting briefly, revising, concluded was completely understandable.

3. He pulls into the Arco station. A coherent mass of McDonald’s French fry containers and 7-Up cans slides with a junky rustle from right to left on the dashboard as the car coasts to a stop in front of the gas pump. A single piece of yellow legal paper has been taped to the pump with a handwritten message in a kindergarten scrawl, “Sorry No Super Unleaded.” The note explains everything with a succinct finality that allows no room for negotiation or compromise. In this way, the clerk or the manager here conveniently avoids culpability, will not have to mumble apologies or detail extenuating circumstances to exasperated customers. He thinks about it and concludes that this approach could have widespread application in a number of irksome everyday circumstances. He considers, as an alternative to tattoos, visiting a copying center, perhaps Kinkos, and placing an order for a set of five hundred business cards with his name, Kalil Franklin, printed in the lower right-hand corner. In the middle of the card in bold boxy letters would be the words “I’m Sorry,” followed by three ellipses to indicate that there is more to the message, that the holder of the card is expected to exert effort, enter the spirit of things, expend energy, turn the card over, participate—all actions that he himself would be disinclined to perform. In fact, he would readily admit, if asked, to being action-averse in a general sense, in relation to the countless minute efforts required to successfully move from one day to the next. No one asks, nor is it likely that anyone will ever ask. But yes, it would be necessary to turn the card over to read the balance of the message and therefore this humble

and lowly business card would have in common with the latest cutting-edge technologies the element of interactivity. On the back of the card, another set of ellipses would dribble into any number of possible phrases: "I'm sorry . . . For my anger at nothing and everything—but enough about me, how are you?" Or perhaps, "I'm sorry . . . For being black in America and not knowing how to define 'black.'" Or even, "I'm sorry to bother you . . . But are you my father?" Comparing tattoos and business cards as methods of communication, it seems clear that while business cards might offer a cost-effectiveness advantage, they would to a large extent disallow the expression of the aesthetic impulse that Kalil finds so attractive in the bold colors of the sound bites tattooed on his body.

The heat is a skittish transparency stirred now and again into exhausted motion by a humid gasp of August wind. He gets out of the car, peeved by fingers of fabric digging insistently into the cleft of his buttocks. Adjusts his wrinkled khaki shorts and walks, splay-legged, to the bathroom. The greasy doorknob refuses to budge or jiggle in his grip. "Key for Customers Only at Counter," a sign says. Yet another sign, another ring buoy tossed out into the sea for those on the verge of drowning. Signs to instruct, edify, prescribe behavior, map out proper courses of action. They are everywhere, for eyes that are trained to see them. Kalil now unzips his pants and darkens the door nonchalantly with an S of urine. No one is looking, it seems. But if someone were looking, it would not matter. Should it? The angel says yes.

4. As a child Kalil watched cartoons every Saturday morning, sprawled on the floor before the television, burrowed into a putty of pillows, eating gummy spoonfuls of Captain Crunch and anticipating the sugary broth he would slurp from the bowl when the cereal was gone. On the TV a talking dog unable to decide on a particular course of action was surprised by a miniature haloed angel and a pitchfork-wielding devil wearing a chintzy crimson cape materializing with a carbon-

ated *pop* in the air, each furiously whispering advice in the conflicted animal's ears. Although Kalil no longer remembers whose advice the dog ultimately decided to follow, those trivial but surprisingly potent polar images of good and evil proved themselves to be ore mined from the deep caverns of his imagination, an excavation of crude archetypes, and they stayed with him all his life, appearing randomly but often when the weight of decisions he had to make threatened him with immobility. As he zips his pants up, the angel hovering over his right shoulder tells him that yes, it should matter, the possibility of someone observing him urinate on the door should indeed matter. But the devil too appears, his breath robust with sulphur, and he makes it clear that Kalil should no longer care about maintaining cosmetic facades of civility. In fact, he should ardently hope that the next time something like this takes place someone will just happen to be watching, because once Kalil's lack of concern is observed by another it will be, in a sense, shared, and thus he will not be alone with it, diminished by it, as a man who stands next to the gigantic bronze monument of some heroic figure is diminished and obscured by the shadow it projects.

5. While working at the corner of Lindley and St. Crane Street with a crew of two other municipal employees responsible for replacing, maintaining, and installing traffic and road signs for the Los Angeles Department of Public Works, Kalil sees a middle-aged black man standing next to a Mercedes, opening the door on the driver's side. The car inhabits its elegant silver sheen in the same way that a woman's slender hand inhabits an elegantly tailored glove. His burnished beige complexion seems a flawless envelopment, an embrace of Armani sleekness. The man and everything related to him suggest neat and flawless containment, an infinite regression of boxes within boxes. At a certain level the boxes would become microscopic, invisible to the naked eye, requiring the use of highly sophisticated scientific instrumentation capable of the quantification

of phenomena on the quantum level. At some juncture in this infinite diminution, the matter composing the human body would finally reveal an inverted landscape of nothingness.

Kalil inhales deeply, checking the air for traces of sulphur.

It seems to him that a long time ago—though an imaginary observer occupying some privileged vantage point from which to view reality might assess a period of six months as not so very long ago—some time ago, then, he was majoring in physics at Cal Tech and at some point during his advanced studies began to see the solid objects of the physical world as phosphorescent subatomic particles. That is, he began to see the very building blocks of matter in their ghostly hip-hop dance, saw everything with the same X-ray vision with which Superman, arms akimbo, penetrated surfaces and beheld the rickety skeleton upon which reality was grafted.

As his two coworkers load a toolbox and ladder into the back of a utility truck, Kalil crosses the street, approaching the man. Wealth reduces him to a heightened awareness of his own ineffectuality at playing The Game. You would think that someone like Kalil, with his spidery dreadlocks, his oversized T-shirts emblazoned with abrasive epigrams, his tattoos, someone speaking a nouveau-millennial hip patois of techno-jargon, street slang, and academic argot, someone with a Nike-propelled bounce in his stride as though a diving board dipped and rose ever so slightly beneath the balls of his feet, you would think that someone like twenty-seven-year-old Kalil with his knowledge that all the players and the props shifted and dissolved and morphed at methamphetamine speeds—you would think such a person would have attained mastery of The Game. (Just as recovery is possible for the addict only if he or she admits the existence of the addiction, The Game cannot be mastered if you aren't aware it *is* a game. "Play The Game as though it is not a game, believe that it matters," coaxes the angel from time to time. "Play The Game as though it's less than a game," counters the devil, coolly.) Instead, he is inclined, even in the face of the most transparently contemptible displays of material success, to feel that he is a failure. My sister B. has told him on more than one occasion that he is conflicted, rising and falling on a seesaw of validation, up for outer, down for inner. But the truth is, winning this particular game, The Money Game, continues to elude him.

"Excuse me, sir." The impeccably dressed man turns smoothly toward Kalil, as though ball bearings facilitate the motion. "I'd like to ask you a question, if I could. What's the secret?"

"The secret?"

"You got the faucet turned *on*. The universe is an ocean of abundance. In this world you are what you make, you are what you spend."

"The secret?" He glances up and down the street furtively as he scoots in behind the wheel. "Money is indifferent to who spends it or whose hands it falls into. When somebody leaves the door to their Mercedes unlocked and the key dangling in the ignition, *carpe diem*."

The car speeds off down the block.

Lesson: Appearances when not established or mediated by signs are without exception deceptive.

6. Kalil is trying to listen to a coworker, but either the devil or the angel is whispering to him. Their voices have lately been braiding together, making positive identification more difficult than ever, but he is certain of the message: it is time to obtain another tattoo.

The young coworker everyone calls Jomo walks with Kalil into a small room on the seventh floor of the municipal building designated as an employee break room and furnished with a Sparkletts water dispenser, a vending machine for beverages, another for candy and gum and chips, a bulletin board where workers post personal items for sale (as a joke someone has posted "best bargain used condoms X-tremely cheap call your mother for more info"), a sink, and a General Electric microwave with a radiation-leaking hairline fissure at the bottom of its plastic window. Curiously, there are no chairs or tables. Jomo is asking Kalil about his tattoos.

"I mean, I'm not one to get all up in a brother's business, but what you've got going is pretty unusual. You've got the tattoo on the back of your right hand that looks exactly like one of those traffic signs and says 'yield,' a tattoo on the back of the other one says 'slippery when wet.' Then, " Jomo says, selecting B17 for a bag of peanut M&Ms, "farther up your arm you got a sign says 'road ahead narrows,' and on the other you got 'danger curves.' Then on your neck you got 'reduce speed.' I mean, that's the same shit we post at corners and shit all day long. You got to admit it's unusual, right?"

Kalil uses the scissors of words to snip little perforated cutouts and prefabricated designs that offer easy one-dimensional explanations Jomo will understand. "There have been times in my life when I didn't travel down the right road, times where the right direction to take didn't reveal itself. In my confusion I stepped off the straight and narrow into strange landscapes. And I always thought, if only there was someone or something to make you hesitate for a few minutes before you were about to commit some giga fuck-up, something to make you just stop and think about what you were about to do. How many fewer mistakes might be made, how much less pain might be caused, how many personal tragedies averted? Follow?"

Jomo munches his M&Ms, nodding cautiously.

"What we need is to be reminded that what we're about to do will result in this or that consequence. We need signs to direct us on our journey. What better way to accomplish this than road signs? Road signs are perfect metaphors for the journey through life. These tattoos are more than just a way for me to remind myself to look for direction when I'm about to lose the trail. They're like monuments to specific incidents that happened to me in the past. If I had only *yielded* that time, I never would have been arrested. Now, when I find myself in a similar situation, I look at that tattoo, and I hope to be reminded to *yield*."

"These signs you're talking about to get direction. Bro, ain't that the same as listening to your conscience?"

"Conscience? Now there's a concept that would definitely cause titters of laughter among enlightened psychotherapeutic practitioners with postmodern theoretical leanings." Kalil, leaning against the sink, ankles crossed in an X, peers at Jomo with skeptical intensity, as though his coworker were a twenty-dollar bill balled up in the middle of the pavement. "You have to be convinced it's your conscience, otherwise there's the possibility they're just voices in your head. Do you know what happens when you listen to voices in your head?"

Jomo appears to think about this. He shrugs and looks away. "No, man. And I don't want to know, neither."

7. The facts suggest that my sister B. led a life that in most ways seems to conform to the cookie-cutter patterns and configurations stamped into the raw dough of the American experience by tradition, societal norms, parental expectations, peer pressure and so on. Even her deviations from these larger patterns of normalcy fit into a kind of well-established sub-pattern of predictable confusion, angst, disenchantment, nonconformity—in short, all those symptoms associated with the anguished and often misguided quest for identity common to so many young men and women.

This became public knowledge: B., twenty-six, graduated with honors from UCLA with a bachelor's degree in sociology and what little free time she had was devoted to community volunteer work with hearing-impaired inner-city children. The following was withheld from public knowledge, for who other than I would know? When she was six she watched her mother succumb to lung cancer. The effect the mother's death had on B. could be compared to the disappearance of a mountain against which desperate shouts aimed across an abyss had once unfailingly ricocheted, returning as an echo to the ears of one attempting to locate her own position in space and time. That is to say, my sister had no sense of direction.

Her father's impact on her life was negligible. Her father, my father: negligible.

B.'s artistic propensities blossomed in an otherwise fallow childhood. Her six-year-old hands waved wands of colored chalk, crayons, pencils, and felt-tip markers that, uncapped, sliced the air with a dagger of vinegary odor and paper, walls, floors were transformed, in my ensorcelled five-year-old eyes, into something magical. After tying my shoes for me while I perched obediently on the edge of my bed, she would use my fleshy chipmunk cheeks as a canvas, painting red and yellow and green swirls and swatches on them, ringing my eyes in monocles of white watercolor. These spontaneous creative acts made a deep impression on me. Some part of me that equated the external world with a pair of unseen hostile hands jerking the strings from which I dangled understood that a scalpel fashioned of imagination could shape and sculpt that same hostile world.

When I was thrown like a scoop of ice cream into the hot skillet of the inner city public school system, my sister waited for me after class to walk me home. How ironic that a child wearing his quiet withdrawn personality like a tattered too-small coat, a child with a fear of everything except books, would attract the belligerent curiosity of his schoolmates, as if he were yelling at the top of his lungs when he was only walking home as quickly as possible with eyes firmly fastened to feet. The boys swarmed about me, angrily demanding to know why I thought I had the right to be different. My sister and I had inherited my mother's almost lemony complexion and not I, but my sister had hair that hung like straight, heavy black rain from her head. The first time it happened they accused me of trying to "act white" and I was beaten. There was no second time because my sister, ten years old, met me after school the next day and when those same three boys approached she acted as my protector. She fought them boldly, fiercely while I stood by and plunged my head into my ostrich-hole of cowardice and fear and when it seemed that she was defeated, her eyes wildly grazed a brick by a nearby fire hydrant and she seized and swung it fiercely, boldly striking on the side of the head the biggest boy, the group's loud, lanky leader. From then on, her reputation soared and we walked home each day unmolested. She filled the void in her motherless world by becoming a mother to me. I'm unable to say who I became in order to fill my own void.

8. Kalil does not really need anything or anyone. This he believes is his strongest and most admirable personality trait. A defeated army of people seems to straggle in single file through his embattled days and nights. Some are looking for a place to pitch the flimsy sagging tent of their lives, as though Kalil's own life were nothing more than a zone of encampment roped off for their convenience. Many, if not most of the people who attempt to do so, are women. They want an area where they can lay out their utensils and little ornamental boxes and envelopes and medicine bottles and hair products and magazines. They are everywhere, there are so very many of them: young women disgorged by traumatic childhoods and single-parent homes; young women who have been raped or molested; young women who have struggled through substance abuse or poverty or clinical depression or some devastation that has pushed them to the brink of emotional enervation—all of them with their useless MBAs and liberal arts degrees, weary with an intelligence to which the label precocious had perhaps been attached when they were younger, a precociousness that in adulthood became a baffling encumbrance, a burned-out intellectual cynicism.

There was a young woman who had tried to force her way into his life when he was still taking classes. She had been in Kalil's conceptual physics class and against his better judgement, he had agreed to meet with her twice a week in the campus library for intensive study sessions. He should have known better and, in fact, he did know better, but he had listened to the angel. He sat on the toilet in the bathroom one Saturday morning, not using it but just sitting there, his elbows resting on his thighs and his forehead buried in his hands, like some sculpture that a Rodin suffering from bi-polar affect might have created and called "The Suicidal Thinker." Hunched with thought, his spine curved with strenuous thought, the tremulous walls of his studio apartment absorbing each sharp-edged thought as a rock absorbs the methodical blows of a pick ax, Kalil was told not to pour the Liquid Drano standing at his feet out of its container and down his throat. The angel ordered him to pour the Liquid Drano down the toilet and to meet Denyce Battler at the library and to connect with her as a fellow student, a fellow human being, a member of the opposite sex—to talk with her, share ideas with her, open up to her, establish intimacy. Oddly, the devil had not materialized at all.

He did try. In retrospect, obviously not hard enough, but he did try. They studied together and afterward went to the student union and then Denyce Battler suggested that they go to a movie. After the movie she asked Kalil up to her lonely cramped apartment for a glass of white wine and after a time she began to touch him, first casually as she sat with her knees angled toward him on the sofa, then more demonstratively whenever she leaned forward or rather collapsed gracefully, tossing pastel butterflies of lacy feminine laughter into the air. She touched his hand, his arm, his shoulder, and the spots where she touched greedily sucked the warmth from her flesh, desperate for some residue of rare tactile intimacy. He could feel the blood pulsing in her fingertips.

All these were signs, inclement signs, because he suddenly understood that if he allowed this intimacy into his life he would lose what little power he had gained struggling through the difficult years of his childhood without a father. Those years had forced him to sharpen his aloneness like a blade and use it to cut a space for himself in the fabric of life in order to survive emotionally and no, no, no, he couldn't forfeit those gains. It was pure foresight and distrust of the angel that had made him put the Drano in his backpack instead of pouring it down the toilet at home and now he removed the bottle and placed it on the table. She looked at him and said, "That's a freaky thing to have in a backpack isn't it?" and he said, "Yes, it is and I'm sorry for the freakiness of it but I want you to drink it," and she said, "What did you say?" because she genuinely hadn't heard and he thought how much easier it would be if he kissed her and so leaned forward and kissed her and she reclined slowly and he was on top of her and her eyes were closed, her mouth was open, and the kiss was a vortex pulling him in. He was swirling in a clockwise, no counterclockwise constellation of crimson down that vortex and barely had time to reach behind him with one arm and grab the bottle and then hold her mouth open and pour a large quantity down her throat *glug glug glug* before her eyes burst open in terror grasping at sight, choking and sputtering and almost vomiting, then screaming or rather crying and bent double sliding off the couch onto the floor with her knees jackknifing up into her stomach and he didn't want to hear her pasty gurgling of phlegm so he plugged his ears with his fingers and sang loudly "la dah la la la lah dah" until she lost consciousness, her consciousness shrinking in the way that an object or a person who might well be someone's father rapidly becomes a dot and then disappears in the rearview mirror of a streaking red Ferrari.

This experience caused him the next day to visit the tattoo parlor called Skin Deep. He had already gotten six or seven or maybe eight tattoos there. He knew there would now be an internecine and protracted battle between the angel and the devil because this qualified as Major Fuck-Up #5. While the battle raged, he would need some tangible reminder of what he had done in order to avoid doing it again. Therefore, the tattoo would be in the shape of a stop sign. The young woman who designed the tattoo, the proprietor of the shop, said to him, "A stop sign this time? Cool," and she laughed. The tiny silver flash of a barbell stud piercing her tongue was what he saw before her laughter died like butterflies withering in the air and she closed her mouth. The stop sign was long overdue. There had been others about whom he would not have been able to say there had been others if only he had chosen the stop sign many months ago instead of the yield sign or the slippery when wet sign.

9. In the Metro section of the *Los Angeles Times* was an article detailing the circumstances of the crimes, the arrest (he had placed a phone call to the police and waited for them to arrive), the unusual legal complications drawing the trial out over an agonizing eight-month period. The article included a psychological profile and analysis that seemed for all its conjectural depth and glossy pedantry to be no more than a recycling of clichés regarding his "loner" status in the community and at work. Also described at length were his myriad misguided involvements and doomed endeavors, his ruined finances (bankruptcy), his abortive absurd attempt to breed brine shrimp and sell them to commercial hatcheries and aquarium owners across the country via the internet, all the twists and turns of a life littered with weird initiatives and haunting failures and disastrous in every way but one—he had, after all, managed to survive.

As a result of this fleshing out process something like a story managed to take shape, so that in spite of the horrendous and incomprehensible things he had done, people began to understand that the monstrous larger-than-life cinematic persona assembled from the detritus of Kalil Franklin's actions was inhabited by a flesh and blood human being who was made to represent, in almost imperceptibly canted media presentations, a man who was emblematic of every man's susceptibility to insanity and evil, as though only by luck or the mysterious grace of God could any given individual escape Kalil's journey into darkness. This implication was all the more startling considering the fact that he is black. What is atypical is media coverage which, number one, suggests even inadvertently that some universal aspect of human nature might possibly emanate from the actions of a solitary black man and number two, avoids intimations that criminal behavior, violence, and their requisite Neanderthal intelligence are inborn racial propensities—but that is a counterproductive line of thought leading down a descending spiral staircase of similar thoughts.

Near the end of the article there was this information about B.: She was born in Milwaukee, Wisconsin, in 19__. In her sophomore year in college she was active in the Actor's Circle, a drama club that twice a year produced the works of local playwrights and staged them on campus. She graduated from the UCLA in 19__. She worked with hearing-impaired children in South Central Los Angeles . . . hearing-impaired children with listening eyes . . . but . . . this . . . has been stated already elsewhere and is redundant. Does this repetition suggest that very little biographical information exists apart from that already revealed to the public? Does it suggest the life she lived was not rich or variegated enough to provide more than a few sketchy superficialities? If anything, let it invoke poverty of the imagination or failure of memory or lack of spiritual clarity on the part of the writer, whose name you will presumably find somewhere below the title of this piece, my name, the brother, the brother here struggling to explain his sister's life without wishing to appear to be struggling. Bear with me. Just please bear with me although if I were you, it's true I might begin to fidget now in my seat, I might stop turning pages and instead glide across the floor and through the door of whatever room I sat reading in to experience the enveloping tilt and spin and twirl of life, life, which is there waiting with outstretched arms, is always waiting there on the other side of the door like a well-dressed, smiling-eyed stranger with welcoming arms, though there is no guarantee that once you step through it, the door, you will ever be able to come back to the place you left. Ever.

10. When my sister was a child, she feared thunderstorms. Great black bowling balls of thunder rolling sluggishly down long lanes of black sky, rumbling and striking a set of enormous hollow pins somewhere in the distance, and night's featureless

face pressing tightly against the bedroom window looking in, and the anorexic branches of the tall diseased juniper tree in the front yard clawing at the same bedroom window as raindrops heavy as the bellies of pregnant women gave birth to small splashes against the glass. My sister would crawl into my bed but she would say it was to soothe me because she knew I was frightened. Trembling all over like guitar strings strummed and plucked in a melancholy ballad, she would pull me to her under the covers, tell me not to be afraid, explain that it was only science. "It's only science happening in the sky so don't be afraid, D.," she would tell me, but I wasn't the one. To admit fear was worse than fear itself and that is something I never succeeded in learning from her.

11. When my sister was eighteen, she had an abortion. She had always loved to paint and her work was scattered everywhere throughout our house. But after the abortion stacks of sketch pads leaned like women brazenly drunk against the walls in the bathroom, the living room, the kitchen. So much paper, so many trees sacrificed to her inner exigencies, a whole small forest's worth of paper floating through the rooms of that house, and on those pieces of paper were signs and symbols limned in a secret language, the runes of decisions and consequences that I could not read. There were pictures as well of unborn babies floating helplessly in dark claustrophobic ambiances, creatures that appeared to be clinging to their safe havens while seeking escape at the same time. Then she abandoned the paper altogether and her body became her canvas and she began to vivify her skin with tattoos. There was a connection between the two things, between the abortion and the tattoos, but I did not know what it was.

Then she opened a tattoo parlor. She obtained the money by cracking the whip of her resourcefulness and making government functionaries jump. The functionaries who were in charge of dispensing grants to minorities, to women, to nightmare-eyed Vietnam vets, to alcoholic white men. She was formidably efficient, street-smart acquisitive, knowing how to ferret out information from many hard-to-access and little-known sources and draw it to the coordinating hub of her brain and then process it there and redirect it back out into the world again in the form of results. She knew how to get things done, she knew how to make things happen. She opened a tattoo parlor with the money and called it Skin Deep.

12. The unruly child of the Santa Ana wind runs through Los Angeles stomping its dirty boots on everything, and on various dust-swirled, grime-whirled corners in Linwood, Pasadena, Beverly Hills, Hollywood, Kalil hands out his business cards. "Have a bidniz card, sir?" he offers, knees bent slightly as he bounces with a sort of mock simian enthusiasm or the impatience displayed by a junkie waiting on a cold-night corner for his dealer, his lips parted slackly, lazily, his pronunciation of the word "business" parodically ghettoized. Stereotypes after all make people comfortable. His requirements for the cards were minimal and as a result he was able to purchase a set of five hundred at a ridiculously low cost at Kinkos. (What aneurysm of genius erupted in the brain of the man or woman who conceived that name, which hints at sexual deviancy in its vague echoing of the word "kinky"? Give admiration freely when deserved, is Kalil's philosophy.)

What he wants to convey to the public or rather to the occasional emboldened passerby who plucks a card from his fluttering outstretched tattooed hand is so difficult to explain. And so he makes no attempt to explain to those who, having taken the blank white card, look from it to his eyes and back to the card again, turning it over and finding no words, no graphics, nothing at all but a wordless white rectangle whose nudity and boxed shape symbolize Kalil's own on an emotional and spiritual level, then repeating the card-to-eyes sequence one last time before moving swiftly away.

13. "A stop sign this time? Cool. I've never had anyone ask me to do a stop sign before. But on your forehead?" B. says, laughing, then walks into the back room. "I don't want to be responsible for your regrets, and I can tell you right now, this is going to be something you're going to regret."

It is 11:00 pm and Skin Deep is closed to the public. The pavement fronting the popular tattoo parlor located in the city's renovated downtown district is no longer awash with mellow lavender, citrus pink, and pale aqua slabs of neon pulsing through the storefront windows.

B. let Kalil in even though the store is closed because he has been coming to Skin Deep for over a year and she knows him. He sits in a chair with a headrest resembling those used by barbers or dentists for customers or patients and waits for B. to return to the room. The blackness behind his closed eyelids soothes him although it is sandpapery and burns like the spices used in Thai food. He is sleeping in a Thai-spiced sleep. But no, actually he is sleeping and awake at the same time, a state of consciousness that he would describe as being somehow quintessentially American, if anyone were to ask him. No one asks, nor does anyone ever think to ask him such questions.

"Hey Kalil," B. shouts, "come on back."

There is a door in the rear of the store that leads to a large storeroom the size of a master bedroom. In defiance of local zoning laws, B. has converted it into her living quarters to save money for a down payment on a condo in the near future. The room contains a bed, end tables covered with scattered knickknacks, a home entertainment center, a computer, bookshelves, a midget refrigerator, and a microwave.

Kalil hovers in the doorway, looking in at B., who is scraping forkfuls of chow mein onto a paper plate from a wilted white carton welted with grease. "I'm absolutely starved. You don't mind if I grab a bite before we do it, right?"

"Oh, not at all," Kalil says.

"Hungry? There's plenty."

"No, thanks."

"Sure?" She puts the plate into the microwave then turns to face him, leaning against the bookcase.

"Go ahead. You should eat. You're very thin."

"One of the not-too-frequently touted benefits of poverty. You don't have to stand there, Kalil. Come on in, sit for a few."

Kalil hesitates. The force of the hesitation is a giant hand pressing against his chest, preventing easy forward motion and entry. Furtively lifting his own hand up to his chest, he pries away the fingers of hesitation.

B. does not see him do this, though she is looking at him. She is looking at his long bulky curtain of dreadlocks. They give him a biblical, acetic look. She is looking at his faraway eyes, which look the way she would imagine pastures and plains on other planets would look. B. thinks now and has always thought that he is very intelligent and that his intelligence encircles him like an island and is the cause of his isolation from others. All the times he has come to Skin Deep she has sensed his isolation and been drawn to it.

But Kalil Franklin has always been oblivious to the perfumed handkerchief of innuendo she has dropped on the floor behind her. Dropping it there, waiting for some old fashioned chivalrous gesture of acknowledgement from him. Not the type to care about such gestures, she nevertheless likes the image—the dropped handkerchief, Kalil Franklin bending down to pick it up and return it to her, bowing deeply. *Je prie votre pardon, mais je crois que vous l'avez laissé tomber . . .* momentarily wandering into the sort of Eurocentric-tainted fairy tale scenario she is typically on guard against. But she has always been old fashioned in that way, waiting for men to make the first move despite the aggressiveness she maneuvers like a sleek red sports car through all other areas of her life, finding all the short fast reckless routes because, except for her dear brother D., whose heavy drinking worries her more and more and whom she loves dearly but does not see or talk to often, she is completely alone in a world that sees her as a young twenty-something black woman woefully handicapped in some irredeemable fashion by her race and largely incapable of reaching her destination.

Kalil sits in the chair next to her bed while she removes the chow mein from the microwave, sits on the edge of the bed, begins to eat. "So why on your forehead?"

"The head is the fountain of thought. All of our behaviors are preceded by thought. Stop the thought, and you stop the behavior. Not now, but in the future."

Now B. chews slowly, looking at him. Immediately the food goes strange in her mouth.

"Too late for now, but there's always hope for the future." Kalil's backpack is on his lap and he opens it. "Are you thirsty? MSG in Chinese food can create a prodigious thirst." He removes a can from the backpack. "I have something here that will quench your deepest thirst."

He stands like spongy grass trampled underfoot that quickly springs upright again. And flowing as tall grass seems to flow beneath waves of wind he is suddenly next to her, holding the Liquid Drano. As if her neck were a tree trunk and his fingertips the beaks of angry foraging birds, his left hand is on her throat and she drops the plate of food.

The sight of the stringy mass on the floor disgusts him.

14. I have taken my position from among many positions available for observation in her converted storeroom near the ceiling, in the corner, out of harm's way, a tiny speck hovering behind a spider's web dotted with the dried brittle husks of dead insects.

15. The kickboxing classes that B. took at Bodies in Motion prove useless against an actual body in motion, though precise methods of execution reliably flash through her brain and faster than she would have believed possible, she is acting on them. She springs up from her seated position on the bed's edge and drives her heel into the top of his foot, but his thick hiking boots are protective and the response she hopes for is

not forthcoming. He does stumble sideways but refuses to relax his grip on her throat. Her flailing arm finds a palm-sized Sony cassette recorder on a book shelf and she grabs it and aims for his face, slicing in an upward arc. The corner strikes the side of his nose and his hands flutter bird-like to nest on his face. Suddenly his skin like a candle melting seems to dissolve in rivulets of blood running between and down the fingers of his hands now cupped over his mouth and nose while the Liquid Drano rolls lopsidedly across the floor.

It seems as though the flame of that wild bold spirit that flared in her that day many years ago when she successfully defended me against my attackers is burning once again and while he is tearing at the veil of blood before his eyes she grabs the present I gave her for her birthday last year, a Casio keyboard with built-in rhythm section leaning against the wall, swinging it like a bat, her stance solidly planted and her entire upper torso twisted by the ferocious velocity of the swing, again aiming for his head but this time missing because he manages to lean back. The keyboard is a toothy smile torn from some macabre face and it seems to laugh as it sails across the room, smashing into the wall. From its now-cracked speaker dribbles a series of repeated automated beats in a tinny malevolent loop, a battery-driven disco rhythm. She darts for the door and he actually leaps with arms and legs spread as though he were some species of flying squirrel thinly spread on the air and gliding on buoyant currents, collapsing around her neck and draping her neck and back with the cape of his body. She struggles forward but the cape of his weight pulls her down.

16. The devil and angel psycho-aberrational archetypes have also been fighting, mirroring the ongoing larger (or, who knows, perhaps smaller) battle between Kalil Franklin and my sister, so that Kalil feels as he wrestles with her on the ground that he is a pendulum swinging wildly between the nodes of two battles alternating for prominence in his consciousness. No matter what anyone says about the world we live in—the

Buddhists, the mystics, the New Age proponents of unity consciousness, all those who maintain that we suffer from and are limited by an illusive perspective rooted in duality and that things are never simply black or white—in the end, it is true that either good has been done or evil has been done, that a monument to one or the other has been created by each and every thought and the progeny of actions those thoughts give birth to, and Kalil knows this—tragically, he knows this.

The outcome of the battle between the devil and angel: the angel slays the devil with a mighty blow that resonates beyond the walls of this room and out into the cosmos. I hear it, I hear the rainbowed note of triumph shake the tympanum of the universe and I'm led to hope against hope—though I know better—that possibly all will be well. In an unexpected reversal of some kind, however, the angel, hovering victoriously over the slain devil, sodomizes the corpse of his fallen enemy.

17. Once again, my sister is on her feet. Things are thrown or heaved, the things that are nearest, the things that can be blindly clutched, a hatha yoga book, a hand-held Revlon hair dryer that is so loud her ears ring after she uses it, a stapler, speaker, clock, nightstand, a red tin can originally filled with Christmas cookies now containing a heavy sludge of pennies—oh, the air is alive with the turbulent weather of objects raining down—a variety of jazz and hip hop CDs, *Essence* magazines, bottles of perfume and coconut-scented hair conditioner for that hair of hers so much like straight black rain; as it turns out, it's a good thing my sister and I never had a mother to berate us on the inadvisability of hoarding every little thing; perhaps that's the silver lining in that dark cloud, and as though invisible seams have burst, the air is animate with toppling, stumbling, streaking, rolling, colliding, tilting, crashing.

18. She continues to struggle fiercely, boldly but his weight again pins her down, down. He has the Drano. And eventu-

ally time erodes her strength so that it virtually melts away as a lozenge is eroded by the tongue. His heavy crucifix of weight atop her erodes her strength. His forearm driving into her throat as a bolt fastens across a latch erodes her strength. And certain thoughts floating in calliope fashion oddly colorfully through her mind erode her strength, diverting it into dissipating channels and robbing her of the ability to disentangle herself from the knot of Kalil Franklin. These thoughts, in bizarre contrast to the surreal horror of the immediate moment, are a frothy waltz, effervesced now in that kaleidoscopic atmosphere where linear thinking in the face of catastrophic forces nears its terminus. Her thoughts have been released and freed as though by the opening of the lid of some delicate music box of accelerated and compressed memory. One of them is of the time that she convinced an uncle not to punish me for an entire month as he was drunkenly inclined to do when at the age of nine I was caught stealing a pack of triple-A Duracell batteries from Walgreen's. He held the belt in his upraised hand while I waited with my pants pulled down and she actually on her knees implored his mercy on my behalf, embracing his ankles.

19. The searing breath of a thousand Drano dragons sighs through her veins as he pulls down her jeans, her underpants, then bends forward, shaking his head back and forth so that his dreadlocks dangle and dance vigorously on her vagina. He sits up and then with his fist punches her vagina in anger, in confusion, as a writer desperate for inspiration punches hard at the keyboard, each fingertip a fist. Then he rapes B.

20. He rapes my sister. He sodomizes my sister. He climaxes quickly, his body shuddering to a halt in the middle of the final raging thrust, the clammy cement of his semen a hardening straightjacket on his dwindling frightened penis.

21. My sister experiences a seismic emotional and physical implosion, caving in as do the roof and walls of a house in an

earthquake. My sister cannot move her body any longer to fight, yet she resists. My sister's resistance is completely internal now. And thus, because of this tiny spark of resistance, perhaps it might even be said my sister lays unraped, unsodomized. For a time, my sister clings to the floor like a ripe tear clinging to the outer edge of God's eye. Then, then the droplet falls.

22. Kalil Franklin sees the flickering of that spark. His eyes blink spastically as if jabbed by shards of that shattered light. He does not leave Skin Deep. Finding the tattoo gun behind the counter in the other room and standing at soldierly attention before a mirror, he watches his forehead scream to life under the biting needles inoculating him with black dye. Crudely he fashions something resembling a stop sign on his forehead with a hand firm and steady. He turns off the lights and sits in the chair with his eyes closed. The intensity of his stillness resembles the one-pointed state of focused awareness known as samadhi, deep meditation blossoming out of absolute silence and cleansed of the goal of attainment.

It occurs to him that once his handiwork has been observed by another it will be, in a sense, shared, and thus he will not be alone with it, diminished by it, as a man who stands next to the gigantic bronze monument of some heroic figure is diminished and obscured by the shadow it projects. He calls the police.

23. I have a fantasy, not now but some time later, in which I visit Kalil Franklin in prison. I sit in a visiting room with a fingerprint-smudged pane of glass between us and look into the same eyes my sister looked into during her last moments. I do not try to find her there. I do not visit him with the intention of forgiving him. I look into his eyes and do not see remnants of my sister there. Neither of us speak, holding the phones to our ears, separated by the glass. I will always have that fantasy.

24. Perhaps my sister would think what I have done is a heartfelt tribute to her, though perhaps she would have wanted the scene depicting her fierce struggle to escape to be longer in order to more fully convey her indomitable spirit. Or maybe she would think I went on too long with it and that I'm nothing but a pimp exploiting her life and her death, searching for the right words to prostitute, the way a john gazes with feline yellow nocturnal eyes through his windshield for the flashiest hooker in the bunch, always searching for the right word, the right phrase, the unique metaphor to keep the Reader interested, to keep the Reader going, keep the Reader entertained, to get the Reader to avalanche forward and say yes. Perhaps she would wonder why the material I wrote about him seemed to be so much more interesting than what I wrote about her, maybe she would wonder what I could possibly have had to gain by juxtaposing her story alongside his diseased perspective, or why I would make the effort to understand or present his point of view, why I would seem to coyly hint at my own sympathetic alignment with his experience of being black in America, why I would squander my imaginative resources telling his story. More than likely she would laugh roundly at my assertion that in the depths of her being she had transcended rape and sodomy and reject it as so much bombastic rhetorical trash, pointing to her torn and bleeding rectum. More than likely she would point out that I could have rendered the value of her life with more depth and honesty had I not been so eager to find an original and engaging point of departure, had I not succumbed to the temptation to sensationalize her story while at the same time ranting in my oh-so-polished way against others who did the same. More than likely she would wonder why for once I couldn't be there to protect her as she had always been there to protect me, always been there for me, not just as a beacon in the lighthouse of the imagination to illuminate my suffering but standing as a flesh and blood presence in the middle of my tribulations and danger. Probably she would say to me, how dare you do what you have done, is this the best

you could do, I hope it was worth it D., I hope everyone is so very touched by your fucking story D., and then she would slap my face hard to brand it forever with the stinging hand print of her disappointment and go on to say more, so much more that might be true that I can no longer bear to imagine what other words she might possibly have in store for me.

Footage

Wave decides to kidnap the man. Out of nowhere, the idea seizes him, coils around his throat, so that there is a slithering pressure at the jugular vein. Coils, a noose of constriction. He actually feels the vein bulging. It bulges as though about to burst open with a great hiss and dapple the air with scarlet confetti. Of course, this does not happen. But if it did, the sight of his own blood clawing through his veins would cause him little distress. That's how ready he is to invite a cleansing idea into his life. That's how ready he is for some broom of an idea to sweep aside all those piled up black Hefty garbage bags filled with the monotony and stasis of his days.

That's how it happens, the idea: A sudden appearance, ultimately mysterious. Sometimes the old clichéd pronouncements are appropriate, beyond and above the novel constructions of language designed to stylishly clothe everyday experiences in a well-coordinated garb of truth. As in the expression "out of nowhere." What other expression, fresh and novel though it might be, could capture so succinctly the birth of an idea whose time has come?

Yes, he really will kidnap the man. Mr. Otto Alexander Davis is a well-respected black man, the vice-chancellor of a top ten university whose numerous philanthropic and political undertakings frequently earn him modest coverage in the Metro section of the newspaper. Yet who decides, Wave wonders, which of Mr. Davis' deeds and accomplishments in the public sphere possess the histrionic heft to qualify as newsworthy? Wave imagines the upper echelons of publication officialdom judging the newsworthiness of Mr. Davis' activities and undertakings, women and men attempting in good faith to make editorial decisions based on a myth of objectivity over cups of near-rancid coffee, stale pastries. They would be ringed about a sprawling conference table 8:00 a.m., drowsily ink-stamping the word "newsworthy" or "un-newsworthy" atop stacks of papers that speed by on a conveyor belt. The racing conveyor belt adds a comic element to the image. In fact, watching MTV on his girlfriend's sofa while he waits for her to return from her shoplifting expedition, Wave laughs out loud. Oddly, the laugh sounds like a canine with an accordion for a throat, barking and baying discordantly at the moon. As the women and men ink-stamp, they gradually blink away the crust of the previous night's tabloid archetypes and hackneyed Freudian symbols, blink away the residue of lurid dreams spangling their eyelashes. However, Wave's own dreams and feverish stratagems, no less lurid, can't be so easily dispensed with.

Wave is once again watching MTV at his girlfriend's apartment. She has just finished showering. Her skin's hue as she stands before him nude seems a dusting of cinnamon jeweled with water. Her seaweed of softly matted hair plastering her face. Her breasts that are startlingly perfect, the nipples at this moment asserting an exclamation, bold punctuation terminating the long graceful sentence of her body. He sees the lips of strangers clinging to those breasts, sees twigs of fingers snapping as they plunge at her flesh, no challenge for the tautness of her twenty-seven-year-old skin. Band-Aids affixed to the knuckles might prevent this catastrophe, but, then again, it might be desirable to avoid the surrealistic air such a remedy would likely impart. Go on. There are petals of rosy tongues blooming as they travel down the stem of her spine, seeking warm cleavage in the steep sweet hills of her buttocks. Beside him on the couch is the video camera that's integral to his impulse to stretch the rumpled sheet of chaos over the smooth surface of everyday life. He sweeps it up, gazes at her through the viewfinder.

"Wave, please, not that damned thing again," she says, exhaling with weariness. Nevertheless, she strikes a series of stances that reduce to cheesy parody the poses assumed by celebrity pin-up girls of the '40s and '50s in calendar layouts. "That thing just keeps popping up out of nowhere, like some sort of pesky-ass erection."

"With this little digital wonder I can see the future. I can see *you*, baby," he says, mutters really, zooming in so closely that the pores of her body attain the elegance of calligraphy. "Alexis Rouge, the hottest, biggest, sexiest porn star of the new millennium."

"What is it, Wave? You've got a communications degree and you work in a damn Blockbuster video store. Maybe I just don't grasp the vision you have for your own life. . . ." In this particular telephone conversation, he experiences his father's voice as a flimsy texture of some kind, a hybrid of water and air, and he can't reconcile this near-insubstantiality with the booming physical presence he's confronted with on those rare occasions when he sees his father in the flesh. The resulting mental dissonance, difficult to explain, momentarily muffles his father's words. It spreads like a fog out of the chasm between the reality suggested by the telephone-miniaturized voice of his father and the reality reflected by Wave's most recent memory of him. Forced to explain this mental dissonance to anyone, Wave might use this example: A young man whose name just happens to be Wave is born as a member of a racial minority in the United States, where the concept of equality is loudly trumpeted in the Constitution. He pledges allegiance to the flag each day in elementary school and comes to feel that it is *his* flag—not his exclusively, of course, but *for him* in some exclusive way. Many years later in a shopping mall, this young man, driving a Ford Mustang, hunts for a vacant parking space. Fireworks of patriotic sentiment swell and burst in his heart, as this happens to be July 4th, Independence Day. He pulls into a space, preempting by mere seconds a red Toyota Land Cruiser, also prowling the lot for parking. Although he has legitimately won the space due to the hair-trigger reflexes commonly attributable to youth, he does not want to be accused of gloating and smiles apologetically to the other driver. In fact, he begins to feel guilty and decides to back out of the space and give it to his competitor. Surprisingly, the conservatively dressed, middle-aged white businessman in the Toyota Land Cruiser leans out the window, screams "That's just what I'd expect from a dirty nigger, why don't you go back to Africa!" and speeds away, tires bleeding a trail of smoke from the wound of the driver's rage. Dissonance now exists in the youth's mind as his belief in the constitutional assertion of equality/belonging and the direct experience of his subordinate outsider status grind against one another like shrill tectonic plates. It is as though he has discovered that he is an American in theory, but not in practice.

But this example isn't necessary because, after all, Wave is not forced to explain this business of mental dissonance to anyone. He's alone. Alexis won't drop by his apartment until later in the evening, well after the department stores in the mall close and her shoplifting expedition is over. It's just Wave and his father's voice, pushing itself through the fog to the forefront of Wave's hearing. "Wave, are you listening to me?"

"I like working where I work," Wave answers. "I get a discount on videos. Otherwise, the five or six videos a night that I watch would be cost prohibitive."

"Look, if I've been understanding this whole thing of yours, you want to make some sort of movie. You have goals and that's good. Let me see what I can do, eh? Let me pull a few strings," his father says reasonably. "I'll talk to Bates, over in human resources. They're contracting right now for a videographer to do some training videos. . . ."

"Training videos." The lack of inflection in Wave's reply kills the question, flattens it into a lifeless statement, draws a chalk outline around it.

"That's right, I forgot. Forgive me, I forgot about all the lucrative experience you've gotten in the film industry since you graduated two years ago."

"I don't need experience. I have imagination. Isn't experience just imagination adulterated?"

"Look, I'm not taking the bait. I won't be drawn into another pseudo-philosophical debate with you, Wave. What's real and what's not. My point is, you want everything on a platter. Wake up, son. You think you don't have to pay your dues, like everyone else? You think you can just get things handed to you on a platter?"

"Would that be handed to me on a real platter or an imaginary one?"

"Be serious, Wave."

"I wouldn't have to pay dues if you'd give me money. Thirty thousand real, not imaginary, dollars. I could get my project off the ground."

"That's right, I forgot. You haven't been working at a miserable Blockbuster video store for the past two years. You're Spike Lee."

A telephone book of responses expands before him. Wave flips through the pages hastily, in search of an appropriate reply. A thumb moistened lightly by the tip of a tongue to facilitate rapid riffling would, without a doubt, be helpful. His father is quicker and the razor-sharp knife of his voice cuts through hundreds of tissue-thin pages with a single efficient sawing motion.

"You're not listening to me. The real world, Wave. Wake up and join it. Everything I have, I earned. And I'm proud of that because in these times, that's an accomplishment only a few black men can claim."

"I'm not interested in the real world," Wave says, and hangs up.

ooooo

The very first time he sees Alexis, she's in Macy's. She's talking animatedly to a tall, jaggedly thin blonde saleswoman behind the cosmetics counter, dressed completely in black, except for a white jacket resembling a lab smock. Wave loves to wander through shopping malls carrying his video camera, a marvel of Sony technology that fits tidily in the palm of his hand. He drifts in and out of department stores, randomly taping the artfully coordinated merchandise hanging from clothing racks, the sleek black stereo components stacked in the aisles, the perfumes and colognes in their asymmetrically shaped bottles scattered across countertops. He wanders through these benevolent mazes, his eyes on the viewfinder. Through the viewfinder he sees Alexis holding a lively conversation with the saleswoman at the cosmetics counter at Macy's. The great honey-hued mass of her hair, parted in the middle and falling to either shoulder in crimped tendrils, bobs languidly as she nods her head, pointing. The saleswoman nods her head energetically in approval, bends down to open the display counter. Alexis, not bothering to confirm the absence of witnesses, quickly plucks two bottles from the countertop and drops them in the oversized leather purse dangling from her shoulder.

Wave walks behind her at a discreet distance, follows her to the parking lot.

"Excuse me, miss . . ."

She turns to face him, calmly meets his gaze. "Yes?"

"I saw what you did in there."

Her arms are crossed at the level of her breasts and she's tapping one foot impatiently. "So?"

"I know what's in your purse."

"You do have a point to make?" she says.

Wave attributes the slightly irritated flutter in her tone not to nervousness, but rather to the prevailing communication style commonly adopted by well-educated, urban-dwelling young women who have found a vocal correlative for their vaguely harried lifestyles and chronic cynicism. "Look, I'm not store security or anything like that."

"No kidding, Sherlock. If you were security you would have nabbed me when I went through the doors. So what is it? You a Jesus freak, a Hari Khrisna, or some other kind of mentally scrambled cultist who wants to give me a morality makeover? You want me to take the stuff back to the store and put it back on the counter so I can avoid bad karma, or so I won't writhe and sizzle in the flames of hell?"

"You didn't even look around in there when you made that move. I could have been security."

She begins walking to her car, but at a pace that doesn't discourage conversation, so Wave walks along beside her. "I would have known. I would have felt it."

"You believe only in things you can feel? I like that."

"I happen not to care what you like. What's the deal," she says, glancing over at Wave's camera, "with the toy?"

"You," Wave says, fixing her in the viewfinder. "You're the deal. There's no one like you. No one anywhere. Not anywhere in the entirety of this great, lonely universe. No one who stands like you, walks like you, thinks like you, sleeps like you, laughs or cries like you." He lifts his gaze from the viewfinder and his eyes enclose her. "You live in a different world, a totally different dimension. You don't look around when you shoplift because you like to play the intuition game. When you do, you're rarely wrong. I know because I play that game myself. You're like a car with faith for fuel. That's what you run on. Not faith in god. Faith in yourself. You're your own god. You never eat breakfast, you don't have a favorite color but if you had to say something, you'd say red. You play a musical instrument, flute or violin. You forget to water your house plants and the poor things are always dying on you."

She stops walking and looks directly at him. Her eyes, like transparent ripe gourds, contain the seeds of all the qualities and traits he's just recited for her. He can feel those seeds taking root in the pores of his flesh.

"You didn't say anything about my sleepwalking."

"I don't think you do."

"On the whole, not bad. So what are you supposed to be, some kind of a snake oil merchant? Trying to start your own dial-a-psychic hotline?"

"Neither. It's just that I've learned to look at what I see. There's a point where what I look at looks right back at me, and at that moment nothing can be hidden. That's why I like this. It never lies," he says, cradling the camera in the palm of his hands.

She extends her hand. She wears rings on the fingers of both hands. "I'm Alexis."

After meeting Alexis and knowing her for a time, the focus chronically absent from his life suddenly informs his every action.

They discuss the idea, the kidnapping. They've had several such discussions in the past week. This particular discussion takes place on the flat rooftop of the university's main administrative building, many floors above city. They are alone but speak in hushed tones that barely rise above the mellow stutter of the rain starting to fall. Looking down, the city at night resembles a circuit board, a grid of micro-activity threaded with tiny blinking dots of multicolored light. Like some mechanism, digitally ablaze, torn violently from the interior of a computer's central processing unit. Alexis had the keys to the utility room, which gives access to the rooftop. She is a faculty member here, an associate professor of English hired to teach advanced composition. Instead, her classes consist of furious and arcane expostulations on the futility and insufficiency of language.

"I want nothing more," Alexis says, hoisting herself up onto the two-foot-wide ledge of the building and looking down the sheer plunge to the street below, "than to become a vagina. At least, at this point in my life. Academia has numbed me from the waist down. Sad but true. I need a remedy. It's time to make that skin flick you keep talking about. Maybe I'd give up all the shoplifting."

"You're sure about this?" Wave asks. "Penises of all shapes and sizes plundering your treasure trove? Engaging in loveless acts of sex with strangers?"

"The thing is, what about you?" she counters. "You say that you'll suffer no damage to your masculine ego, that possessiveness and jealousy and so on aren't issues for you. But given your level of sophistication, that assertion is pretty predictable. The question is, what will you actually *feel*?"

"Shattered, at first. Then maybe turned on."

"And what about the kidnapping? Are you ready for that, too? Given the identity of the kidnapped? Baby, I'm sorry, I don't think you're ready. You're still trying to think your way through this shit. But if we pull it off like *this*. . . ." As if to illustrate she jumps onto the narrow ledge of the enclosing wall and stands with her arms outstretched for balance. Wave is watching through the viewfinder and sees that her eyes are closed. Arms extended, she begins moving along the ledge in heel-to-toe fashion toward the corner of the building, a few feet away. She neither stumbles nor sways, moving forward with the slow implacability of a glacier. When she reaches the edge, she pivots smoothly left without hesitation, places her left foot squarely on the intersecting ledge, and continues walking. She opens her eyes. "See what I mean?" she says.

"I'm ready," he says. Given the identity of the kidnap victim, he's as ready as he can be.

Wave is as ready as he can be, given the fact that Mr. Otto Alexander Davis is quite an influential figure not only at the university, but on the local political scene as well, although he prefers to maintain a low profile. As an independent consultant in the field of image management, for example, his cunning reconstruction of white Republican Alan Specks' formerly drab public persona resulted in the election of Mr. Specks to the mayor's seat. Trailing slightly in the polls behind the incumbent, Mr. Specks was able to edge his way to victory by attracting a small but significant percentage of black voters who had seen, and responded positively to, the anti–affirmative action commercial conceived by Mr. Davis in which Specks had appeared, lifting a black infant in both hands (though there was some speculation as to whether the infant was, in fact, biracial) triumphantly over his head toward a sky kaleidoscopic with stars, while the announcer's voice intoned sonorously "Michael Jordan, Sammy Davis Jr., or Colin Powell didn't need affirmative action—who among us would dare imply that *this* child is incapable of rising, on his own, to even higher levels of greatness?!" For his conceptually audacious handiwork Mr. Davis, a Republican himself, became the target of criticism from black leaders and voters who claimed that the interests of the Republican Party and those of the black community were as a whole incompatible. When criticized by these hostile factions for his orchestration of the commercial, Mr. Davis, in a newspaper article, was quoted only as saying, "Frankly, I am truly dumbfounded."

Wave knows these things and has recorded them in a notebook:

- Mr. Davis enjoys Thai food, for the reasons that it is "Generally inexpensive, yet substantial enough, and rescues the palate from, as the poet said, the malady of the quotidian."
- Mr. Davis frequently dreams of falling, his body jerking alarmingly as he plunges from some awful height in the dream.
- Mr. Davis finds it impossible to resist his habit of returning two or sometimes three times to his parked car after

he has left it on the street, simply to ensure that the alarm is truly engaged.

- Mr. Davis has a tendency to respond to certain questions with the remark, "I don't know what you're talking about. Don't be ridiculous."

Alexis wants Wave to elaborate on the last point, and Wave uses this example: an eight-year-old child whose name just happens to be Wave is visiting his grandparents in Rockwell City, Iowa. There, the child spends his days more or less pleasantly, if uneventfully, his experiences a porridge of rural sights, sounds, smells stirred lazily together by the sun's sweltering hand. One day his father drives the child to the public swimming pool downtown, called—mysteriously, to the child—a "natatorium." The father then leaves, promising to return in approximately two hours. Attired in bright red swimming trunks, the seven-year-old child stands self-consciously and at something of a loss on the lip of the pool, blinking into the spectral blue water at a group of children of varying ages, splashing and yelling. A group of about five children climbs out of the pool and stands around the lone child, whispering in low tones among themselves at first, then becoming alarmingly bolder. Finally one boy points and exclaims loudly, "Look, a nigger!" (Eight hundred people reside in the town of Rockwell City, Iowa—all white, except for the child's grandparents.) Not knowing the word "nigger," the child has a sudden full awareness of something that had previously danced, in an ill-coordinated fashion, as though on an icy floor, across the surface of his mind: that the entire town, with its meager population of eight hundred, was filled with people who in some fundamental way looked nothing like his grandparents, or his father or mother, or him. And, of course, this had something to do with the designation "nigger," now hanging vividly in the afternoon's heat and sudden stillness. One blonde girl, older than the rest, probably fourteen, steps forward toward the tittering group, and says, "He's human, too." Sadly, this remark increases the child's sense of acute isolation and shattering embarrassment, when it was only meant to effect moral edification.

The child's father picks him up in more or less two hours, as promised, and on the way home, the boy asks him, "Dad, what's a nigger?" His father stares unblinkingly forward while driving, and after a long deliberation, answers, "I don't know what you're talking about. Don't ask me ridiculous questions."

"Imagine this child," Wave says to Alexis. "The resentment he feels for this man who not only didn't explain the way things were so that the kid wouldn't go stumbling out in the world unprepared for what he'd find, but then totally denied the validity of the kid's experience by saying 'I don't know what you're talking about.'"

"Maybe what he meant to say was that he refused to invest the whole concept of 'nigger' with any validity and that it was ridiculous to act as though it had any reality. So the only legitimate response he could have was a nonresponse."

"Bullshit."

She may be right, but Wave doesn't want to feel ambivalence regarding the kidnapping. He wants to proceed coolly, calmly, as though Mr. Otto Alexander Davis was not his father at all but merely a means to an end.

Wave checks his wristwatch and skulks in the shadows near a dumpster in the parking lot. His father, who since Wave's mother's death always dines alone, leaves his favorite Thai restaurant located one block from the university and is now heading toward his car in the lot where Wave waits. From the back door of the restaurant and across the lot to the car: two minutes.

They leave nothing to chance. How crowded will the streets be when his father leaves the university? In these fairly early evening hours, the sky overhead spreads its deep russet blanket of winter, suggestive of hibernation, ennui, sleep. No students enliven the streets as Wave and Alexis near the restaurant. His hand twitches for the video camera, but Alexis, walking behind him, is carrying it. "Think of the camera you're entrusted with as a precious navigational tool. Think of Sulu at the helm of the U.S.S. Enterprise on *Star Trek*." Did he actually admonish Alexis with this analogy moments ago, or has he only imagined it? And if he has not said it, should he?

To prepare for the kidnapping, Wave exercises his employee discount at Blockbuster and brings home, for instructional purposes, dozens of videos where the commission of intricate crimes sweep the plots along on a rollercoaster of violence, mayhem, bloodshed. He and Alexis watch them through the weekend, discovering a mind-boggling array of techniques surrounding the crime of abduction. Wave is particularly interested in the crucial moments after the victim is accosted, when the sheer physicality of the abduction becomes most problematical. Should the victim be punched in the spleen, kicked in the groin, shepherded with a cattle prod, lashed with a cat-o'-nine-tails, reasonably persuaded, laughed at, shot in the kneecap, tickled under the armpits, slapped in the face, slyly cajoled? A burlap sack tossed over the head, and then forceful jostling until the victim finds himself in the trunk of the Ford Mustang that will be parked nearby, is settled upon.

Shadows have the effect of dematerializing the deserted parking lot. Wave attempts to toss the burlap sack over his father's head. As though endowed with some finely tuned sixth sense for danger, his father whirls around, sees the sack descending, steps lightly, almost jauntily, to the side. Wave is jarred off balance and stumbles to the ground, falling on his side heavily. Alexis stops taping and sprints to the waiting Mustang, burning rubber as she exits the lot in screeching haste. His father spends a few moments straightening his tie, needlessly it seems to Wave, for the tie appears to have escaped any dishevelment that might have been caused by the brief commotion. He looks down at Wave pityingly. "You should be ashamed of yourself, Wave. I know you blame me for not teaching you certain ugly social realities, for instance, that America for the most part will always see you as an outsider and that you might, from time to time, hear the so-called N-word, on the milder end of the spectrum. It's true that on the harsher end of the spectrum, there might be certain unfortunate and dangerous circumstances in which you could be beaten, spat upon, tarred and feathered, lynched, dragged through the streets with your wrists affixed by a rope to the bumper of a car or truck—but I was only trying to protect you." Wave begins to weep in shame. No, wait.

Shadows have the effect of dematerializing the deserted parking lot. Wave tosses the burlap sack over his father's head. Alexis stands off to the side, taping while Wave maneuvers his father, stumbling and careening like a drunken man, toward the car, the engine already humming and the trunk open. His father drops the doggie bag of Pad Thai he was carrying on the ground. When he begins to scream, Wave is violently startled, never having heard his father, in particular, or any man, in general, screaming in stark, unmitigated terror. Wave reaches under the burlap hood and tightly cups over his father's mouth and nose a cloth copious with ether. His body goes limp and Wave scoops him off the ground and staggers to the car. As though nodding in assent, the car bounces when Wave tosses his father's body into the trunk. He closes the trunk with trembling hands. Alexis jams the camera in her purse and runs over to Wave, grabbing his hands. "Jesus, baby, take it easy. You're shaking like a proverbial leaf." They get in the car. After a moment, Wave gets out of the car, runs a few steps back to the bag of pad thai, picks it up, then runs back to the car. When they pull out of the lot, Alexis burns rubber, although the streets are almost forlornly empty.

His father sits slumped in a chair. His ankles are bound to the legs of the chair, his wrists bound behind him, his eyes blindfolded. He has been told that he is being held for $50,000 ransom in an abandoned warehouse on the outskirts of the city. In fact, they are in the living room of Alexis' sprawling, frenetically disarrayed apartment.

"We want you to contact someone who can get the money to us. We know you have a family—or, at the very least, a son." Wave's voice is electronically distorted, rendered unrecognizable by a signal-processing device strapped to his throat. "We've done our research."

"I don't have money like that on hand," the father says in a fearful tone.

"Don't lie to us," Wave accuses with appropriate harshness. "You've been under surveillance for quite some time. We know you have a safe in the house where you keep a substantial amount of cash, bonds, jewelry, pornography, and so on."

"Please," the father says weakly. "Please."

"You know, Mr. Davis, that pornography provides a conduit for the expression of psychic or unconscious content, in the form of fantasy components that would otherwise remain dangerously occluded," says Alexis, also speaking through an electronic distortion device as she gazes through the viewfinder.

"We've contacted your slacker of a son," Wave says, winking at Alexis. "We want you to talk to him. Tell him we want $50,000 cash from the safe. Give him the combination. We'll arrange a trade with him, pick up the money, and drop you off. You won't be hurt unless something unexpected happens."

Alexis places the phone to the father's ear. Wave leaves the living room and now speaks to his father without the device from an extension phone in Alexis' bedroom.

"Wave? They've got me."

"Who?" Wave asks. "What are you talking about?"

"I believe I'm being held by a black extremist group trying to fund their subversive activities."

"Black extremist groups? That was a sixties thing, wasn't it? Weren't they all killed off?"

"Don't argue with me, Wave," the father says heatedly. "I don't have enemies among white people. It's only my own people who have been jealous of my status in the community at large. They and only they have tried to undermine me over the years, reduce me to a position of ridicule and scorn, accusing me endlessly of Uncle Tommery and so on."

"Look, whoever these people are, how much do they want?"

"Fifty thousand dollars in cash."

"So give it to them. It's a small price to pay for your life."

"Wave? I just want you to know that if anything should happen to me—no matter what people may say, I've always done my best."

"That's enough with the true confessions," Alexis says, hanging up the phone. She kisses the hostage lightly on the forehead, apropos of nothing. "It's time to do this thing, Mr. Davis."

The huge tri-level house where Wave's father lives is immaculate, a test tube into which efficiency, organization, and orderliness have been poured in equal measures. The cold sheet of daunting sterility draped over Wave's childhood floats over him again as he kneels before the safe in the bedroom closet, spinning through the combination. His father sits on the edge of the bed, his head bowed dejectedly under the hood of burlap. Alexis stands by, watching through the viewfinder, taping. As his father finishes giving the last number, he begins coughing and sputtering dangerously, as though choking.

"Pull yourself together, you old bastard," Wave barks in his harshly electronic voice. "I want that last number."

"Where is Wave? You said he'd be here." His father sits stiffly on the edge of his bed. Though he had complained that the restraints were too tight on his wrists, Wave hadn't removed them. "I can't breathe," he says, gasping. Alexis is holding him by the shoulders but he begins writhing violently. Suddenly he slumps and falls back on the bed. She puts her ear to his chest, then lifts his hood. There is a frothy bud of saliva sprouting from the corner of his mouth.

"What the hell are you doing? Leave his hood down!"

"Damn, Wave," she says slowly. "I'm not sure, but I think he's had a heart attack or something."

An attorney sitting behind an oak desk reads the last will and testament to Wave, who leans forward in his seat slightly as he listens. Along with the contents of the safe, which amount to $48,560 in cash, Wave inherits real estate, investments in municipal bonds and T-bills, stock and stock options, mutual funds, and miscellaneous assets totaling $979,000.76.

Alexis wears a pair of reading glasses that lends to her flawless nudity a scholarly aura. She stands before a blackboard scribbling what appear to be complex mathematical equations with her back to the camera. Glasses, black high heels, a piece of chalk are her "wardrobe." Four burly males, also naked except for the football helmets they wear on their heads, sit at desks positioned in a row near the blackboard. A fifth male, naked also, wears a dunce's cap rather than a helmet. Two men holding hand-held cameras are positioned strategically to capture and create propitious angles. Wave sits in a director's chair with a clipboard on his lap, discussing the scene with a woman who, with an air of frazzled concentration, thumbs through a sheaf of coffee-stained papers. After shooting *The Naughty Professor,* Wave has plans to use the footage of his father's kidnapping to complete a documentary illustrating the poignant, "real life" ordeal of an innocent hostage. Footage which, Wave explained, had been inadvertently left behind by the abductors and which provided a kind of heart-rending documentation of his father's last hours. Wave's official statement to the police and the press was that he had attempted to telephone his father over the course of the weekend, became concerned when his calls went unanswered, and finally forced entry into the house along with Alexis to determine whether the elderly man had slipped and fallen in the tub, or perhaps taken a spill down the stairs. At this point he found his father's body, along with the tape. "This is a black man," Wave explained, "who was perhaps misunderstood because of the political stances he took which were not in vogue, but who was morally earnest, and I would hope that he will be appreciated and missed by the community he so selflessly served for most of the years of his adult life."

"Wave," Alexis says petulantly, without turning around, holding the chalk as though she's writing on the board, "it's cold in this damned room."

"Of course. Slate. *Action*," he cries sharply, and because this is a word that he has longed to utter in just this fashion from the earliest days of his childhood, chills spill down his spine.

My Father's Penis

Unsettling exclamations spill from lips of neighbors, their mouths welling with rancor and affection as they reminisce over my father and his penis: What an angel of rapacity, what a demon of purity that man was!

ooooo

They gather together and light bonfires of primal gossip hotter than flames, tongues ignited with stories about my father, filling the air with the laughter of morbid speculation. Until I arrive with my comic seltzer bottles filled with water, the water of my animus, spraying them with shushing rebukes that break up their huddled clusters on my brittle lawn. As they leave, I rail at their scandal mongering but they ignore me, leaning into haughtiness as into canes. They take their time, departing in canoes of shadow, moving into the apricot light of this fading Monday, paddling away slowly.

ooooo

Valeriana, one of my father's former lovers, walks up the path, approaching with slow and heavy prominence as I sit on the porch of my father's condemned and penis-haunted house. "You need to go in there and clean out your father's house, but you're not ready," she'll say when she decides to speak. She meanders me down long avenues of regret, she maketh me lie down in pastures of languor. She explains, pitying me as though I were a ragamuffin child instead of a man of thirty-eight, that all my sighs and regrets are nothing but an evasion. I won't understand but I'll be content to drink the wistful wine of her words. I'll choke and sputter as I gulp, lips gaping like those of fish choking on the silent thunder of oxygen. Shrouded as I am in my own Freudian dramas, I sometimes forget that it hasn't been easy for Valeriana. Listening to the diabolical speculations of neighbors has added to her gravity-clawed face an overlay of memories as of weary widowlike lace. As with any war-roughened general, her eyes are hard as scars, and she bears upon her breast the silver medals of her battles, my father's campaign of casual atrocities.

ooooo

Valeriana tells me about my father's penis because I want to know. Every man should know whatever it is possible to fathom regarding the regal penis of the father, and in particular every black man. Little lambs of that legacy await slaughter by revelation, decapitation delivered with the guillotine of steely aperçus. And what she tells me is never enough; I need to know more, always more. I cajole her with my eyes, they swell with rivers of solicitation. I enjoin, insist, but she recoils from the fangs of a craving anticipation that slices my smile carnivorous. If I threaten her with violence, she simply absorbs and releases it, the boomerang of my vehemence bouncing back in my face. Remembering she is a woman, I soften my approach, release the golden pollen of my wishes, dust her yellow with a passivity of whispers, and she unpremeditatively succumbs, a sudden soft and girlish incarnation of her seventy-seven-year-old self, relenting, mellowing into silky coquetries of memory that parade like strippers on my starstruck stage.

ooooo

"Your father's penis," she says, "was a memorable contraption. It was as the mist, as the wave crested with spume, as the drum, pounding with rhythmic officiousness. An officer's baton, enforcing injunctions of passion, a monolith of expanding membranes, a wire ripping through my melting insulation, a thing slender as a greyhound's ribcage, and more. It was a newborn kitten mewing for milk of feline teat, it was a pendulum swinging in all directions, a compass with eighteen cardinal points, it was a telephone that rang and when answered delivered a voice apologizing through static for having called the wrong number. But whatever it was, it was never a key, the latches to my deepest chambers were bolted fast. If yours is an odyssey of emulation, you'd do well to remember that. It was also an instrument, a dither that laid songs of malaise in strips like black masking tape across my cinnamon wounds. It was, primarily, his cage, his incarceration, his dead man walking, but this he never realized or cared to know—blissful ignorance!" Valeriana's words taper to cessation. She then asks to see my own penis and as my fingers flutter the zipper down, the sensation of shrinking that skates through the ice rink in my stomach communicates itself in blades of embarrassment lacerating my loins. She extracts it, a pitiful thing, a mere son's penis, and from a purse the size of a small bush she removes a magnifying glass and tweezers, Playtex rubber gloves like mockeries of condoms. Latex snaps with snug finality against her wrists after flexing over fingers. A brief distasteful examination commences. I know already that the comparison will be comical, inauspicious. "I see traces of similarities," she announces with diagnostic crispness, "in the scroll of flesh surrounding the hood like a little girl's rolled up sock, but there it ends, all else is overshadowed by insufficiency and woe." Though I know better, I ask her what recourse I have to supplemental bulk, girth, and beefiness. "Take two aspirin," she answers, "and call me in the morning—or measure your manhood in other ways."

ooooo

Well-spoken and resonant like an orchestra populated with French horns of wisdom, piccolos of prudence, cellos of logic, but more difficult done than said, for every boy-man knows in the deepest catacombs of his descending heart that other ways of measuring his manhood are travesties of quantification that would not be necessary in the first place had the son been gifted with the regal endowments of the father. All manner of gambits and strategies have been pitifully adopted by the son as substitution for monumental flesh: decadent exercises in overcompensation, such as the acquisition of advanced degrees, the cultivation of aesthetic sensibility, various ruses of compassion (e.g., head cocked slightly and ear tilted mouthward in a mimicry of empathy and listening as one woman after another, potential paramours, divided their well-glossed lips with wounding words). All these trappings would prove to be the outwardly convincing gestures of an elaborate puppetry, excellent facilitators of relationships with the daughters of other regal fathers, but ultimately useless. For these could hardly compare with the legitimate exigencies contributing to the yardstick against which manhood was rightfully measured in my father's heyday. Those were the days when my father served the troops of offspring and wife the hardy soup of his mentorship as they stood in a regimental line holding shallow bowls, humbly awaiting the more substantial second course, the bloody scraps of his tutelage, the gristle and sinews of the world's flank he sank his teeth deep into, bit off, chewed, then regurgitated selflessly into our plates. We saw little bits and pieces of white people floating there, for example the hands of job interviewers he twisted off at the wrist because he read in their eyes refusal, rejection, janitorial assignments. And the eyes in which he read silent smug superiority, those were far from tasty morsels, rubbery as calamari, difficult to swallow as splintered squares. The father examined my stool to ascertain that the meal had indeed been swallowed, digested, not squirreled away into the pouch of the cheek to be disposed of later. No chicanery of ingestion would be tolerated in his domain. He was the warrior king at battle in the arena of the wide wrong world, the black Ulysses returning to the encampment of family with tales of brutality endured, of traps and snares narrowly avoided, of the swarthy nightsticks of porcine policemen dexterously dodged, of Wild Turkey-fueled flames of KKK crosses he extinguished with the fire hose of the penis when sources of water officially sanctioned were mysteriously withdrawn and made unavailable by the off-gazing officials of Pentecostal hamlets. Striding with gigantic steps to match those of Martin Luther King Jr., the father marched next to the exemplary Father of the Civil Rights Movement through the sweltering streets of Selma, Alabama, and once, skulking among a copse of dogwood trees that composed a tableaux of static dread and banked the slumping waters of the Mississippi River, the father slid snakelike through the imperiled night to act in accordance with common decency and cut the rope from which a mob-bludgeoned black man dangled at the end of a noose. By these stories—apocryphal, so say some neighbors who claim to have known him well—an appropriate awe, respect, and fear of the father were induced. The boy-man yearned to be tested by similar Homeric trials but by the time adulthood enveloped him like a monk's hood and cast its shadow across his face the world had changed, paradigms had shifted, the vulva of American consciousness was in the process of expanding to accommodate a new, a spasmodic, a laborious birth. Once it came about that the boy-man took his place at the checkout line in Target and was told by an older white gentleman "you people are so pushy"—this incident could hardly compare with the epic exploits of the father. It must be noted that he, me, the son of the regal father, was with a group of six other raucous male youths, youths sprinkled in a spice of various races over the disapproval that turned on the slow rotisserie of elders dripping the simmering juices of their censure, youths who, each in his own way, perhaps hoped to plumb the mysteries of his own father's penis.

ooooo

Valeriana leaves, retreating into the fog left by her words, and a neighbor named Crystal Mary, unlike the other neighbors in deportment and lacking in cruelty, glides swift up the walkway, moving like a reverie of gazelles let loose in a bed of reverent flowers. She'll spill her pillowy anecdotes before me so that I might recline a moment, relinquish my posture of bitter expectations. For I've grappled so long with immensities while reclining with only superficial comfort on the sofa of my quests and disasters. In her approach she nimbly avoids the holes I have dug in the ground with the red toy shovel I unearthed from the mausoleum of my cobwebbed childhood, that trunk of memorabilia my mother had long ago relegated to the attic of this house. Yes, Crystal Mary dances around the holes I have dug in the futile search for my father's penis. The autopsy report I had received some time ago documenting his death stated that the penis was mysteriously missing from the body at his time of demise. These holes now mumble dark reproaches, for I have not found the buried treasure I foolishly thought I might exhume from the unforgiving earth. "The neighbors are watching," Crystal Mary tells me now in a racing whisper, "watching now as always, watching you, just as they watched when he was alive and would stumble up this ruined flagstone path in the middle of the night, holding the hand of some woman of ill repute. The two would finally reach this porch, clutching each other to stay upright as they waited for their carousal of drunkenness to slow to a manageable whirl. Then they dove into one another off the high diving board of lust, swam in mingled spittle and sweat, the gong of their moans alerting those who weren't already watching with faces sticking to ardent panes of glass like press-on stickers. With his thick fingers and shrill teeth he would knead her flesh into a sculpture of lewd contort, his lips consuming in oblivious haste the gourmet feast of her happy nipples, then with his penis, so like a skyscraper ripping the belly from the bottom of the moon, he would begin his high-storied plunge, while her legs yawned in earthquakes of accommodation. Neighbors with entrepreneurial aspirations would rope off an area around the porch, set up booths as though selling homemade lemonade, break out folding chairs, attempt to sell tickets to passersby from other sunless neighborhoods. To this very day he has his defenders and detractors, your father. There are those who contend that as a black man he was a disgrace, nourishing stereotypes of the insatiable Mandingo buck, the savage primate from the jungle who had, through his indiscriminate appetites, almost single-handedly ushered the world into the epoch of AIDS. Then there are others who claimed he was a visionary, foreshadowing in three dimensions the national obsession with one-dimensional cathodic sex that the makers of HBO movies would ray into voyeuristic living rooms and from which they would build the vast empires of inexhaustible commercial success. Still others insist he bore an uncanny resemblance to Marcus Garvey, Frederick Douglass, even as some maintain with equal intensity that he was the spitting image of O.J. Simpson, Stephen Fetchit." I ask Crystal Mary, "All that speculation, spawned by my father's penis?" And she answers, "Oh, yes," eyes gliding from mine like words in a sentence with no period to wall the rush, "as a black man, his penis was very much the subject of widespread speculation." As if to illustrate this, she produces a popular tabloid publication, with cartoon representations of barbaric penises above tawdry captions: government studies black cons, findings suggest length linked to hard time, recidivism, and so forth, so on, so forth.

ooooo

I had a wife whose name now eludes me and who told me that in the beginning, before the sweet locomotive onrush of our courtship, before the subsequent derailment of our marriage, she would watch through the timorous peephole of her apartment door as I entered my own apartment across the hall, my hands dripping with the honey of respectable purchases from the hives of mammoth malls: shaggy ferns to exhale green solace into the jagged air of the cube I lived in, bags brimming with sensible vegetables inimical to the typical bachelor, a cage that housed a fuzzy ball of hamster I named Sisyphus, bohemian literary journals from Borders suggesting that the buyer was the rare man able to tame the lion of primal philandering with the rarified whip of eclectic intellectual pursuits. For even then I was compelled to prove to myself that I had found avenues that would lead to a kingdom of glory greater than the one established by the regal father's penis. What a poor misguided soul I was! For the man who endeavors to transcend the insuperable influence of his father's penis without confronting it on its own terms, howsoever those terms might be defined, is he not doomed to forever remain the boy-man effete with longing? Ever in search of definitions and in self-fulfillment of prophecy finding them, I failed—and still do where it counts, in the deepest Cyrillic windings of viscera—to understand that defining oneself in relation to what one rejects is to fail to build the myth of an authentic identity. My future wife saw me and her thoughts loosened in a panoramic sweep, drawing her out of the teeming city that was the architecture of nerve-raw loneliness where she had long been quarantined, drawing her toward what she had always imagined in pastel masturbatory fantasies but never encountered: one who wore his man's flesh with outward command but whose little boy's bones were soft and vulnerable beneath the surface, visible to eyes gifted with X-ray discernment. In the brushing of her knuckles across my door was released an illness of noise like a dove seeking the solitude of rotting eaves in which to roost and die. Against the chorus of better judgement singing a cappella in my brain, I let her in; she had come to borrow double-A batteries for what I later discovered was the not-too-large phallic-shaped instrument of pleasure I would find hidden on the rear shelves of her home-entertainment shrine, behind a collection of DVDs she had received as a gift from her mother, episodes of *Julia* that had been aired and taped in the insomnia purgatory of 3:00 a.m. TNT. "Syndication," I said drolly, in reference to the DVDs she proudly displayed to me on our first date, "the media's embodiment and trivialization of Schopenhauer's theory of eternal return, divested of nineteenth-century Europe's lacy dignity." Such remarks endeared me to her, were a safe harbor for her, instances of sandpaper wit thinning the thick slabs of Neanderthal virility, instinct. Oh, there was lovemaking—how could there not be that?—but it was of the tasteful variety, full of restrained etiquette, like one who drinks tea with the little finger protruding from the cup in decorous salute, and our bed was a veritable bunker surrounded with boxes of Kleenex like sandbags, the tissues white flags of surrender to be employed for sop and seizing of smear. The tissues themselves over time became associative visual cues and triggered in the both of us finicky orgasms that allowed us to eschew altogether the annoyances of sticky physical contact. One, two, three—go! Simultaneously, for we were believers in the notion that greater intimacy was to be found when couples were able to achieve their orgasms at precisely the same moment, we each snatched a tissue from the box, shared a platonic shudder. Before that, we had coupled with intent to procreate. For she had announced one night that her womb was hungry for a son as we dined on frog legs at a restaurant called Les Battements du Coeur, an establishment where waiters like gliding mannequins struck falsely obsequious and vaguely hostile poses before taking orders. I smothered the terror in my eyes with half-lowered eyelids, nodded in grim concurrence as she watched me . . . studiously. I could only continue to chew my mechanical food by imagining the tiny body of the boy-to-be as he emerged wet and finless from his aquarium of seaweed membranes and coral-red blood, imagining my hand gripping the crown of his head and screwing it back from whence it had strenuous come. That I should sire a son, who would turn to me for direction and counsel as he hobbled down the shifting cobblestones of manhood; that I should have nothing to tell him about the ways and means and proper utility of the penis, how to befriend it and harness its random power as one without sight lets sighted canine lead him, skirting dangerous serrations of landscape and flesh; that, finally, in the end, in fury and frustration, he might loom over me with his eyes flashing dull blades and hand brandishing one duller for carving off the withered turkey wing of an old man's penis—no, this could not the nightmare be. And as though my very cells had been feast for the insectile mandibles of this bug-eyed anxiety, doctors with stately movements of mouth told us that both motility and sperm count were almost nonexistent in the watery paucity of specimen I thinly labored to collect. I wanted desperately to tell her, as she retracted the anchor of her love from the shallow seas of our domestic charade and, laden with Versace luggage, walked through the door, that she had erred by way of adulteration; that if you straddle the line you cannot cross it; that in the future, as she searched for perfect male and mate, she must embrace the very thing she seemed to fear; for in fears, not dreams, reside your deepest desires: hers the scepter of the penis, regal and upright, heedless, antediluvian, never shrinking from embroilment with the strife and destruction wreaked by other regal penises as they battled to slice the world into fiefdoms, man attached to phallus like incidental afterthought.

ooooo

Suspended so in a marmalade of thought, the objects in my vision glazed orange with that marmalade as though smeared over toast, this township brittle as burnt rye toast, this orange an unnatural tint as though the sun's sinking effluence were digitally engendered, I'm dimly aware that Crystal Mary, who when I seek her company always seems to unleash a delirium of acceleration in my blood, is gone, and long gone at that, I think. Clouds like eraser smudges on parchment of sky are scribbled darkly. Wanton the rain, falling without discipline, as neighbors unfazed by the downpour stride in aimless to and fro, some carrying signs of protest with slogans that declare *Power to the Penis*, others hoisting high above their heads effigies of my father aflame. But none cross the property line, as though all are able to sense that trespassers would be summarily executed by father's son in a trance of nine-millimeter abandon. To my left, though such spatial coordinates seem to me increasingly a mockery as I scramble to discern points of reference and meaning in the search for my father's penis, then—no, why not—to my right, something in a crumpled embrace of disreputable brown paper prompts my hand to purpose. I have always considered the hand to be a mysterious contraption, for the bio-electrical triggers of thought that determine its course for the most part take place below thresholds of awareness, so that without cognizance of the origin of its motion, the hand can only appear to its owner to be a thing observed, and when so observed, seems autonomous and cannot fail to strike the owner as an alien mechanism, ridiculous, grotesque. And so it is, after all, with the penis, that puppet dancing blind on strings. I have never been able to call it my penis; I have never been able to own it, as my father was apparently able to establish ownership of his regal penis. Might that not be a clue to my estrangement in relation to this, the son's hapless penis? After all, it extends from its host like a hand, nothing like the intrinsic and enviable vagina (contradicting that theory of genital envy by the august Father of Modern

Psychology) which harbors its maiden secrets within, like a musical composition that reveals and justifies in the ineluctable coda motifs transparently submerged in preceding movements: organic. Enough. I look in the bag, rather the bag looks into me, and there, here, is a long plastic cylinder sadistic with clamps and hoses, advertised portentously as Doctor Dick's Amazing Penis Pump. No doubt my father, anticipating my quest, has left the device here to mock me.

ooooo

But this comes too late; the son has researched to satiety pump devices purporting desperate miracles of enlargement. Slumbering within its sausage-like encasement of skin, the ever-aspiring penis is a bold conjunction of blood vessels, exquisite threadings of nerves, bundles of fibro-elastic tissue, smooth muscle—a mystic mandala of flesh. A triad of cylindrical bodies of tissue fills with blood like a vampire sponge when and if the temperamental erection is exacted. There is largely an absence of bone, discounting meager skeletal muscle at the base of the protrusion. Some books advocate exercises practiced since times ancient to enrich the penis with greater length, but in reality these exercises are little more than onanistic techniques elevated to the realm of the exotic. Have not such "techniques" been compulsively employed by boy-men the wide world over with no lasting effect on the dimensions of the penis? For example, "Jelq" has been touted as an "Arabian" technique of enlargement: encircling index finger and thumb around the root of the organ, then pulling up or pinching the phallus. So "Jojido," too, is advertised as an exotic technique of Asian provenance. These exercises all are undertaken on the premise that the penis is a muscle similar to the bicep and can be toned and tempered, disciplined into mammoth expansion. Unfortunately, the smooth muscle of the penis cannot be exercised.

It is true that penis pumps may enable those stricken with embarrassing flaccidity to achieve honorable erections, by means of a vacuum which draws blood into the organ as air is pumped out. When a satisfactory erection results, the cylinder may be removed and a rubber tourniquet applied to the base of the penis, retaining the glut of blood without which tumescence and premature ejaculation for boy-men engaging in coitus would not be possible. (The constrictor band should not be kept in place for longer than twenty minutes.) Penis pumps do not permanently increase penis size. To permanently increase the size of the penis to kingly proportions, the quantity of tissue must increase, a phenomenon no amount of vacuuming or manipulation inspired by ancient wisdom can accomplish. Weights to stretch the tunica albuginea, the membrane surrounding the erectile chambers of the penis, have been the subject of much speculation, but results are not encouraging. Surgical enlargement, still in its nascent stages and considered investigational or experimental, involving fat injections and tissue grafts, seems to extend legitimate hope to those with less than regal penises, but these procedures can leave unsightly scars or even result in a lumpy member, since the injected fat is reabsorbed into the body; and snipping ligaments that tether the otherwise unruly penis to the pubic bone often results in an erection that points downward, due to the loss of the organ's anchor to the pubic plate. Nerves can be cut and damaged during surgery as well. All is inefficacy, dashed hopes, unfulfilled expectations in the matter of augmenting penile length. Yet oddly, the American Board of Urology, the only certifying board of urologists in this country of dissatisfied penises, has taken no official stance or issued unequivocal pronouncements on the surgical enhancement of the disillusioned boy-man's best friend.

ooooo

The slow barge of my memory is an empty vessel, buoyed by currents inert as sidewalk saliva, and with only hearsay as river, I navigate toward no shore. It is not possible for me to remember my father's appearance, whether he was tall or short, fat or thin, nor is it possible to recall mannerisms such as a signature way of walking, whether he strode to rhythms of dignity or limped as though lame to metronome of defeat. For my father insisted that when I was in his presence I wear a blindfold, sensing perhaps that I could not be trusted to lower my gaze under humility's gray veil when he granted me audience. His explanation to me was that his own invisible face would force me to imagine in the faces of black men I would see all my life on certain streets terrible possibilities of kinship. Of an evening, as I lay in my child's restless bed and floated like a fly in the soup of my existence, of an evening, watching the idle play of shadows on the ceiling honeycomb my eyes in shimmering imitation of an infinity of avenues, I would struggle to secure the slippery eel of my own interpretation—that perhaps he meant me to understand that he was everyone and no one; that, by extension, I too was related to every man and no man, and going the step further that would no doubt have incurred his wrath had he awareness of that unsteady step, that I might be related to every white man, too, for do not all men, straining muscular thighs, struggle forever to heft upright the heavy barbell of the penis which dares aspire to regality, even into vain old age and death? I do remember the textures yielded by touch, the way he gripped my boy's loose Silly Putty wrist, spreading the fingers wide to grip and measure and test the firmness, the ripe width of the trunk of his loin's tree. I do remember the liquored breath, I do remember the liquored breath, I do remem

ooooo

ber that, and that I thought at the time his choice of intoxicant was odd, the same Wild Turkey I'd been told had been used to fuel the flames of KKK crosses, if indeed there had been KKK crosses, a proposition that some have seemed so eager to introduce by way of elements of doubt, I do

ooooo

what must surely be apocrypha introduced by diabolical neighbors projecting onto the blank screen of the boy-man's father (as though ever he could be blank screen) all the grainy light of evil imaginings, surely that, the wives of husbands seeking to forge an alliance with my mother based on the collective sorrow of women who believe they are made to bear witness to the havoc men wreak with the mighty penis, for in all probability these women, watching from behind the fluttering crack of secrecy afforded by curtained windows, or spying from behind a copse of dogwood trees, would misinterpret the tableaux of the father's regal penis in the grip of the child's hand, an act which was a form of instruction, but the eyes never perceive intent, their eyes suffered in evasion of that noble intent, I do try

ooooo

do not remember my hand made to grip my father's penis as he attempted to, to educate me so that I might experience the transition from flaccidity to unbridled up, so that I might learn to mimic the proper manufacture of sounds with which to inaugurate the end result of that transition, instruction in huffing and puffing as the lungs contracted and expanded, his ragged wheeze, his scratched seventy-eight of breath skipping back beneath the dull needle of arousal as needle labored to escape its gummed groove, as of an evening,

ooooo

or my father darkly aflame, but strangely whatever pleasure of edification the son could have extracted from instruction reversed itself, ran like film backward in the maze of the father's sudden commandments. For of an evening that seemed not to take place outside the head, but inside where memory like wild game may be slaughtered and gutted, the son beneath his fingertips felt the fretwork of penile veins standing out like the color red against a backdrop decorated in blue decay, just as the Spartan interior of our house was decorated by my mother, modifed to reflect the house inside her, but I do not speak of the mother, I do not have affinity for the mother, for this is my and my father's saga, this is the saga of that most arduous quest to

ooooo

my father sliding snakelike through the imperiled night, nor remember the failed-marriage eyes of my former wife, and certainly not the female eyes of neighbors, who probably bore witness to nothing more than Jelq, than Jojido, and could not be expected to morph empathic, or to understand that this was instruction and nothing more, the instruction of augmentation. The penis pump of my little boy's palm was slick and slow as though webbed indeed with an elaborate dew. Enough.

ooooo

Or if not father, then uncle, or grandfather, or third cousin who would later die alone of AIDS, the Father of All Diseases, in a library-quiet hospice, or the male babysitter, something of a local hero for his displays of athletic prowess that reduced gravity to groveling slave on sweat-glossed floors of high-school basketball courts. Or the baker, the postman, the priest. Enough.

ooooo

Lysergia arriving, the youngest of those who were both neighbor and concubine to my father, is so colorful in her calliope of garments. Her delirium of hair tumbles down her shoulders in a cacophony of dreadlocks, each appendage dyed a different color, as though the bands of a rainbow have been peeled from their archway and laid across her head. Never one to waste words, Lysergia moves straight to the point, though my attention span is fraying like a madman's cape. "Enough," she says, "I have a gift for you from your mother who, like one who works for the darkest branches of government, is in deep cover for her crime, hiding in a foreign country. In this box is your father's penis, severed and preserved, it's what you've been looking for all these years." The shape and size of the box cannot be discerned beneath the checkered cloth draped over it. It is checkered, I surmise, in a display of parsimonious symbolism meant to suggest the high and low exploits of my father. Standing on the uppermost stair of this porch, a shipwreck of sagging wooden planks and posts, she extends the parcel with both hands, but when I reach for it I'm forced to rise, stumble forward, for she takes a step backward, smiling, pulling box to breast. Again she falsely extends the parcel, as though offering me a gourd filled with my own thirst, and again I reach, again she pulls back. Nearby, neighbors stand like infants presiding over sand in a sandbox. Some cheer and others cry out in soundtrack horror as Lysergia opens the door and, stepping backward into the darkness of my father's penis-haunted house, teasing and tempting my flailing fingertips, draws me deep incrementally in.

The Serial Killer Museum

The Serial Killer's right foot measures, from rough heel to spatulate tip of big toe, ten inches. If the protrusion of a bunion is included in the measurement, the length of the foot may be recorded as ten and one-eighth inches.

The bunion had entered the orbit of the Serial Killer's attention at the age of twenty-two in the diffuse way that all such changes engineered by the body usually intrude upon awareness—so gradually they seem to appear suddenly, overnight.

Vigorous debates reveal that opinions divide equally into two camps: those who affirm that the bunion is intrinsic to the foot and can no more be viewed as failing to contribute to the whole than a mole can be discounted when considering factors that contribute to the overall beauty of a woman's face; and those who believe the bunion to be an assault on the flesh, marring what would otherwise be the perfection of an inviolate specimen. The Serial Killer, in the open and gregarious manner that the public has come to expect in the stark surge of his responses, straddles the line on this issue, cannot honestly align himself with either point of view, can only offer to an audience of worldwide connoisseurs leitmotifs from the symphony of emotional dissonance playing in heart and head.

"Maybe the bunion is integral, m-m-maybe it's not. On the one hand—or m-m-maybe on the one foot, I should say,"—listeners' or readers' or viewers' appreciative laughter for wit that sandpaper years of captivity have not completely shaved thin—"the bunion is a bother, especially when it seems to sort of flare up at night, it's just one more thing for me to deal with, and I can see how there are those who think it's not a part of me, per se. Then again, the bunion is how it all began. When I first noticed it, I was reminded of a mole. Not the kind of mole you'd find on an old person's chin, unsightly, vaguely evil, vaguely East European, covered with tiny hairs. I've always been a bit of a dreamer, m-m-maybe have a bit of an overactive mind. At any rate, at the time, Madonna—who, I think we would all agree, was quite something, a vamp and a vixen, a fiery slut when you come right down to it, my apologies, M, for telling it like it is—Madonna was really popular, and I was fascinated by her. She's not what I would call beautiful, but I became fixated on the mole, the mole just eclipsed everything else, day in, day out, I couldn't stop picturing the thing, what it would feel like between my fingers or on the tip of my tongue; I had to have that mole, and, of course, you can't get anywhere near Madonna, though believe me, I tried. I did get close once, she was on a world tour and it was in Australia, where I had gone to see her. She pulled up to the venue in a black limousine and was getting out, somehow I had fought my way through the crowd, and I had a scalpel I intended to use for the slicing off of the mole, but it was hidden in the pocket of the army jacket I was wearing; after all, even I knew, despite the voices in my head telling me the scalpel was invisible, you can't walk up to Madonna with a scalpel in your hand, not even an invisible one, without calling attention to yourself.

So I approached with a piece of paper such as an autograph seeker would have in his possession, and m-m-maybe I didn't look right, or rather normal, or m-m-maybe too normal, because one of the bodyguards—of course she was surrounded by them—saw me walking up and reaching out with the paper, the pen, and the guy, this big bald-headed bastard, in a completely unnecessary display of brute force, punched me in the face. My face, it was incredible, I could feel it deflating like a tire with the impact. I would expect that sort of thing from that other guy, Sean Penn, but this guy was supposed to be a professional, and here I am just a member of the public, just a fan, for all he knew I could have really just been after an autograph, the fat bastard. Furthermore I think he had something in his hand when he hit me, because my jaw was unhinged, the blow . . . m-m-maybe brass knuckles, the blow was such that I lost consciousness. So Madonna's mole was an impossibility, and still, I had to have the mole, only now, it was any mole.

And the rest, well, sadly, we all know the rest, so in a way if not for the bunion, there would be no mole, no rampage of mole-seeking and mole-acquiring acts, and no opportunity for the world to know what drives a person like me beyond the line that separates darkness from light, no opportunity to know and learn or understand how it's possible for one person to go so far astray."

The Serial Killer's highly organized and methodical approach to scheduling daily activities might have frayed to failure without the Wirebound FranklinCovey Executive Planner seen on pedestal above right with simulated leather wallet featuring pen loop, interior pockets, and high quality cream-colored paper with a page size of 3¼" x 6½", item #23453, available at a cost of $19.95 and small enough to fit neatly in shirt pocket.

The binder's cover, originally dove-white, had been plucked off by the Serial Killer on December 24th, 2001, at 12:02 a.m., when a corpuscular snowfall consumed the viral darkness overspreading the city, and his eyes, stitching around a single flake's intricate lace with the precision of a tailor's needle as he stared out his bedroom window, traced and then transposed that pattern into a transparent finery of thought: the notion to replace the cover with black silk billowed around him.

This substitution of black for white is a matter of lively speculation for those who have found faith and avocation in the arc of the Serial Killer's career. Many believe that the Serial Killer, one of the few black perpetrators in a pantheon still dominated by heterosexual white males in their twenties or thirties according to FBI Behavioral Science Unit profiles, was determined to symbolically fashion a statement whispering with subtle political resonance: That by replacing white with black, he was announcing an intent to add his own not inconsiderable crack to the comparative meager few made by black killers in the glass ceiling of sociopathology, and that while he was at the mercy of succubi inciting him to fornications with havoc, he was not unaware of the role he would play in shattering stereotypes at odds with this enlightened age.

"The binder is very attractive in any color. The flair of the format, with the inserts, the sections with the daily motivational quotes, Weekly Record of Events, the Monthly Task List I made use of for my own disgusting purposes, the Two Page Per Week Weekly Pages, including the removable address/phone pages . . . really, the people at FranklinCovey have done an exceptional job in their line of organizers. And, m-m-maybe if something could ever come of all the damage I've done—which it can't, not really—I would say that the FranklinCovey corporation, by increasing production for many more thousands of units featuring the black cover, and with those proceeds starting the Foundation for the Families of Victims of Unspeakable Crimes, has helped me to pay back society for all the evil I've wrought." The FranklinCovey corporation has, to date, donated $895,000 to the Foundation for the Families of Victims of Unspeakable Crimes.

The Serial Killer's mother's empty bottle of Listerine, featured above.

The decision to display the bottle empty was hammered out by museum curators after discussions with the Listerine corporation's public relations director, in consideration of the pros and cons of filling the bottle with water bearing pale yellow dye to simulate its original contents (original in relation not to the manufacturer but, in a manner of speaking, to the Serial Killer)—11.3 ounces of the Serial Killer's urine.

The problem was not, the director maintained, that the product would be linked in the public's mind with the Serial Killer, whose quest for oral hygiene, after all, was as legitimate as the non-serial-killing population's; indeed, that the product would recommend itself to one living in a lurid fantasy world, piercing the darkness of his storm-swollen mind like a lighthouse beacon, attested to the reality of the product's wholesomeness and the compelling power of brand recognition, masterfully engineered.

Rather, the possibility that the product might become unreasonably linked with whatever distasteful associations urine held for the public were not to be encouraged or condoned. Nevertheless, patrons of the museum, well-educated and effortful, today's patrons and tomorrow's, certainly know the bottle had once contained the Serial Killer's urine and strive to decipher whatever meaning or symbolic import the act of urinating in the mother's Listerine bottle might possibly disclose.

Once again, opinions flourish and fork in diverging branches of contention: Those theorizing that the bottle as receptacle, appropriated by the Serial Killer from his domineering mother, and the positioning of the penis above the bottle's open mouth as though in an act of alignment preparatory to intromission, were elements that combined to limn a subconscious dramatization of Oedipal proportions, demonstrating the Serial Killer's submerged castration rage for his mother and for all women; and those insisting that if the bottle as receptacle symbolized the vagina, reason dictated that there must be a corresponding phallic symbol; and that this symmetry suffered subtraction since the Serial Killer's penis, as he urinated in the bottle, was simply itself—a penis, affording no corresponding symbol for the phallus.

The Serial Killer's response is opaque: "The active ingredients in Listerine are thymol (0.063%), eucalyptol (0.092%), methyl salicylate (0.06%), menthol (.042%). Inactive ingredients are water, alcohol (21.6%), sorbitol solution, flavoring, poloxamer 407, sodium saccharin, benzoic acid, zinc chloride, sodium benzoate, FD&C blue #1." The active ingredient of thymol in Listerine, however, has actually been computed as 0.064%.

A connection between the chemical composition of the Serial Killer's urine and his habit of alternating, every seven seconds, fork from left hand to right, then right to left, in a continuous lateral of juggle and jactitation, while eating his favorite meal of Salsbury steak, mashed potatoes cratered with gravy, and stringed beans, has been proposed by those for whom the bunion is seen to be intrinsic to the length of the foot. Results of urinalysis, seen below, indicate the chemical composition of the Serial Killer's urine on the morning of his arrest as falling within the normal parameters of 95% water, 2.5% urea, 2.5% other. "My mother loved the color black. All of her undergarments were black. M-m-maybe, I don't know, I've often thought that she would have been like one of those insane women who make their male children dress up in mom's panties and bra. I think she sensed I wouldn't go for it, but I always suspected the notion was in her mind."

SERIAL KILLER FACTOIDS, BELOW CENTER

- The Serial Killer believes in the historical reality of Jesus Christ but it is not clear whether he has accepted Him as personal Lord and Savior. Jesus With Children Nightlites are available for $14.95 on the Internet, at www.___.com. An inspirational tableau casting runes of radiance onto the floor of night, a translucent jade porcelain scenario featuring Jesus with children. UL-approved bulb and cord; accidental electrocution of boys and girls highly unlikely. The apparatus 5 1/8" x 4 3/4" x

5 3/4” high. “Keep your lamps trimmed and burning”: Luke 12:35-48.

- The temperature in the town of Y___, where the Serial Killer was born, is currently seventy-four degrees with rising barometric pressure; barometric pressure rises and declines suddenly in Y___, at all times tinting air to tones of the unsettled, indeterminate indigo more commonly seen at twilight; thus the air seems a conduit of temporal dislocation, suggestive of something it is not. An upside down tricycle, all motion kidnapped from unspinning wheels by a criminal absence of wind, is propped on its seat as though sidewalk were rider. Tiny brown birds flock to fountains in long-lawned yards, beaks busy with worms of water. Janice Johnson’s fountain, she of the mole. Darcey Moore’s fountain, she of the mole. Lana Puig’s fountain, she of the mole. Fountains.

- The Serial Killer writes with a blue Bic pen. The four-color retractable Bic ballpoint pen, blue barrel, is available at Staples at the low, low cost of $1.49.

- The Serial Killer enjoys chewing ice. Ice is, in a sense, free.

- The Serial Killer is capable of holding his breath 3.9 minutes.

- The Serial Killer is not ticklish.

Readers (or viewers or listeners) nod thoughtfully before displayed factoids and when chimes chitter to signal that the line must move, move.

It is 4:29, p.m. Above, moles preserved, and scalpels.

Scalpels were the instrument of choice used by the Serial Killer to extirpate the moles, and he had demonstrated a fondness in particular for Ribbel surgical blades, comprised of fine stainless steel and high carbon steel, sterilized by gamma radiation at a minimum dosage of 2.5 Mrads or 25Kgy; sterility guaranteed for five years, as long as packaging remains unbroken. Wheels of icy silver light rolling down the runway of blade and lifting toward the eyes' horizon, the spokes extending and reaching beyond all that the Serial Killer remembered or would ever come to remember, paradoxically recall former and similar saturnine days and times . . . but all this, blade's cutting kiss and smileless slice, the screams and cries of loud-dying flesh, the sing and swirl of sick sensation, the waltz of killer adding victim to serialized blur, the blood like an outmoded carbon copy of previous day's blood—all this has been recorded by the Serial Killer, in his own unyielding hand.

His diary may be seen by backtracking four pedestals left, halt at FranklinCovey Executive Planner.

Serial killers do not obey the rules; they do what they want, having little impulse control; they do what they desire to do, though sources of desire are not transpicuous; the rules dash down to play in the mysterious valleys of the brain's limbic region, skipping through the sprinklers, and are never seen again. The FranklinCovey Executive Planner is not the FranklinCovey Executive Diary, but the Serial Killer has made it so, attaching to it the reins of his own renegade will and breaking the wild stallion of the FranklinCovey Executive Planner—the Planner virtually neighs in its broken state. Some entries have been edited due to violent content, but these passages are not without edification; disappointment is disallowed and is in fact precipitous, for unexpurgated versions are immediately available at www.____.com in exchange for donations, all proceeds allocated to the Foundation for the etc.

"The man with a mole adjacent and below the bottom lip, if such a man exists, I haven't seen him. I have nothing against women. My choices seem to have been made for me, by biological determinants regarding gender and mole placement. My sense of control disappears into the scalpel, is just sucked right in. The last one, by that I mean the very last one in the series—you know which one—pleads with me to take the mole and leave everything else. 'Just take the mole, perhaps that would suffice.' I don't like the suggestion, but she fortifies it with plea and prayer, and told—tells—me she's the mother of three. 'You'd be doing me a favor to take the mole, I never liked it anyway, my boyfriends claimed to like it at first, then, when they had their fill, said it made me look whorish! Take the mole and something else I don't need, a thin strip of fat from the left buttock, which is slightly larger than the right one.' It occurs to me that she's really in no position to bargain, hanging naked by the ankles from the hat tree. I object that the mole is firmly attached to the face. 'Well, I certainly need the face,' she says. I'm not able to tell whether this is an attempt at humor. 'What about the mole and the little toe?' But the little toe is ugly, I tell her. I tell her she doesn't understand the gravity of the situation, and she points wryly at her feet, as though to say, 'I'm upside down, I think I know more than a little about gravity.' I'm silent, for a time. 'Well, you're definitely not an innovator,' she says, and then she surprises me by pulling the race card. 'You select your victims from your own ethnic group. Your methods are a bit passé, don't you think? I read some remarks the other day. They may be of interest to you.' Probably not, but I don't say so, the balance of power, precarious at best in such situations, seems to have subtly shifted. She goes on, 'Philosopher (Objectivist) and author Greg Johnson, and I quote: "Serial killers are not impulsive. They are not stupid. They are not unimaginative. Otherwise, they would never get past their first killing. Therefore, there is a natural tendency for serial killers to be white, because these characteristics are more often found in white criminals end quote."' She goes on, slyly, 'People have called me nigger. Have you never been called that? Have you ever wondered what white folk would do without that word? White writers, for example—novelists and short story writers?' I don't know where she's going with this. 'They use the word cavalierly, in dialogue and exposition. Of course they put the words into their character's mouth because it reveals something about the mind state the character represent. When it appears in exposition—who knows.' If nothing else, I'm patient to a fault. 'Without that word, whole books would be devoid of meaning. *Light in August* would be the condensed Reader's Digest version if you struck that word.' What is the point, I ask? 'You have an opportunity to break the mold. I have feminist leanings and I'm not comfortable saying this—all women are my sisters, after all—but you might better be served by letting me go and replacing me, here on the hat tree, with a non-woman-of-color. Maybe even, god forbid, a man.' And m-m-maybe this would go on for days, I see, if I were brave enough to let it.

But my bravery is in the scalpel, and I stab her several times, starting at the throat and in a line traveling opposite north to navel.

This one is too startled to scream.

Her blood is like the very marrow of sorrow, and I think in the last of her transmarine thoughts she must have seen floating in farewell the faces of her innocent children."

Readers' (or viewers' or listeners') faces coalesce in a vast stadium of reactions—outrage, disgust, morbid fascination, sexual arousal—none of them unpredictable.

Serial Killer Factoids Cont., Below Center

- The Serial Killer's 591 copies of *Light in August* were purchased subsequent to the murder of M____.

- Insects found by the Serial Killer in his home were not crushed and disposed of in the toilet, but herded into paper bags, taken outside, and set free.

- The Serial Killer's favorite meal: Denny's Grand Slam Breakfast, $5.99.

- The Serial Killer's favorite color: baby blue.

A single page from the FranklinCovey Executive Planner, seen immediately right (It is too late to return to the makeshift diary; it is 5:00 p.m. and the museum is closing; the guards, behind the line of people ever moving forward to the next artifact of the Serial Killer's life, move like shushed acolytes in their boxy institutional shoes, collect displayed items from their unshakeable pedestals.) "At a certain point I saw that it was all a big mistake. The moles lost their allure and like beady eyes stared up at me accusingly from the album in which I'd mounted them like butterflies. My childhood was not scarred by violence. My parents had tried to do so much for me. 'These are days and times when a young man of color can aspire to and achieve anything.' He then spoke of holding high offices in the government, and I told him my dream of being elected the first black president of the United States. 'Well, what I meant was, almost anything,' was his comment. Still, it could happen, I thought, never guessing that a young black senator from Illinois would rise from the ranks of relative obscurity, fulfilling my dream and overturning my father's cynicism. I've failed miserably at everything, but dwelling on failure is not a fine thing—you could say I hold a kind of office, have a kind of constituency. M-m-maybe it hasn't all been a waste. I've given what was left of my life, m-m-maybe that's worth something. Because you need to know that we walk the streets right next to you, sit next to you at church, coach your kids in little league, wear clothes from Banana Republic to look like you, bag groceries for you at Vons, use the same words you do to make ourselves understood. And, if it's not inappropriate to quote oneself, you need to know what drives a person like me beyond the line that separates darkness from light . . . to know and learn or understand how it's possible for one person to go so far astray."

This need to know notwithstanding, according to the FBI's Behavioral Science Unit, no universally accepted typology for violent serial offenders exists.

Speck of lint from the Serial Killer's baby-blue carpet; therefore baby-blue lint, below left. Opinions on the lint have yet to be formulated. Tickets are nonrefundable.

Reverse Gender

Yell her name and thoughtlessly toss the duffle bag on the coffee table where junk mail and overdue bills are steepled and strewn across the surface. She will complain about the mess as she has done almost every day of this three-year marriage that relentlessly trembles toward the impasse of irreconcilable differences, like the hand of a drunk man at 3:00 a.m. striving to fit the key in the lock, scratching and scarring the darkness that the niggardly porch light cannot dispel. Do not use the word "niggardly" because it is a transparent husk through which the dark seed in the middle glows with malevolence, threatening to burst into ugly prominence and spread spiky suffocating leaves. Laugh dolefully, bitterly, because it would occur to no one else that, for example, the odious word "kike" would most assuredly never have been inserted into a legitimate synonym for parsimonious called "kikeardly" and been tolerated, neither that nor any other racial epithet. Let this thought whither before it blossoms into a wild garden of hopeless societal indictment. Look at the duffle bag stuffed with comforting accoutrements of masculinity: jock strap in its humid fetal twist, keg-like container of Creatine, Nikes fashioned with NASA bulk and sophistication to crush and flatten gravity in the chunky threads of pounding soles, sweatmooned T-shirt sleeveless to reveal thistle of armpits and accentuate biceps because there is nothing covering them. Consider removing the workout bag as the sort of small but significantly effortful "gesture of accommodation necessary to ensure the longevity of any healthy relationship" that the marriage counselor speaks of in the weekly Friday night sessions. Do not think of the marriage counselor's legs as she crosses them and the gray Anne Klein skirt slides higher to mold thighs voluptuously before her fingers fret the hemline down—a despicable observation given the context of the sessions. Consider therefore removing the bag but instantly erect a Tinker Toy architecture of rationalization, imagining a tiny city where one segment of the citizenry, over the course of three years, has become obsessed with imposing an ever-lengthening list of rules and regulations on another segment of the citizenry, reducing them to compliant automatons, stripping them of independent action and thought. In a trivial act of rebellion, leave the workout bag where it is and wander into the bedroom. Let the current bedroom evoke another bedroom, a ghostly bedroom from boyhood, and then wonder briefly at the cheerless centrality that Tinker Toys occupied in a childhood spent avoiding other kids who scribbled the streets with the chalk of their cruelty, marking off territory until there was nowhere left to run, a childhood spent sequestered in the bedroom to escape their taunts ("proper talkin' sissy"), their always airborne fists. Brood on the fissures this may have left in the foundation of self-image while taking note of the black lacy maze of panties, bra, slip, sheer Hanes nylons left on the bedspread. Fail to see how this is any different from the duffle bag on the coffee table. Sit on the doughy edge of the bed, hear the telephone on the dresser ring, do not answer it but listen as the machine engages with a modest beep: "You home? Guess not. Me and Tricia are gonna stop off at Acapulco's for some salsa and chips, maybe a margarita." Once again, hear the tone beep, this time with something disconsolate and dimly ominous about it. A mere year ago the invitation to join them was always extended, the last word heard in the message was "sweetheart," but that was then and now, now the absence of endearment and invitation nervously fingers some trigger of aloneness and regret, the barrel pointed straight at the chest like a mugger's gun. As though struggling to lift some barbell straddling the heart, make an attempt, rendered feeble with the weight of something like emotional exhaustion, to remove obstacles and find the clean clear space below the causes and origins of so much spite and so many recriminations. Think, don't feel. Dismiss the suspicion that the reasons for this growing estrangement are self-generated, a cataract of neglect that has been allowed to film the eyes, dulling the sight of her, or no, crushing the nugget that initially sparkled in her, the inner diamond allowed to revert to a lump of coal. But mull over how it is impossible to see another person day after day and retain that freshness, the sparkle—just shrug, attribute it to human nature. Do not think, What kind of man have I become? Decide to take a shower—this may, or may not, prove to be therapeutic.

When the doorbell rings, feel solar plexus contract in a knot of anxiety and walk back through the living room slowly, each step a freefall from a high ledge crumbling into air. Jerk the door open.

See no one. See nothing. No visitor, no solicitor, no arrogantly apologetic Dominos delivery boy trying to find the right apartment. Detect neither scent nor subtle displacement of air's volume, which would leave the shimmer of another human being's recent departure. Calculate that this has been happening off and on for a month, and only when Paula is not here. The doorbell ringing. Jerking the door open. There is no sound of children running, no evidence of youngsters playing pranks. No flyers have been left on the welcome mat, no advertisements, no newspaper. Listen to the dreamy tinkling of wind chimes from somewhere, an airy confetti of toy-like tones. Whisper something that has no meaning, an expulsion of vowels and consonants, a phrase unstructured by syntax. As though being watched by eyes that are everywhere, nowhere, stand very still. Say aloud, arms hanging impotently at sides, "Fuck you," but say it softly, without conviction. Do not use the word "impotently" for obvious reasons, especially in conjunction with the word "fuck."

The ringing of the doorbell, then nothing.

Take inventory of all the things that have failed to make an appearance over the course of this lifetime, the absence of the providence or luck that seems to lead others to the right place at the right time, no welcome embrace of life-altering events, no sequence of moments combining propitiously in the lottery of the random world . . . suddenly forget what has launched this spiral of thought. Remember again, like fingers snapping.

Someone had been here, someone perhaps with a message to deliver, someone who would extend a box gift-wrapped in vapor, a broken alarm clock, a withered branch. Someone who, if convinced to stay and stand and stare unblinkingly at this man holding the door open, would whisper hoarsely that the time has finally arrived or already passed, then turn and walk quickly away with lowered head. Wait, dear god, don't go, what is it? Watch the figure retreat. Come back, please, no more of these fucking charades, all this useless mystery, say something; what's the meaning of the broken alarm clock, the withered branch, the box gift-wrapped in vapor? Silence, like thick slices of bread and these thin thoughts sandwiched in the middle. Close the door now and follow the trail of heartbeats that had fallen like fairytale breadcrumbs back into the bedroom. Think, What is all this business with bread? so that laughter like butter can smooth the walk to the bedroom.

Begin to remove clothes, though with no intention of showering. Women stand before long mirrors and seem reconciled to the reflection. Paula, disrobing, always watches herself, wishing for less weight here, more there, reading the body dismissively as though it were a Sidney Sheldon novel, merciless in self-assessment but never questioning the echo of herself in the mirror.

Try doing what she does.

Naked now, gaze into the mirror. Biceps seem permanently flexed from weightlifting, the thighs from running seem a sturdy trellis for vines of vein. Stare at the pubic hair as though it were a dark corridor leading to a door any sane man should be afraid to open. Look at the valve-shaped penis, recalling that Paula and her female friends laughingly refer to it—not this particular one but penises in general—as "package" or "unit." Suppress opinions because isn't self-image suspect and therefore unreliable? Realize that something is missing, some filament essential to irradiate understanding, this void now enjoining the hand to assume the shape of an examination table with the penis placed on it carefully like a sedated patient. Reflect on the pain that people inflict on themselves, especially young girls who burn forearms with cigarettes, slice thighs with razors, whittle themselves away with the stiletto of anorexia, and imagine the unit's pain if skimmed forcefully with a scalpel.

This is what Paula did to herself when she was younger, a troubled teenager living in Detroit, or so she had explained: Hurt yourself before others have the opportunity, savor the irony of the preemptive strike, because no self-respecting guy finds a serious challenge in further mutilating already damaged goods. She had said, Better to hurt yourself rather than to give that power to a stranger. She had said, Isn't this at the root of the appeal of virginity for men? She had said, If it's fair to say a woman is nothing but a parody of a man, something stripped by castration of an inalienable power, and you add the dynamic of race, then do you know what a black woman in America is?—A black woman in America is a just nigger without a dick. She had said. . . .

The doorbell rings, followed by a soft melting thud, like a dome of ice cream slipping from cone to floor before it reaches a child's mouth.

Snatch a towel hanging from the bathroom doorknob and wrap it around the waist, then run through the living room.

Towel trailing in flap and float enhances the impression of gliding, moving ghostlike forward. Glide on, the balls of the feet skimming carpet.

Jerk the door open.

Feel without hearing the rake of wind as though gusting off a tumbleweed prairie far away. Refrain, restrain, suppress. Looking right and left, see nothing, no one, then catch in the pinched periphery of the right eye a dark object, a shape. Command head to turn and drop. Allow vision to spear the tiny body of a bird, dead from impact against the living room window to the right and above the mailbox.

A box gift-wrapped in vapor. A broken alarm clock. A withered branch. A dead baby bird.

She had said, Better to hurt yourself than to transfer that power to a stranger.

The messenger has departed, leaving silence and secrets and a counterfeit currency of stillness.

Recall gliding through the living room ghostlike.

Peer down the row of identical townhouses and notice that at the very end there is something happening. Squint to pull everything closer. Observe what appears to be a family of four people with expressionless faces standing over a stretcher as though they are suspended in an aquarium of gelled muted activity. Two paramedics lift the ends of the stretcher and bear it away so that the wheels, spinning helplessly in the air, grieve for contact with solid ground. Step out, around, careful to avoid the sparsely feathered baby bird lying in the center of the welcome mat, its new nest of forever thwarted flight. Stare at the body on the stretcher, tucked cylindrical in a sheet, the mummy sheet pulled over the head.

Try doing what she does and stand nude before the mirror. Do not ask where the towel is or at what point the towel became problematic in this respect. Where is the towel? Where is the box, the broken alarm clock, the withered branch? They are perhaps with the bird, in the bird. The location of the bird is most certainly known. Recall the words of the marriage counselor, "Embark on a journey of empathy, not a journey of refusals." Postulate that knowledge of the unknowable, an alternate identity, might be achieved by an act as simple as the rearrangement of anatomical parts on an unremarkable flesh-and-blood mannequin. Conclude that the body, this body standing here that resembles a mannequin, is perhaps good fortune, a lesser omen, and might be a place to start, a point of departure and arrival both. Start with the obvious.

It's obvious now, isn't it?

Walk to the bed and sit on its doughy edge, picking up the black nylon stockings.

Think about the guys, why twice a week the chessboard-in-motion of the basketball game played at the YMCA should be so important, a ritual that bridges the gulf between boyhood and manhood and achieves quintessence not on the sweat-puddled court but in the locker room, where rough palms and rough wet towels slap a Morse code of dire camaraderie on muscular asses.

Does this ritual have anything to do with the box, the clock, the branch?

What would the guys think of what's about to be done here in the bedroom? Men are natural explorers, venturing from the place they know to discover other regions, while women embark on expeditions to arrive deeper into places they never left. Wonder which this is, how the guys, busy bouncing basketballs, would see it.

Reverse gender.

Try to remember the order, like seasons, in which Paula dresses—stockings first, then shoes, next slip and then panties and bra . . . something like a spring, summer, winter, fall of undergarments?—but fail to recapture the sequence of progression, experience instead a brief jumbled autumn of confusion. Improvise, try to imagine what would be natural. Take the spineless eel of the nylons and lay them as though on display across the palm of one hand. Mash one of the stockings into a bunch, point the toes and insert the right foot, begin to tug. When Paula does this the stocking is already compressed into something like a ball and then she neatly unrolls it up, nothing at all like this collapse of effervescence in the hands. Pull. Feel the hairs of the calf snip and snag at the fabric, read the biting alphabet of hairs scribbled beneath the black papery translucence of the stocking. The calf is a pregnancy of flesh, a pendant gourd around which the stocking with difficulty spills its stretch, but then it slides easily over the hard anger of the kneecap and begins to rise nicely around the football bulge of the lower thigh. Compare the thigh to the widening bell of a tuba, but hear the ascent of the nylon as a slurring flute. Do the same with the other leg and stand, the stockings tight and clinging desperately to skin like a raft that clings with all its might to waves as it splinters and sinks.

Note with relief that there is no enjoyment other than that which attaches to a dry determination to see this complex pantomime through.

Avoid as yet reflections that lurk in the mirror. As though watched by eyes that are everywhere, nowhere, look around the room. Feel, don't think.

Suddenly remember how, many years ago, Uncle Elroy came every Saturday afternoon to the house when the family lived in Milwaukee, offering advice and instruction in self defense, an ex-middleweight boxer on the amateur circuit who was the masculine fulfillment of Mother's hint of broad shoulders and sturdy musculature, a promising talent until battles with alcohol took the place of opponents in the ring. Uncle Elroy, wearing the long Navy pea coat he always wore even as the smoldering viscera of August summer squeezed a last cramp of sweat from the body. See again the first thing Uncle Elroy does when he enters the house, which is to find the Tinker Toy boy hiding in the bedroom and sweep back the wings of the unbuttoned coat, thrust his gigantic stomach into the boy's face, and with his great sculptured fists, beat upon the booze-bloated keg of his own abdomen in illustration, bidding with baritone bark the child to similarly strike it.

This right here and now for your pummeling pleasure is those other kids out there waiting for you, he says, those other little black heathen bastards. Mother watches, uncertain as to the validity of the wisdom being transmitted. Bounce, bounce the stomach closer to face. They call you punk, do they not? I'm told they call you a proper-talking sissy. Bounce, bounce the stomach closer to face. Flash of pint bottle like a fang from an inner pocket of the coat. Because you know the difference between a noun and an adjective, you have to TAKE THEIR SHIT?! But the Tinker Toy boy loved Uncle Elroy too much to assault the stomach and never did as he was exhorted.

Look now into the corner of the room. Mightn't Uncle Elroy be over there, hiding behind the curtains?

Reason that if theologians are right and death is but a passing over, then there must be dead who do not pass over, for reasons the living will never understand, and that those who do not are here, because where else could they go?

Decide to stage a belated exhibition for Uncle Elroy, who must always have been secretly disappointed that the boy's fist refused to pummel the keg-like belly. Curling upper torso into a defensive crouch, begin to shuffle, tensing in and out of tentative rhythms. Weave and bob, swiveling from the waist to dodge the blows of the opponent: the box gift-wrapped in vapor, the broken alarm clock, the withered branch, the dead baby bird, the man on the stretcher. With heathen glee cry out and throw punches hard, feinting and dancing backward, slicing with jabbing arcs, sweat skipping down the face like water beading on a hot tilted skillet. Coast with a tic-tac-toe of flurried footwork back to the ropes and lean into them, unable to evade the enemy's furious barrage. Anticipating the terminal blow that will catapult consciousness beyond the barrier of the head, cover up, tuck elbows in and hide. Catch a glimpse of Uncle Elroy, who has seen enough, and who buttons his coat, waves sadly goodbye.

Realize that once again a failure has taken place, a diversion has been allowed to wedge itself between intention and accomplishment, and return to the matter at hand before it's too late and the mind burrows back into its molehill.

Pull the stockings up, out of their forlorn droop below knees. Step into the slip and feel the elastic band stretch stubbornly to accommodate this larger waist, sense the tissue of static-cling in a weak force-field about the thighs and think about searching for the can she keeps in the kitchen pantry to spray the airy electricity away, then decide against it. Take the bra and do what she does, fastening the four hooks through the eyelets first, then slipping the entire apparatus over the head and maneuver arms through the loops. Make shrugging adjustments and pat. The cups of the bra are twin badges of deficient volume, flattened against the chest like kites against sky. Do the job right if it is to be done at all. There is toilet paper in the adjacent bathroom, get balls of it and stuff the cups. There is a donut of white medical adhesive tape on the edge of the sink. Go get it and return, sitting on the doughy edge of the bed. When the penis, the unit, the package, is firmly taped to the thigh, the legs crossed, study the mirror and muse that in a certain negligent light the effect of the reflection might be that of a handsome, solidly built woman.

Is it distressing that the reflection in the mirror suggests a person who might have been a better looking woman than man? Don't answer that question.

On the dresser is a small lavender makeup bag, rimmed with beads meant to resemble pearls. Paula has never been given pearls as a gift and now it's surely too late. Carefully apply lipstick, of a brand purporting to be for "women of color," the phallic rise of the dark red tip protruding ironically as the tube is twisted, then find deeper in the bag a tiny brush with powdery bristles and a dime-thin case which when opened reveals a rainbow palate of small squares, tiny television screens tuned each to a different pastel frequency. Use the diazepam-blue and brush it on eyelids, smearing it in with the finger's tip. This association brings to mind her bottle of Valium in the medicine cabinet, find it quickly and read the label "one every four hours for anxiety" then place one of the aqua tablets on the tongue and chew.

Anxiety.

All that is needed now is a wig but there is no wig. Open the closet door and find a pair of black high heels, force toes into the tapered cavity of the shoes. At least five inches of heel overhang the edge so it is not possible to tie the trailing straps. Walk now. Experience how with every step she takes, even without the excess counterweight of heels, she must struggle to maintain equilibrium.

Uncle Elroy has returned and is hiding behind the curtains, watching from the corner of the room.

The doorbell rings.

The baby bird in its new nest of death.

The impulse to glide ghostlike across the living room and jerk the door open is an almost palpable magnetism. The messenger of everything unresolved has returned and this time, this time would not flee if the door was jerked open. The heart begins to hurry in the chest, unloading beats like gravel from a dump trunk. Hurry with the heart. Finish this.

Think what the guys, ceasing to bounce basketballs, mouths agape, might say if they saw this, their lips wet with scald of invective, the word fag like chewed matter between the teeth, although they know there is not a gay bone in this body. One of the guys is Middle Eastern, one is Asian, one is Jewish, one black, friends of all colors and cultures, Americans all. Speculate why it is that the black community in particular seems to despise gay black males. Comc to no conclusion regarding this observation . . . or rather, come to myriad conclusions—same thing. Continue walking, even though one ankle and then the other seems to snap free of the socket, rolling painfully before reconnecting.

She had said, Better to hurt yourself rather than to transfer that power to a stranger.

The doorbell rings. If that ringing were weather, it would be thunder followed by lightning.

Continue walking to and fro before the mirror. Try to let hips loosen, imitate the motion of water left in the wake of a sailboat, think of sails filling their aprons with air, of glaciers in their drifting ballet, of wheels turning within wheels, of a seismograph needle measuring an earthquake that curves gently, of children turning in bed as they dream of pink smoke, of red wine pouring lushly from a bottle. Think sinuously and let the thoughts extend down strange avenues of realization: That perhaps this should have been done years ago, that it should be mandatory, at least once, to dress little boys like this for purposes that have nothing to do with the sexual, but perhaps as a preparation for ringing doorbells, unseen messengers, a broader rite of passage. Conjecture that if the bedroom door of the Tinker Toy boy had been jerked open to reveal him wearing Mother's bathrobe he would have been whipped (for the punitive blows of the belt were not called "spankings" back then and "time outs" had not yet been invented) by Father, with Mother watching, uncertain as to the validity of the wisdom transmitted by belts. And words, begin to dwell on words as well, the difference between nouns and adjectives, the encyclopedia of words hurled as adjectival substitute for the noun "woman"—bitch, slut, whore, tramp, ho, cunt, pussy, and so on, so forth, so on. Listen to Uncle Elroy remind you that the doorbell is ringing insistently now and that the messenger must be confronted, that these clothes must be taken off, take off the shoes, the stockings, the slip, the bra, quickly smear makeup off with the back of the hand. Do not think about finding the towel, there is no time for that, and barely time to tear the tape off the unit and glide ghostlike through the living room, when the tape is ripped free blood seeps from the outraged head of the unit, but ignore this and jerk the door open. Jerk the door open on the final ring.

See.

Look out from a face that suddenly feels exposed and vulnerable without makeup. The purpose of makeup, beyond the ornamental, is obvious now, isn't it?

See Paula. She is always misplacing her keys. She is holding the baby bird in the towel that was left on the welcome mat. It is not clear whether she is resigned or is grieving for the bird because her eyes are screened behind stylish sunglasses. She is about to take those sunglasses off.

Do, or with whatever words are left, say something.

Shot in the Head

You are here again, Jarrid, in this déjà vu of darkness, the ambient diapason of voices snarling with testosterone and booming through powerful high-tech speakers. Your ears throb with a chorus of tires shrieking like a bow sliding sideways over violin strings, your eyes riveted to geysers of metal and flame as cars collide and their collisions produce a gritty midnight of smoke and fumes. You can taste soot and gasoline coating your tongue and, as a countermeasure, you suck short bursts of Sprite up through your straw, your throat muscling the prickly liquid down. Everything is a rich tangle of cuts and dissolves and close-ups and dizzying pans, intestines of images almost spilling glossily into your lap as though the screen were a stomach split open. You slump low in the seat, letting this putty of relentless action smear itself into the holes and cracks and craters in the graffiti-strewn wall of your life. You've seen this movie twice and you don't even remember the names of the actors, even though they're mega-stars who are household names. You don't care about that. What you want is what's at the heart of the stories themselves, which is pure potential and possibility.

In the same way that you're able to clearly see the workings of fate in the lives of characters on the screen, you conclude that your own life, from a different vantage point, must, too, display a pattern. The observer of the pattern in your life isn't God but something closer to a cosmic motion picture camera, far enough away to take in the entire picture, see where everything is headed, see the end of the story. Without the cosmic motion picture camera, Jarrid, the story sinks into darkness. You're certain that if the motion picture camera had been invented thousands of years ago, there would have been no need to invent God.

Of course that's not the way you would explain it because you've decided that explaining yourself is too much trouble. You know what the right words are, it's just that putting them together requires too much energy. You always struggled to get passing grades in English, even though your composite score on the Stanford-Binet IQ test was nearly two standard deviations above average, a score attained by only about 2.3% of the population.

You are twenty-four, Jarrid, with both everything and nothing unspooling before you.

You had just enrolled for your second year at the local community college when you decided to drop out and devote all your time to the band you played guitar in, Boy Storm, a band you were certain was destined to crack the local music scene wide open. Jarrid, it breaks your heart to admit it but your parents were right about your pursuit of the hip hop stardom fairy tale.

You did exactly what your mother, an overworked teller at Wells Fargo, advised you against and "put all your eggs in one basket." And you ignored the embittered counsel of your father who, working all his adult life as a bus driver for City of Los Angeles Public Transportation Department, tried to communicate his experience as a hapless blue-collar worker contending on a daily basis with the ignorance of the general public and the ignominy of a paltry pay check. Both of them tried to dissuade you, maintaining that the lack of a college education for a young black man was a virtual death sentence in these days when bachelor's degrees were a dime a dozen.

"You can't get a job pumping unleaded without a BA," your father, with his blackboard-dark face emphatically pushed close to yours, prophesized darkly. "Ask me. I should know."

But you didn't ask him, did you? And when Boy Storm crumbled like a boulder of glass struck with a sledgehammer only three months after the band's inception, you moved in with your girlfriend Akema and her grandmother rather than admit defeat, acknowledge your parents' prescience, and resume your education.

None of that matters now anyway. This is the third time you've seen this movie and your favorite scene is coming up. One man presses the barrel of a gun against the temple of another man and pulls the trigger. The back of the head ruptures and the camera lingers on shards of cranium, welts of gray matter, a pulpy bolus of blood plastered against the wall.

How does it feel to be shot in the head? You can't answer this particular question, but there are other related questions based on what happened earlier today that you may be uniquely qualified to answer.

As you sip your drink, you notice your hand is shaking, Jarrid, because certain thoughts are threatening to nudge their way back into your awareness. Those thoughts want back in. They're like wide-eyed children pressing palms and faces against the window of a store displaying alluring dangerous toys.

You decide not to fight the direction your mind wants to move in. Close your eyes, Jarrid, just for a few seconds. Your eyes are sprinkled with a grainy pepper of fatigue and you need to close them.

Earlier this evening you're sitting in the disheveled living room watching television with Akema and her grandmother. The broad doughy elfin face of game show host Regis Philbin dominates the screen. His eyes twinkling conspiratorially, he awaits a contestant's fretful assessment of multiple-choice possibilities for the correct answer to a question concerning the average cranial circumference of female anthropoid apes.

Grammy DuPont sits in a recliner whose lank shabbiness reminds you of a weeping willow tree, although living all your life in a part of the city that has been held up as a paradigm of American poverty and crime, you have never seen a willow tree. From what you've observed on the Discovery Channel, you think you could perhaps relate to nature if, for some reason, you were actually out walking around in it, although the only thing nature seems to be good for are catastrophes and natural disasters, and as far as you're concerned the world would probably be better off without nature at all.

Occasionally Grammy scribbles with the nub of her pencil in the boxes of the crossword puzzle grid in the *National Enquirer*. From time to time she comments approvingly on some aspect of the quiz show luminary's appearance or comportment.

"That Regis is not half bad-looking for a man his age. Now, for me to go out of my way and say that about a white man, well, you know he's got to have something on the ball. But irregardless of how much charm Regis is got, I say something's wrong with that Kathy Lee for staying."

"Kathy Lee? What does she have to do with anything?" asks Akema.

"Well, I say Kathy Lee is a damn dumb bitch for staying with Regis after what he did, just couldn't keep that nasty old wrinkled ding dong of his in his pants, and all that public humiliation he put that poor girl through."

"You mean that other guy, not this guy," you say, then without waiting, you explain further. "You mean Kathy Lee should have left what's-his-dude's-name, Frank Gifford. This dude on this show here, that's Regis."

"Is he married?" Grammy asks, vigorously rubbing the Enquirer with one of those bubble-gum pink block erasers you haven't seen since you were in grade school.

"If he is, it's not to Kathy Lee," you say.

"Well, if Regis was married and cheated, his wife would be a damn dumb bitch to stay with him, even if he is well-preserved for a man his age and he knows how to make a good impression," Grammy says, and though you're able to swallow the lumpy oatmeal of her logic, it takes a moment to digest it.

You sit on one end of the sofa and on the other end Akema reclines with a pillow under her head, her good leg stretched across your lap. She had earlier removed the wooden peg attachment that had been purchased from a pawn shop and modified to accommodate the stump of her right leg and now it leans with piratical rakishness against the television set where she placed it. She absently massages her hip and with a sly look takes advantage of Grammy's preoccupation with the crossword puzzle by pressing into your crotch with her heel. The soft mass coiled between your legs stirs tentatively and those familiar golden pins and needles of sensation threaten tumid arousal, but you preemptively nudge her foot away.

"Grammy?" Akema says, and you know by the quaver of resentment in her voice what she's about to say. "What about my leg? You promised."

"I'm working on it," Grammy says vaguely without looking up from the crossword puzzle.

"You promised. You said you'd hook me up months ago. I lost my fucking leg for you, Grammy."

"I don't appreciate that kind of goddamn language in my home from somebody who'd be nothing but a everyday street urchin or a little whore in training if it wasn't for her grandmother's pity and how I let her live off my good graces."

Akema has admitted to you many times that she would have become a ward of the state were it not for Grammy DuPont, who took her in two years ago, but for some months now she's been complaining that the old woman's mean-spiritedness has been escalating slowly to something bordering on dictatorial cruelty. Akema had been fifteen when her mother one evening two years ago left the tiny apartment to drop some clothes off at the dry cleaner and never bothered returning.

Shortly after moving in with Grammy, Akema had accompanied her to the Social Security office downtown to resolve some problem the old woman was having with her monthly check. While they had been walking along the sidewalk, a lanky teenaged boy with thorny blonde hair had crept up behind them and snatched Grammy's purse. As he took off running, he tripped and the purse had cartwheeled out of his hands and landed at Akema's feet. She bent down to scoop it up and when she stood up the thief had returned and with a sweep of his arm managed to grab the dangling strap. She held the purse and he pulled. She fell to the ground and held on, encouraged by Grammy's hysterical exhortations not to relinquish her grip.

"Don't give it to that dirty white trash punk, I got all my money in it!" she cried.

Akema held on even though she was dragged across the sidewalk, over the trash-strewn curb, and into the street while she desperately splashed the sonorous acid of her screams for help into the faces of onlookers. There was the blast of a horn and a pneumatic crush of brakes and the youth let go of the purse and leaped aside as a city bus rolled over Akema's right leg and crushed the bones into animal-cracker bits and pieces.

Now you try to change the subject and extinguish the fuse burning down into Akema's powder keg of resentment. "Hey Key, that sounds like a question you'd know the answer to. It's an animal question."

"Yeah, but the cranial circumference of female anthropoid apes of what average age?" Akema asks irritably. "How can you answer that question without knowing what age?"

"They said something about that already," you contend.

"No they didn't," she insists, "I've been watching it."

"Well then you missed it."

"You are an asshole," she says, "who never pays attention."

You're about to respond to this essentially playful accusation, but the matter of the cranial circumference of female apes strikes the neat triangular formation of your thoughts with the bowling-ball impact that only synchronous events and situations can, Jarrid. Apes, cranial circumference, skull, and once again, head.

Everywhere you look, you see that a particular form of violence stands out from the usual assortment of violent acts reported or portrayed in the media. What you mean—and you've explained this to Akema while the two of you sit at Starbucks in the late evenings having discussions that skate in looping figure eights over the slippery floor of topics ranging from the goofy to the sublime, she sipping a latte and nodding, on the verge of understanding you but not quite there, as when you are both having sex and she is momentarily framed and suspended in that narrow window of opportunity that separates imminent orgasm from no orgasm at all—what you mean is there seems to be a strange trend in how people are choosing to kill each other.

Lately you've noticed what you call the shot-in-the-head thing. Reports of people shot in the head, dramatizations and depictions of men or women with their heads agape and extruding vivid watermelon-red: a gag of images so profuse that they can't be swallowed or digested, an endless barrage of references and reportage in newspapers and magazines, to say nothing of the glut of fictionalizations on TV or in the movies. And don't forget computer games, theater, sculpture, toys, the Internet. You saw a man wearing a T-shirt the other day with a cartoon picture of Elmer Fudd slanting the barrel of his shotgun against the head of Bugs Bunny, who shuddered in incontinent fright.

You're more than idly curious about this, Jarrid. What exactly is going on?

You have managed to put together a modest collection of shot-in-the-head photos and images from serendipitous browsings through books, magazines, newspapers, websites downloads, videotape scans, and so on. The photos, neatly clipped rectangles, adorn the walls of your and Akema's small bedroom. Your feeling is that perhaps with solid information at your disposal, you could arrive at certain conclusions that would increase your understanding of society in general and your place in it, the role you're expected to play. And what role are you expected to play?

There is the role of the embittered black kid who's not smart enough to gracefully accept his intellectual inferiority to anyone with white skin. There is the role of the black kid trying to find a way out in the world of professional sports or music—this is the one you played with the intention of tweaking, right, Jarrid? There is the role of the black kid engaging in acts of destruction, clinging to vestiges of jungle savagery, the inability to adapt to civilized society. Irresponsible absentee deadbeat father, Uzi-toting drug pusher, misogynistic bejeweled flagellator of low self-esteem, crack-addicted streetwalkers. The only remaining option is to create your own role through sheer audacity, stupidity, genius, or some combination of all three, a risky business, you suspect, whether black or white, resulting in ostracism, persecution, incarceration, insanity, death—or fame.

But you're getting off the track, Jarrid.

The shot-in-the-head thing. It must be significant in some way, at this unique time and place in history, in this media-generated reality that surrounds you and holds you tightly in its embrace. You've wondered what it would be like to shoot someone in the head or to be shot in the head yourself. How can you not wonder?

"How can you not wonder? In a way," you explain to Akema, the two of you having left the house to escape an evening of Grammy's headachey non sequiturs and the side of her personality that morphs into viciousness without warning, the two of you sitting now in Starbuck's and drinking lattes, "it's like society approves of it because to be against something is, in a weird way, to approve of it."

"Maybe not *approve* approve," Akema says.

"Okay, right, not approve, but . . . you know."

"Not approve of this whole shot in the head thing you're talking about, but more like society has acknowledged it, made it legitimate in a weird way. It's all over TV all the time.

I mean, forget about you are what you eat—you are what you watch. Okay, so it's a part of us, right? But what are we supposed to do with it? Resist it, accept it, what? I mean, all along you've been right about this shot in the head stuff. It's a part of the zeitgeist. Cool word, huh? It was on Oprah." Akema looks down at the tabletop and lowers her voice. "They put it there, and the question is, what do we do about it, Jarrid?" Her eyes, still fastened on the surface of the table, seem to bore deeper into it. "Can we use it to our advantage?" When she looks up the pupils of her eyes widen like drops of ink hitting the still surface of water in a glass. "Maybe we should get serious about what we talked about."

For Akema, it's all connected to getting a real prosthetic leg. You've even researched various manufacturers' products with her to show her how supportive you are. You've both decided to go with the Mauch knee unit for its high quality machining and the greater overall mobility it would deliver, the Total Shock Pylon by Century XXII, (narrowly usurping the less wieldy and heavier Otto Bok torque absorber after much comparative analysis), and the Vari-Flex model foot, reputed to be more forgiving on uneven surfaces than the Flex-foot VSP. She attempts to make the best of the current situation, decorating her peg leg with plastic army men, costume jewelry, condoms, coinage, candy canes, key chains, dog whistles, and other intricate eye-catching trinkets and colorful ornaments, but she's getting tired of that.

When you moved in with Akema, you promised to help her raise the money to buy a customized prosthetic.

Boy Storm had just broken up, and you had decided you wouldn't return to your parents' home. Remember how it was before Boy Storm had turned against you, when the group practiced in the drummer's dank mildewy garage, the four of you chain smoking cigarettes and arguing over how "political" the band should be, the kind of image to establish, the lyrics and chord changes (you maintaining that the keyboard player should refrain from using extensions like ninths because the harmonic structure of the songs became too "jazzy")? Those were good times, Jarrid, perhaps the best days of your life.

Girls in the neighborhood began hanging out on the weekends to listen to the rehearsals, sixteen-year-olds with apocalyptic tattoos and tongue studs and dyed hair, girls with thin angular coat-hanger bodies and haunted eyes who wore bulky utilitarian boots, leather wristbands, T-shirts too small to cover their coquettish navels. Some of these girls were singers who hoped to win auditions with the band. Others were looking for someone or something to absorb the furious bravado and glittering empty energy they radiated, something or someone who would allow them to escape for a time the growing bewilderment that was beginning to overshadow their days and prefigure the unhappiness of impending adulthood.

These girls were cookie cutter replicas of one another, walking representations of some marketing teams' concept of youth and style. They had a generic quality about them and were devoid of imagination and you had no interest in them, Jarrid, none at all.

There was a girl though who appeared one day and hung on the fringes of the more aggressive girls. There was something about that girl, wasn't there, Jarrid? When you saw her you felt something strange was happening and you were drawn to her laid-back aura of hostile arrogant disengagement. Talking to her you discovered that she had her own completely unique jagged vision of life that grew out of what she had suffered in her one-leggedness. You recognized that her outlook on life had been drastically changed by her consciousness of herself as an outsider. When you told her about your observations and findings and how you were spending more and more time in movies theaters watching the screen run red with cranial explosions, she didn't laugh.

When the band occasionally had practice sessions that were closed to outsiders, you began inviting her as though she were your girlfriend. When you were alone with her, she sang to you and you thought she had an incredible unearthly voice. How to explain it? It was as if her throat were lined with blisters and the blisters were being scraped off with a razor when she sang. The raw emotive power of her voice made you think somehow of a female monster of some kind singing a monster lullaby to its monster baby.

You tried to explain this to the band but their ears hungered for aural pabulum, a sound smooth and palatable and innocuous as Gerber's baby food. In fact, they told you she sounded like shit and impugned your motives, suggesting that you were a pawn whose judgement had been clouded by sex.

"Listen, what you do with your dick ain't none of my business, but who would be sick enough to want to screw a one-legged bitch anyway?" Scratch or Fontelle, you forget which one, blurted out during a band meeting where you nominated Akema for the female lead singer spot. "Are you fucking nuts? How pathetic would that be, some peg-legged bitch hopping around on stage trying to dance and shit?"

You picked up your Fender Sratocaster and became the calm center in the airless storm of rage that descended on you and you smashed your instrument into a pair of expensive Alesis studio monitors stacked on a shelf next to some empty Pennzoil cans. You walked out and kept walking and Akema said, "I want you to live with me and Grammy," and so you did.

You owe her something, Jarrid. As you reach across the table at Starbuck's to take her nervously flitting hand in your own, something in you swells in appreciation of all she's done for you. You can't say that you love her because you do have this much self knowledge: you have no idea what it means to really love anyone. You love things, yes, but not people. For example, you love television, the movies. In fact it seems to you that what you see on a screen, any screen, is colored by an energy and life more vital and vivid and multi-dimensioned than your own. Perhaps it's not love, but the two of you are together now and she believes in your guitar playing and has encouraged you to do something with your observations on the shot-in-the-head thing, though neither of you know what that might be.

And so in answer to her question "What are we going to do about my leg?" you squeeze her hand and say, "We're going to get you that leg, Key—I mean, if you're serious about what we talked about."

"She gets my disability check and she's got power of attorney over it just because I'm under eighteen. It's not fair. She's got her own Social Security every month. I lost my leg because of her. I mean, I love her and everything but fuck that. She doesn't give me shit. She doesn't give us shit."

The two of you finish your lattes and return to the apartment. You and Akema stretch out on your usual spots on the couch and watch TV. In the middle of an HBO movie she says in a dreamy voice, "You know what I just figured out? If you're not famous, you're not real."

You feel the camera that's with you at all times panning to emphasize the commonplace bathos of the living room. It hesitates knowingly on the solitary crack in the wall over the doorway to the kitchen and the very act of lingering transforms that tawdry fissure into an image for the pain beneath Akema's glibness. What would be a good image for your own pain, Jarrid? The Goodwill end table holding the fishbowl with the dead goldfish floating on the nacreous surface of week-old evaporating water?

Grammy is sleeping. Her snores seem to drift out of her bedroom in cartoon dialogue-balloons. Akema puts her finger to her lips and rises from the couch, balancing expertly on her one leg. Finger still slanted across her lips, she hops to the bedroom doorway, leans there against the frame, then gestures for you to follow her as she slips through the partially opened door into the dust-stale darkness of the bedroom. The numerals of a small digital clock on a bedside table throw a soft emerald phantom of phosphorescence onto Grammy's face.

The camera zooms in, Jarrid. Framed now are two hands, yours and Akema's, jointly gripping a .38 revolver. Your larger hand, a rind of flesh inside of which her own childlike hand is a pod of clammy warmth, steadies and cups hers, and both your index fingers curl lightly around the trigger's curved tusk. You stand behind Akema and she flattens the feathery weight of her upper torso into your chest, balancing stork-like on her leg. The two of you lean forward in a perfectly nuanced ballet of slow motion, extending the gun through some thick special-effect medium of aborted time until the barrel almost kisses Grammy's forehead, and it's as if you've become one with the camera as it begins to pull back and slowly up—as if, when the trigger is pulled, you're not a person so much as a nameless presence commanding a perspective that someone else will edit and unify into a whole at a later time.

The final action sequence is over. The music is a percolation of strings mutedly plucked, nervous dabs of percussion, asyncopated rhythms, ricocheting snippets of atonality, skittish atmospheric jabs and sweeps, cool raindrops of metallic resonance. You wish Akema would get here.

When it was all over, you had both changed clothes. On the way out you kicked in the door to make it look like B&E. The plan called for the two of you to separate for a few hours. You would go to the movies and Akema would go to her best friend Diane's house. Akema had already told Diane everything and Diane had promised to testify to the police that you and Akema had spent all day and evening with her. In a few hours Akema and Diane would meet you at the movies and then the three of you would return to the apartment and call the police as though you had walked in on the scene.

When you and Akema left the apartment the dimly-lit streets seemed to be tunnels carved crudely through the surrounding darkness and the few people lurking around looked like gang members or drug dealers who, if they had heard a shot, would be disinclined to volunteer information to authorities. She kissed you tenderly at the corner when you separated.

"Now we'll be able to get my money," she whispered, "and we can buy me my prosthetic, and you a new guitar."

Over the past months when you had both fantasized about shooting Grammy in the head, Akema hadn't explained how it would be possible for her to collect her monthly disability payments as a minor, but she always implied with a confident wink that this was a small detail.

You don't know yet what you'll be able to add to the shot-in-the-head thing now that your knowledge is first-hand. But it wasn't what you expected it would be, Jarrid. What you've seen hundreds of times on the screen was far richer, more intense, the technicolor blood more urgently red, the lifelessness of the corpse more stark and existential and horrible. You wept when it was over, Jarrid, standing over the bed and looking down at Grammy's alphabet-soup face. Akema put her arm around your shoulders and told you how very sweet you were to shed valedictory tears and tried to comfort you by pointing out what a long life she led, but you didn't tell her that it was disappointment and not sorrow spilling from your eyes—disappointment at the thin pallid watered-down nature of life as it was experienced every day, moment by moment.

But that's all right, Jarrid, that's okay. You have a treasury of observations; they just haven't coalesced into jewels of insight yet, that's all. For example, you've noticed that stray bullets often strike innocent bystanders in the head. Why is that? Why would a bullet seem to be magnetically drawn to the head. Everything that enters a person from the world beyond does so through the eyes, the nose, the mouth, the ears, all of which are portals residing in the head.

You don't know what to do with this information but you may write a song about it—one so powerful that it would compel the reunion of Boy Storm.

But it's okay, Jarrid. And it's just possible that whatever insights are spawned by all of this might shed light on the condition of your twin brother Alan, who less than a year ago was shot in the head by just such a stray bullet and now floats with fetal obliviousness in the womb of a coma, buoyant in unseen liquescence. You don't count on it, but anything is possible.

Someone taps your shoulder behind you. You turn and it's Akema leaning forward over the back of the seat. "What's up?" she says, smiling. "Diane's outside. Let's bounce."

Your Sprite is empty and you bend down and place the cup under your seat. You don't turn around to look at the endless column of credits as the two of you walk up the aisle, nor have you ever understood how some can sit staring raptly at a meaningless list of strangers' names rolling by so rapidly as to be almost invisible.

The Relationship Handbook

1.
Relationship Dissolution—An Overview

Friendship may yet be possible if individuals formerly a couple have been prescient enough not to ruin one another, steering the troubled relationship off its rutted track, allowing it to safely coast to a complete halt, and decisively abandoning it before it bursts into flame. It stands to reason that friendship will be impossible if either partner falls into the pattern of blame, recrimination, spite and enmity that threatens lovers who find themselves in the unenviable position of dissolving their relationship.

Remember, the ultimate goal for the dismantled couple should be to stand together, united in precarious survival. "We will always be friends," should be the key phrase that the couple holds before them like a shield against pity, jeers, accusations of failure on some deeply human fundamental level.

2.
Scenario #7 with Study Notes and Key Questions

"In the final analysis, falling out of love is not much different from falling in love," Dick declares. "There's that sense of being a part of something you can't control, the terror of adrenaline untethered, the junkie's rush toward the unknown."

"I disagree," Jane says mildly. Her voice as ever seems to launch at sentence's end the questing inflection that lifts declarative statement into the fluctuant atmosphere of a question.

"Of course she disagrees." Dick widely addresses the group with an amused, conspiratorial tone. "Thus we are friends and no longer lovers."

He references what is now well known to the group, that he and Jane could only come to an agreement after tediously plucking quills from the porcupine of opposing opinions, a prickly little beast of impassioned debate creeping through sheets night after night when they should have been making love or sleeping. As a sort of addendum to this revelation he enigmatically states to the group that while idle minds are truly the devil's workshop, it is not always possible to extend the logic of the adage, for the carpentry of accelerated minds often succeeds in fabricating mansions that transcend the angelic. *What is the meaning of such a remark, nudging enigma toward the unfathomable? The group absorbs this epigram with blank stares. Other data elements: the couple Genna and Keith, the Pizza Hut countergirl, Terramaine-Tammy, who will prove to be instrumental in pushing Dick to precipitous behavioral extremes and who appears in upcoming scenarios and has, as of the current scenario, been fired for absenteeism; the boy of fleece, also a catalyst, similarly appears in a forthcoming scenario, as does the hapless mathematician, Richard Wayside.*

Dick's remark triggers careful laughter from Genna and Keith, who both take another slice from the pepperoni pizza in the middle of the table. The four sit in a Pizza Hut booth.

"What I mean," Jane clarifies, "is that to say it's like a junkie's rush trivializes. Love, falling in or out of it, isn't just sensation. After all, we're talking about a connection that, even when it's broken, never completely disappears." *Jane's remark seems to indicate a wistful desire to rekindle former intimacies; at the same time, it exemplifies the couple's inability to strike a chord of agreement and underscores the utter inadvisability of daring to contemplate a reunion.*

Hours later, alone in bed, Dick forages through the scrap heaps of Jane's remarks with a tinny rake of sleep, the scratch of its tines on the rubble keeping him awake. His mind palettes past pastels, painting peaceful sleep into the acrylic white of wide awake.

3.
Scenario #8
with Study Notes
and Key Questions

Telephone. Serving an essential function as a relationship-facilitation device in the lives of happy couples who have yet to cohabitate, the telephone retains its importance in failing and failed relationships, enabling the couple to lay the building blocks of a new and satisfying liaison as friends. For this reason, it is important to pay the phone bill in a timely fashion to ensure uninterrupted service. Ready access to the telephone ensures that fractured couples may continue to dissect the corpse of the dead relationship, analyze motives, launch questions like toy boats to float and drift in a feeble sea of sudden tears. The telephone is an excellent device; users may pour all manner of rhetoric and oblique phraseology into the mouthpiece, so like a miniature manhole cover. Users may talk and say anything at all they wish to say, with facial expressions that slash words to shreds, while the tone of remains deceptively placid.

On the phone, Dick lets slip to Jane that he has forgotten how she looks without clothes on.

"How could you forget something like that?" she asks, her tone unguent for the injury he has inflicted.

"We broke up three months ago. That was at the end of not having sex for two months previous to the three, and I seem to recall during that time you were mostly sleeping at your mother's. How is she, anyway?"

"We just had a kitchen table confab. She said that the only thing we accomplished was to reinforce the negative perception of the fragility of relationships between African-American men and women. That both of us working on master's degrees in anthropology should have been smart enough to figure out how to make the thing work."

[The introduction of ethnicity may be seen by some to be unnecessary, arbitrary and jarring in a text which purports to examine a topic as universal as relationships. The Relationship Handbook has chosen to portray Jane and Dick as African American, since relationships between African American men and women may be perceived by the public to be particularly problematic. Please keep in mind that the governing logic applied here does not depend upon the truth, but on that which is perceived to be true. It is hoped that analysis of relationships whose chances of survival in a cultural milieu hostile in general ways to the couple depicted here will inspire and hearten non-African American readers, who will perceive themselves comparatively as facing extraneous pressures less insistent—i.e., as having a higher likelihood for success in all phases of their relationships, including dissolving them.

In the complete absence of description of either Dick or Jane, some readers in a dim grisaille of imagination have no doubt ghosted together physical characteristics for the couple; this is only natural. It may, however, be fruitful for these readers to consider the following questions: *Was some measure of surprise experienced in discovering that Dick and Jane, constructs though they may be, are African American constructs? If so, why?*

The aforementioned cultural milieu is examined at length in The African American Handbook, which is recommended reading and probes a number of questions, e.g., *How do African Americans Love? Is the manner in which African Americans love offensive? What do African Americans mean by the word love?*, etc.]

Dick says, "Double dysfunctionality. One set of problems because we're African American, another because we're simply men and women. Absurd. African Americans are as lost as anyone else."

"Of course. But we're held to a different standard. We're watched a bit more closely."

"And because of this we're supposed to be motivated to find the right way to love?" This quasi-cerebral banter is what he loved about them when he was not infuriated by it, but less and less he had experienced infuriation's absence. What Dick is unable to leave cleanly behind is not a sadness, but a high-strung engineer's exasperation at not being able to reconfigure problems into solutions fast enough, the problem of discovering a design that would accommodate the new shape their relationship should assume.

"Dick, I want to let you know I won't be hanging out with you guys Friday. I have a date."

Something avalanches through his skin, an overdosed niacin of curiosity flushing through startled limbs. "Someone I know?"

"No." Jane pauses, long and significant. "But I wish you did. You see a lot of things I don't. You know, Dick, you can be difficult much of the time. There's something in you that can't be found but isn't exactly lost, either. I have to admit, though, you raised the bar, and now I'm afraid it's very, very high."

"The bar can never be raised high enough."

"I mean, you really are a brilliant sort of a person. But I don't think you quite know what to do with it."

"My head is expanding and simultaneously deflating." It is, diastole and systole, but not with the stroke of flattery. It is the familiar piston of thinking, the smooth facilitation toward action. "Keep the bar high, Jane. Don't ever sell yourself short. Men are relatively easy to figure out—if you're not a woman. I might even be willing to offer an objective point of view. "

"Strange proposition," Jane says faintly.

"Is it? Just because we're not together—in that way—doesn't mean I'm no longer concerned with your happiness."

"It seems," Jane probes, "somehow almost incestuous."

"Think so? I should get a pat on the back for being concerned with your happiness at this point, given the bitterness of our breakup. I'm offering to lend you my judgement, and in return I ask for only one thing."

Jane, he knows, is both suspicious and intrigued. "Which is?"

"If I'd known I would never see you again, that it was the last time, I would have remembered every detail of your body. I want to remember that, Jane. I don't want the memory of that part of our relationship to become unreal. See me tomorrow, please. Let me see you that way once more. Just see, nothing else."

Before proceeding, the following questions should be considered: *Is this an encounter that would be better served by face-to-face interaction?* The telephone presents challenges of impenetrability and trust; users are disembodied, loosed from the constraints of the flesh, are forced to invoke hidden resources in order to negotiate the mystery of Self and Other. *Has Dick made full and effective use of the telephone as a relationship-facilitation device? Has Jane?*

4.
Scenario #9
Circumstances in the Past Contributing to Dissolution with Study Notes, Key Questions

Saying the sentence to hear it sing, Dick with arm resting in a proprietary collar around Jane's habitable neck so near his roaming lips, the press of their bodies in the small booth seamlessly Siamese twinned, their relationship at full bloom, its petals not yet leprous with spores of decay, the pizza like a mandala with the power to soothe at the center of the Pizza Hut table, Dick had answered in the caramel days when they were still sweet together, "Michelle Pfeiffer's pyric eyes of icy blue." The group had been discussing movie stars and the question directed by Keith to Dick was what attributes, if any, he thought unusual about Michelle Pfeiffer. Dick had decided to iron his response to a flat unadorned plane, a plain stiff shirt cut from neutral cloth. He deliberately skirted assessments of beauty he feared would appear like holes in ice, dropping them deeper into the murk of the assumptions on which conceptions of beauty floated.

"Beautifully expressed. But do you think the Pfeiffster is hot?" Keith asked.

Keith had met Dick at the university's freshman orientation when they were both new students, their eyes rounded into cups as the tall campus buildings seemed to tilt like teapots, filling them with the exotic flavors of their future. Keith came to admire Dick, his eccentric intellect, his synaptic snap and sizzle. He often wondered how he, Keith, would have fared without the skin he was wrapped in, the white-sheet complexion—especially when he considered that as yet he had achieved nothing, really, of distinction (he did not see obtaining a degree as an achievement). He knew that Dick's background was solidly middle-class like his own, Dick's mother an orthodontist, his father the manager of Blue

Cross's Policy Administration Department, their large two-story house regal on Lake Michigan's affluent lakefront, the family's financial portfolios well-padded, the money afroth like piranhas in frenzies of discretionary spending. Yet how, he wondered, must Dick have felt to be visibly and inescapably different, to be judged a priori, to be foremost seen and so held in thrall by the most superficial of the senses; seen as related, even if distantly, to Crips and Bloods, to O.J. Simpson, to fat gold-toothed rappers; seen as slinger of marathon adjectival oaths and expletives; seen as the beater of America's countless Reginald Dennys or as the beaten, one of America's countless Rodney Kings; seen as mangler of English and carrier of the nation's viral slang; seen, even when rich and successful, as clowns, like that fellow Don King . . .

[It must be pointed out that other names, classifications and characterizations drawn from African American history or current events could have been as easily substituted for those Keith had chosen to cite in his litany; it may be significant that these did not readily occur to him.

Keith has also given primacy to the vantage point of Caucasian observers, and does not consider that the existence of African Americans may extend beyond the realm of being seen to include the realm of actively seeing; that Caucasians might be similarly seen and judged intruded at no juncture as a reality for him. Keith depends, as do the majority of the American population, on television as opinion-facilitation tool; it is not a tool conducive to the development of critical thinking. *To what extent is Keith's point of view his own?*

Is Keith's point of view damaged to the extent that his understanding of Dick has been compromised? If so, on what foundation has Keith built his relationship with Dick?

Are there degrees of racism? Benign Racism? Degrees of culpability in the personal sphere? Benign culpability in the personal sphere? In considering these questions, please keep in mind that Keith, when all is said and done, is Dick's good friend. Does the author of The Relationship Handbook express a particular cultural bias or alliance? Does the author have a hidden agenda to promote? Is the fact-driven tone of The Relationship Handbook a thinly disguised façade for the sort of didactic undercurrent that seeks to establish a high moral ground?

The Relationship Handbook adopts the position that these questions are of sufficient importance as an aid in understanding relationships to warrant closer consideration and covers these issues in greater detail in The Enlightened Caucasian's Handbook; for African American readers wishing to enhance their understanding of this dynamic, The African American's Guide to Understanding The Enlightened Caucasian's handbook is suggested.]

. . . seen as egregious in utilization of state and federal correctional facility resources; seen, and not invisible as Ralph Ellison declared—*Invisible Man* being number three on Keith's list of top-ten favorite books of fiction—but seen and seen and seen. How must Dick have felt?

Genna, Keith's girlfriend, said to Jane across the pizza's carcass, the preyed-upon table, "I think what Keith really means, is how screwable is Michelle Pfeiffer? Isn't that what you're asking, Keith? Is she kill-your-mother screwable? Or just moderately maim-your-sister screwable?"

Keith and Genna's relationship was in the brittle state that precedes crumbling. "Did I say that?" He seemed startled. "Who heard me say anything about screwing?"

Genna said, "Please."

"It's always about the women," Jane observed to Genna, "so let's flip the script. Let's do hot male movie stars."

"You're right," Keith said to Jane. "Then let's not be sexist at all. Why not discuss hot male gay movie stars?"

"Brad Pitt," Jane said to Genna. "Brad Pitt is definitely hot."

"I don't know," Genna replied. "Sometimes he looks like he doesn't bathe regularly. He looks like he might sort of smell bad."

"Point taken," Jane conceded. "So buy a bar of Dial and make him take a bath before you nail him."

Keith, ignored, continued to goad. “Come on, sizzling hot male gay movie stars.”

“Pierce Brosnan,” Jane suggested. “Sophistication’s epitome.”

“Only looks really good in a tux,” Genna countered. “I saw him once in some movie where he was dressed in regular clothes. Jeans and a checkered flannel shirt. He looked like a dressed down mannequin. When’s the last time you screwed”—she tossed a look at Keith as though it were scalding water—“a manikin?”

“Val Kilmer,” Jane offered, slapping the table. “That man’s voice is like a lullaby.”

Dick listened. He began to centimeter away from Jane.

“We’re not talking voices here,” Genna qualified.

Keith forgot he was aggrieved. “If I were a woman—were, was a woman?—I might go for George Clooney.”

“Were, unless you’re seriously thinking of a sex change,” Dick said with a slight edge no one heard.

“I might be,” Keith said, looking at Genna.

The blonde countergirl was passing their table. “Mooney drunk-boy Clooney,” she suggested.

“No, wait, if I were a woman,” Keith revised, “I’d go for Eminem.”

“Chick,” Genna corrected. “You said woman. I think the word you’re more comfortable with is chick? “ She looked at Dick and Jane. “Keith and I have been lately discussing the fact that, much like his old man, he has definite sexist tendencies. He denies it, of course.”

“Eminem? Not a movie star,” Jane objected. “He’s only been in one.”

Genna stated, “54.5 million for opening weekend of *8 Mile* says he’s a movie star.”

“Kurt Russell,” Jane exclaimed, slapping the table.

“I guess he’s not bad,” Genna said dismissively, “if you like grown men who look like they lost their skateboard or something.”

The blond countergirl passed the table again. “Benicio del Toro,” she proposed.

When the countergirl was no longer within earshot Genna remarked, "I think our waitress has attended consecutive raves over a four-day span. Maybe she met Benicio on the intersecting cusp of one of them. He certainly looks like he might benefit from a whole fifteen or, god forbid, maybe even twenty minutes of uninterrupted sleep."

Jane said, "Jesus, Genna. Then what about Alec Baldwin?"

"Alec B!" Keith cried, slapping the table.

"Big and bloated in all the wrong places," Genna declared.

"My vote goes for what's-his-name—those eyes, you know, Melanie Griffith's *inamorata*—Antonio Banderas," Genna submitted, slapping the table.

"At long last," Jane sighed, "we concur."

"That would be inamorato," Keith said proudly to Dick, looking to him for confirmation, "if I'm not mistaken."

"Sure," Dick said.

Keith only now realized that Dick had failed to fully participate in the game and attempted to draw him in. "Dick's gotten off easy. Dick, you wily bastard. Here I've all but admitted that I may have latent tendencies by saying I might find these guys hot, and you've kept silent. Your turn. If you were a woman, who?" STOP. *Before proceeding, re-read the dialogue with an aim toward ascertaining Dick's forthcoming response. Those who predict that Dick's reaction will be rooted in garden-variety jealousy receive partial credit for being correct; however, is there evidence in the seemingly innocuous dialogue of larger issues that lend themselves to interpretation in a broader context? Readers unable to anticipate Dick's reaction are urged to obtain both The African American Handbook and The Enlightened Caucasian's Handbook as an adjunct toward understanding the more challenging aspects of interpersonal relationships.*

Dick said slowly, "Well. Let me think. Denzel Washington? Samuel L. Jackson?" He paused, then went on pointedly, "Laurence Fishburne? Will Smith?" Shifting in his seat, he faced Jane. "Cuba Gooding Junior? Mario Van Peebles? Blair Underwood? Tupac?—Eminem was allowed, so Tupac's fair game, or would be if he were alive—Lorenz Tate? Wesley Snipes?"

All three, Genna, Jane, and Keith, were chained together in silence; had any of them moved, the links might have jangled.

Again, the blonde countergirl passed the table and winked down at Dick. "Blair sure as hell gets my vote."

Is Dick's response valid or invalid?

7.
Scenario #11
Modalities of Jealousy
with Study Notes

"For I am afraid that perhaps when I come I may find you to be not what I wish and may be found by you to be not what you wish; that perhaps there will be strife, jealousy, angry tempers, disputes, slanders, gossip, arrogance, disturbances." 2 Corinthians 12:20. The Relationship Handbook adopts no position on religious orientation. The quote cited above has not been chosen in advocacy of the Christian perspective over any other; rather, it seems the perfect illustrative prescription: the capsule, precise and compact, inside which Dick's emotions swirled, like a blizzard of toxic time-released granules, swallowed on the evening of Scenario #10. Jealousy is the dagger held in the heart's left hand, while the right clutches the cloth smeared cardiac red to further staunch the self-inflicted wound. Those under jealousy's sway were long ago depicted as displaying a threatening countenance, a lowering aspect, gnashing of tense teeth, froth of words, and a hand poised for the violence of slaughter.

That evening after leaving Pizza Hut, Dick drove while Jane sat in the quintessentially female posture, the heels of her feet tucked under the buttocks, inner ankles kissing and inner knees, legs' parallelogram slanted toward Dick; her upper torso too was angled toward him. Her fingernails she sawed asunder with sweeps of a hissing emery board. Dick parked the car without responding when Jane asked why they were stopping and jumped out, disappearing into a store called Mangled Masks always crowded with students from the nearby campus, returning five minutes later with a bag.

"What were you doing?" Jane asked, slightly annoyed. "What's in the bag?"

Her annoyance ignited his anger. "Why is it that they always assume that their standards of beauty are universal? And take it for granted that we'll find them beautiful? That we have no choice but to see them exactly as they see themselves?" Dick tried to ask this contemplatively, calmly. But a trembling tone had crept into his voice, an appoggiatura of grief. *The lesions and wounds of jealousy are secret and hidden, nor do they admit an anodyne or the remedy of a healing cure, since they have shut themselves in suffering within the dungeons and skulking places of the conscience.*

Jane pulled her eyes up into an astigmatic squint. "They? What are you talking about, anyway?"

"Yes, they. Don't pretend you don't understand. They means white."

"Who?"

"Keith, Genna."

"Our friends? You're calling our friends 'they'? Why are you talking like this?"

"You were there. You were right there, going along, in fact you led the pack. Every movie star named was white, until I said what I said."

"It was just a stupid game," Jane said hotly. "It was a game, you know? How can you can turn a game into something so ugly and hateful?"

"Just a game. You don't understand what I'm saying?"

"What, a stupid game? All the movie stars got ripped apart! You would have felt better if we'd have ripped apart African-American movie stars?"

At that snowballing escalating moment, Dick wished he were the brutal, remorseless sort who would have thought nothing of slapping her. "Do you understand what I'm saying or do you not understand?"

Dick had stopped the car in the middle of the street. Cars in a swerving wishbone swished right and left around them but did not honk.

A cellophane hood of anger fell over Jane's face, a grave asphyxiation. "I won't have this conversation with you."

"It's too late," he shouted. "We're already having it."

a.) Is Dick's position valid or,

b.) Does his elaboration regarding socio-racial dynamics merely smoke screen his own jealous motives or,

c.) Both or,

d.) None of the above.

"I know *exactly* what Dick thinks," Keith said. Genna and Keith were sitting on the uppermost row of tiered bleachers ringing a rodeo arena at the Pomona State Fairgrounds, where they had gone after leaving Pizza Hut. Dust like floaters in the eye dangled in the equine-scented air. "And I hate it. I hate he would think that about me. He should know me better. I'm not some kind of blunt-brained redneck . . ."

On the word "redneck," Genna yelled, "Yeeee-haw," then, seeing Keith's furious expression, pointed at horse and rider bounding brutally out the chute.

"That's so fucking funny," he said.

"You don't understand?" Dick persisted. "That they, and you, never thought to include among all the beautiful people a single African American? Why shouldn't they pick themselves as an image of ultimate beauty? But they expect us to do the same, while it never occurs to them to pick someone black. And you—"

"Look, Dick had a point to make, a valid point, so he made it. So accept it and move on," Genna argued mildly.

Keith said, "The point he made contained a wrong judgement of me. And you. You don't care about that?"

"Well, when you get right down to it, Keith, I don't remember any names of African-American stars falling off your lips."

"What the fuck? Look at Halle Berry. She's as beautiful—no, more beautiful—than any white actress. Dick knows I'd . . ."

Genna laughed. "Screw her in a second? Hello. But you weren't a guy in the game. You were a woman. And you didn't pick any African-American male stars. Period."

"That's insane!" Keith almost yelled.

Jane shouted, "Just drive the car, Dick."

Dick reached in the bag and removed a blonde wig. He jammed the wig on his head. "How's that? Better?"

Jane began to weep in frustration. "Drive. Drive this goddamn car. Drive!"

Again Dick plunged into the bag and dangled a second blonde wig with long tangled trembling tresses. When he placed the wig on Jane's head as though it were a crown, she did not bother to remove it. Jane wept. "There," Dick said. "You look good. Hot. Not that you weren't before. Now I'll drive."

"Yeeee-haw," Genna exclaimed.

[Note that Antonio Banderas and Benicio del Toro, actors of Latin descent, have been lumped into the category "white" by Dick without consideration for ethnicity; while Dick would bitterly object to the homogenous grouping of black persons based on a common denomination of skin color which ignores nationality, (i.e., a black African is not a black Frenchman, etc.) he appears to be blindsided by the same reductive tendencies.]

8.
Scenario #12
Modalities of Jealousy, Cont.

On the night of Scenario #11, as though they had sketched upon the bed an image of bodies entwined in reconciliation with a pencil of troubled lust, Dick and Jane dropped into a scribble of arms and legs to grapple toward the sense of union that had eluded them earlier that evening; but it was simply, in the final analysis, connect-the-dots sex, flat and uninspiring, a chalk outline delimiting lifeless bodies. Eyes closed in the toy-drum thud of an orgasm that left her hollow, Jane had not seen Dick with one hand groping to find the wig sprawled where thrown on the floor next to the bed. As he swam in the steep of his own weak-broth release, Dick covertly placed the wig atop his head, then slumping, spent, covertly removed it.

This would be their last shared sexual experience, though they continued to live together in the solemn rooms of the apartment. They would continue to say the words, "I love you."

A month later, on Saturday, Dick took Jane to a party.

In a warehouse not far from the docks of the Queen Mary, in Long Beach's harbor area with its forlorn tumbleweed feeling, Dick strolled with Jane through an auditorium-sized room. Bodies ricocheted wildly, bullets fired from an AK-47 of dance: Beneath a ceiling so vaulted it appeared black as night, they danced; in clusters before a bar long as a racetrack selling water, they danced; as though the music with its deafening bass line were a flagellation, they danced. Wearing a surgical mask reeking of Vick's Vapor-Rub, red hair fanged in moussed extrusions, a young woman pressed into Dick's hand a pill bearing the Addidas logo as she passed. Dick smoothly passed pill into mouth as though shyly shielding smile or yawn. Some time later they had found a smaller room where a dozen or so partially or fully nude people lounged, languished, or loved on puffy cushions beneath black lights. The countergirl from Pizza Hut rose from blonde entanglement with another girl who could have passed for her twin and whose upper torso was covered with angel tattoos, approaching Dick with the rubber nipple of a pacifier plugging her mouth. It popped out when she spoke, dangling on its candy-beaded string around her neck.

"Glad you could make it," she greeted, hugging Dick with an extravagance suggesting complete absorption into luxury.

"Wouldn't have missed it," Dick responded. "I was telling Jane that it would be educational to expand our horizons, that we'd settled into a rut."

"You guys came to the right place to expand your horizons." Looping her arms around Dick's neck, she kissed him with friendly languid intensity. His face now dewed with perspiration, he returned the kiss, stroking her arms, his eyes sliding like oars beneath a wash of rippling lashes to find Jane standing next to an iced keg sprouting plastic bottles of Evian, staring at them. Despite her unflinching stare, it was obvious that Jane did not know what was happening, that she had expected a party and not a rave, perhaps wine or beer but not Ecstasy. She stood like cold iron until the purple sofa behind her with a magnet's pull drew her into a sitting posture. Next to her was a shirtless boy wearing dark glasses, hiking boots, below-the-knee flabby surfer's shorts, his skin the color of lamb's fleece. Dick asked the countergirl her name. Terramaine, she said, or maybe Tammy—Dick heard the T's wispily as though they were smoke rings.

"Have you ever raved?" she quizzed.

"Only against the dying of the light," Dick riffed, then realizing she had not said the word rage from Dylan Thomas' poem, he laughed as they slowly looped down a barber's pole of sensuality, ribboning around each other. When they reached the floor, a cushion soft as an infant's flushed fontanel rose, magically, to meet them. After a time he became conscious that his clothes were gone and he was on his back, the countergirl positioning herself above the second heart beating hard below his waist. Body a thesaurus of touch, the girl finding all the synonyms with fluttering fingers, Dick remembered Jane and turned his head to seek her face, wanting to find the expression he imagined and hoped he would read there; for in his own obstructed way, Dick believed he loved Jane and wanted to confirm her love for him in her eyes' shattered stare. But what he saw was the boy of fleece taking her hand and gently pulling her up, saw him place a pill on her outstretched tongue, leading her through another door into a deeper room. The beating heart below Dick's waist subsided, then flat lined.

She moved like CPR, then stretched herself with eager resignation fully upon him.

"Doesn't matter," Terramaine-Tammy whispered. "Oh my god, just, whatever you do, just keep touching me."

9.
Scenario #13 with Key Question

Posit that Dick still wants Jane, her rare and clinquant quiddity, without the superfluity of relationship. *Is possession without relationship possible?*

3.
Recap—Scenario #8

["If I'd known I would never see you again, that it was the last time, I would have remembered every detail of your body. I want to remember that, Jane. I don't want the memory of that part of our relationship to become unreal. See me tomorrow, please. Let me see you that way once more. Just see, nothing else."]

Judgement a jigsaw of mind and emotion, Jane has accepted Dick's invitation and is sitting on the bed's edge. Dick, standing in front of the shuttered French-style closet door, can no longer remember what she was wearing when she swept through the door of room 251 here in the Ramada Inn, the rendezvous' imposed condition of a rented room's "emotionally neutral territory" Jane's idea and unbending insistence. In the noon-colored light that seems a template for all bright and uncomplicated days streaming through the windows, her nudity is his amnesia, striking his eyes as though it were the stunning surface against which he had fallen, a cruel concussion inflicted. Legs crossed, thighs sandwiching a slice of shadow tightening to shaved fork of flesh that holds a feast's invitation, leaning back into her arms so her honey-hued shoulders round into a prominence suggesting double-jointedness, a hunched ripeness, Jane watches Dick with fetchingly tilted head.

"This is it," she announces gravely, "the whole package. This sums it up. Do you remember now?"

"Now it seems impossible I could have ever forgotten."

Here is the Dick she remembers, words right, eyes awed, his presence shining her into immortality. How sad, she thinks, that these things die as though destined. But Jane finds the official tone she needs to continue, the tone that like a needle that somehow severs as it sews. "The breasts, as you can see, are small. I've often thought of remedial augmentation but never told you that. The right one appears to be smaller than the left because I was in a car accident some years ago and they ended up removing a rib. Why they felt this was necessary, I'm not exactly sure. The hips are too wide for a five-foot five-inch frame."

"Nonsense," Dick protests with authority, moving to the bathroom's doorway. "Child-bearing hips. They bespeak fertility."

She purses her lips dismissively. "Please, don't make this harder than it is. This is the kind of frank confession from a woman you'll probably never hear again. The ass"—swerving to stomach, back arched in a supple valley, vertebrae snaking skin's toffee-hued stretch, legs pressed together and jackknifed in classic '50s pinup fashion, for Jane has always been a bit of an exhibitionist—"the ass is fairly shapely. However. There are the beginnings, very faint, of stretch marks. Now"—flipping over onto her back with agile energy and sitting up again, stretching straight her legs—"the legs I like. The legs are long." She springs to her feet standing hands on hips. "But the knees could be a little less knobby. I have a scar on my abdomen, as you know—the abdomen, as you can see, is flat, another good point—tiny, next to the navel. Same aforementioned accident. So. This is my imperfect body. This is the body you'll probably never know again in the biblical sense." She begins to dress. "So. Your end of the bargain. But first, I lied about you not knowing my date. You do know him. It's Freddie Wallace."

"Mistake," Dick says.

"I want us to be friends, Dick. We had issues that made it impossible for us to be lovers, but I still want you in my life. Maybe it's crazy, but I just can't imagine you completely and forever not there, like a sudden death. I've never known you to be a liar. You have issues like anyone else, but . . . what I'm saying is, for us to stay in each other's life, I need to trust you."

"Fair enough."

"Starting now."

"Starting now," Dick says solemnly.

"Why did you really want to see me in the nude?"

"Simple. A little embarrassing, but simple, really. I won't be dating for a while. Frankly, this whole thing has drained me. But I still have needs." Dick sits on the bed, headboard jostling against his back.

Jane sits next to him, dressed now in jeans and sweatshirt. "I'm not sure I understand."

"I mean I don't intend on sleeping around. You don't do that these days."

"Well, neither will I be . . ."

Eyebrow rakishly raised, Dick cups an invisible shaft in his hand, sliding up and down. "Needs." Jane laughs, delighted chimes sounding high in her throat, and thuds Dick with a pillow. "Hey, I'm just being honest. If and when that moment arrives, when I close my eyes, I want to see you. If I'm forced to retreat into onanism, I don't want to be sitting there with a pathetic stack of adult movies, drooling over some big-breasted bimbo."

"Jesus, Dick," Jane says, still laughing. "Your mind works in such odd ways." She touches his face affectionately. "I guess I should be flattered or something."

"Be flattered."

"Next true thing. Why is Freddie a mistake?"

"Fast Freddie the track star—such an impatient young man. His dad was the first black manager back in the '60s to crack the glass ceiling at Pepsi and zoom up to the executive echelon. He was promoted to international VP of R&D,

or marketing, something like that. Freddie inherited daddy's good looks but not the brains, apparently. Still, he wants to make daddy proud. I wrote papers for him when I was an undergrad and charged him an arm and leg."

"Are you kidding?"

"I would wish, for your sake. He goes for the glory, all right, but doesn't want to do the work. The two-twenty? He broke those records with a little help from his friends, as the song goes. Steroid speed. Impatient guy. And in matters of the heart, impatient too. Cuts right to the chase: roofies."

Assume that the information Dick has shared with Jane is substantively true and accurate.

[Like a diminuendo, The Relationship Handbook from this point to the conclusion of the friendship chapter will gradually recede, with the confidence that the information presented will prove useful in guiding a relationship through its moribund stages has been provided. It is hoped that the chapters preceding this one, i.e., mind-set preparatory to seeking an appropriate partner, courtship techniques, compatibility factors, sexual intimacy, cohabitation, and finally dissolution, have prepared readers to effect a synthesis of the key elements that have been so far presented; that readers will be able to formulate informed conclusions regarding the relationship between Dick and Jane, avoiding the impediments to cultivating friendship after an intimate relationship has breathed its last gasp. This chapter has been particularly dense in its presentation of a welter of factors shaping interpersonal relationships, and readers are to be congratulated for their willingness to untangle the strands of the tapestry The Relationship Handbook has woven. Readers who have found this handbook helpful are encouraged to investigate other publications in The Handbook Series.]

"Roofies. The date rape drug. Great." Jane locates her anxiety on the tip of her fingernail, inserting it between her teeth, beginning to thinly nibble. "I was about to go out with a subintelligent rapist daddy's boy loser."

Dick tugs her finger from her mouth and lays his arm around her shoulders like twilight falling frail on stained glass: he hopes she will feel it as something almost religious, an aperçus of touch, a pureness contrasting with Freddie Wallace's demonic darkness. "Don't worry, Jellybean"—nickname he had given early on because of the sweet citrus taste of her tongue's tip— "I won't let you end up with someone like Freddie Wallace. I know what your type is, Jane. I should—I was that once."

"Don't make me sad and sentimental. You still are my type."

"Then you need someone like me. Only without the glitches. I can do this. It'll be my act of contrition, it'll be like protecting something precious. If you still want me in your life, this practically guarantees the guy won't be jealous. He'll be indebted to me."

Jane says faintly, "This is so strange."

"I think it's being very mature."

"No one will believe this."

"We'll boldly go where no couple has gone before," he says, stroking her hair. "I'll get the guy, you go on the date, you tell me what happened. Dick as professor determines the grade. No grading on the broken guy's curve."

Dimly, hesitantly, Jane agrees. She stands as though her legs are tearful. "I have a class to get to. Are you coming?"

"In a bit," Dick says. "Lick my wounds. Trip down memory lane. That kind of thing." When her hand is on the doorknob, Dick stops her by calling out, "Tell me something." She turns. "That night, when . . . at the warehouse . . . when you left with that guy . . ."

"Don't ask me anything about that," she answers. "Please. You hurt me, Dick, and I wanted to hurt you back, so I hurt myself. End of story."

"End of story."

But it is not the end of the story. Dick imagines Jane that night standing with palms pressed against wall somewhere in a dark warehouse room, the boy of fleece standing behind her with fingertips tuned to hips' strong signals (radio KFUK, Dick actually thinks laughing acidly aloud), the bats of their moans bouncing off the ceiling.

10.
Scenario #12
Warehouse
Discontinuous, Cont.

The boy of fleece is nineteen, serotonin-deficient, decadently anemic, with washed out eyes that Dick, had he seen them, might have mistook for pyric eyes of icy blue. Had these years of early manhood taken place during the '60s, the boy would have been effortlessly absorbed into the astral bloom of young people the dominant culture had referred to, with wistful disdain, as the "flower children." Where that generation had espoused a philosophy of free love, the generation to which the boy of fleece belongs participates in a promiscuity devoid of pretensions to higher philosophical value; thus, the boy of fleece may be both more honest and unknowingly cynical when, placing the tablet in her palm, he tells Jane that E (Ecstasy) is "all about sensation" and speaks of becoming "more open, other-focused, more about connecting." They sit on the floor while talking. Jane gives the tablet back, "If I were anymore open, I'd be a wound," she declines. He laughs. She does allow him to hold her hand paternally as, for the next hour, she tells him about the problems she and Dick are having. He listens sympathetically, nodding.

It may be possible that the combination of projected fears and mildly hallucinogenic properties of the Ecstasy Dick had ingested on that night were responsible for the manufactured tableaux, now horrifically warehoused in his mind, of Jane's outstretched tongue, the pill placed sacramentally upon it.

11.
Scenario #13
Ramada Inn
Discontinuous, Cont.

Since learning that the time had come for Jane to emerge from solitude and grieving, as a patron swathed in a movie theater's gloom must inevitably step into the light of obliterated illusions, Dick has burrowed deeper into imagination's cocoon. He sees a merry-go-round of faces and features, personality types, physiques, mannerisms, hears their voices, Dick's heart walking in a drunken stagger, chest a heaving hill. The swirl of men resembling Antonio Banderas, Brad Pitt, Kurt Russell, Pierce Brosnan. Even now, as he rises from the bed, Alec Baldwin, Val Kilmer, Eminem, George Clooney, all swirling, and the boy of fleece, followed by a flock of similar young men from the university.

"I'm alone now," Dick says.

The voice from the closet answers, "I think I took some good ones, considering the angle afforded. Can you open the door? I think the door is stuck."

Dick tugs the closet door and a tall young man with stooped shoulders, a dull complexion like poorly polished onyx previously packed in dry ice, steps into the room. In his large dwarfing hand, the fingers dangling on medallions of knuckles, he loosely clutches a digital camera. His eyes, fawn-like, seem to take their focus in sips from a quiet spring of inner pleading. Gesturing toward the bed, Dick takes the camera, watching Richard Wayside, a thirty-one-year-old math instructor at the university, tip tentative in the manner of one testing ground around puddles before slowly sitting on the bed.

"Her body is amazing . . . she's so beautiful." This genie of praise rises through the bewitchment his voice barely bottles. "I doubt seriously she would ever be interested in someone like me."

"Nonsense. You lack confidence, Richard," Dick contradicts in tutorial tones. "I know better than she does what her type is. I'll tell you what she likes, what she abhors, what makes her laugh, what brings tears to her eyes. You're a mathematician. Think of Jane as a classic problem—say, the irrational number *e*. What do you need to construct a proof, Richard?"

Without hesitating Richard answers, "There are three preliminary steps needed to construct a sound proof. First you have to be aware of the definitions of each of the terms associated with what you're trying to prove. Next, understand previous proven theorems related to what you're attempting to prove. Finally, know the basic rules of logic . . ." Excited now, he jerks a pen from his pocket. "Do you have paper?"

"I'm afraid not," Dick replies. "My point is, Jane is *e*, and I can provide you with the proof."

"But isn't . . . wasn't Jane your girlfriend?"

Sitting very close to Richard, Dick strives to look in his eyes, which dart and drop. "Don't impugn my motives, Richard."

Huge hands flutter up, cooing ebony doves. "I would never . . . no, no, you misunderstand . . ."

"Let me make it very clear," Dick says slowly, "that what I do, I do out of my love for Jane. That love will outlast even my body. It will outlast yours. It exists in the realm of pure spirit. We're not together anymore, but I consider Jane to be my dearest friend. Can you look at me, Richard?" Dick lifts Richard's chin. The mathematician's entire head trembles in the powerful current of this proximity, which must seem inescapable to him. "For I'd like you to see the seriousness in my eyes. My task—maybe mission would be a better word—is to make certain she's not exposed to all the evil, the flotsam and jetsam, the shit out there. I want her to be with someone who meets my highest standards. Does that seem so strange?"

"When you put it that way," Richard almost whispers, "no, it doesn't."

"You're among the elite. If you listen to me, Richard, if you really listen to what I tell you, then yes, you stand a chance.

A very good chance. You're a brilliant mathematician, or so I hear. You have a bright future ahead of you. Jane admires intelligence above all else. But you have to be able to follow instructions. Are you capable of that?"

"Yes, I think so."

"That's good, but I don't want you to think. I want you to know."

He declares more firmly, "Yes."

"Good." He gently releases Richard's chin. Immediately, his eyes dart and drop. "You'll have to trust me. Jane can sometimes be very eccentric. No matter what I tell you, no matter how strange it seems, you have to do it if you're going to win her heart. If I tell you to put a fucking wig on your head in public because it will amuse her, you have to be willing to do it."

Richard nods.

"And what is this opportunity worth to you?" Dick asks.

The mathematician stares blankly at Dick for a moment. "Oh. Yes." He hastily pulls a check from his pocket. "You mean . . ."

"Yes, we discussed it. Everything worthwhile has a price."

Richard gives Dick a check for a thousand dollars. Dick explains that there he would be dishonest in guaranteeing the outcome of Richard's adventures with Jane; that there can be no refund of Dick's fee as relationship broker if Richard's expectations are not met.

Richard does not ask what Dick will do with the pictures he has taken. *Will Dick indeed use them as visual aids in the sporadic bouts of onanistic succor he has alluded to with Jane? Will Dick post the photos on the internet as an inducement for others who would find Jane an attractive prospective partner and who would submit to Dick's tutelage?*

12.
Scenario #14

Time has passed. Dick and Jane meet for lunch at Jane's favorite restaurant in Santa Monica. She looks, to Dick, more beautiful than ever, though slightly worried, slightly weary. Fatigue lines thin as tarot cards viewed edgewise are stacked beneath eyes yielding the gaze of a baffled seer.

"Who am I seeing tonight?" she asks.

"I can't keep track of your life for you. It's wearing me out, you know that, don't you?" Dick says, though his tone, kindly humorous, is such that Jane feels, for the moment, less troubled.

"I know. I'm sorry, this is turning out to be harder than we thought. Maybe I should declare a boy moratorium."

Nevertheless, they go on to speak in an intoxication of choices not made, of decisions perversely withheld. They segment the future into little squares, a domino row of probabilities and possible outcomes; they tease themselves, stretching out a forefinger of words that hovers in readiness for the first irrevocable tap.

Chantelle's Braces

You say that, instead, we could look out that window. That the Hollywood sky, clouds whipped by Santa Ana winds into a frothy parfait, is nothing like the ashen sky you left behind in Bedford, Ohio.

You say that we could stay inside and listen to the romantic murmur of nearby branches, and you remind me that I said I would show you joy.

Yes, I did say that five hours ago, when you first emerged from the stale gloom of the Greyhound bus, and it may be that you've reminded me because you're beginning to have doubts, though I would prefer to think it's simply that you can't see how the scenario I've proposed could one day become a treasure box of retrospection you could plunder during those times when you might otherwise yield to the temptation to rest your chin in the broad palm of boredom, stare into the poverty of empty space, do nothing. Isn't boredom the arch-nemesis of every teenager—in fact, of every man and woman?

Try to imagine the exciting details of my proposed scenario: the door to the room I'll rent for an hour down the hall slamming open upon indecent caresses as I burst in, playing the part of the wolf from streets like wild woods. Imagine bolting upright off the mattress, the poor john tumbling like a rockslide from the slopes of your body scant seconds before he can fit himself snugly between your holstering thighs. You'll clutch wildly at the sheet and pull it up to your neck (behind this salacious bib will dangle the silver crucifix that was a present from your incest-loving father), while I snarl and snap at his sodden crotch before beating him senseless. How will I know when to kick the door in? I'll know because you'll take this tiny black box, a simple transmitter, and you'll press the button a moment before the arrow of his lust finds its target. This receiver I hold will blink its tiny red eye; my response will be instantaneous and brutal.

Won't this be pure exhilaration, and without a doubt the opposite of bloodless boredom?

ooooo

It's true daylight lessens in imminent exit, the hour seems to be latent with the spent sexual immobility you think we could share and not regret. But we need to make money to eat, to pay rent, to establish our modest household . . . no, none of that, to hell with those lies, Chantelle. I won't lie, I'll just make promises I can't always keep.

What we have to work with is the tree beyond the window, your eyes, and this room.

If I could capture the dew of even your most disillusioned of glances in jars, sell them to other sly peddlers, they would only distill them to a stasis of black petals. I know that's lovely to hear, but what would such glances be worth to us? And as for this room, we could pretend to recline in a parlor not filled with cheap K-Mart lamps, our tarnished maimed brass servants, but this light will never be our fortress. For that, we would need protective walls of light remote as the moon, terrible as the efficacy of cactus. And the tree—we'll peel with our eyes the pastel shadows of that tree beyond the window as though it were an orange; there's no great harm in pretending to enjoy it for now.

But you must choose your illusions carefully. You have so much to learn, Chantelle, and there are so many things I can teach you.

Think back to that first little skin-popping prick of the needle I administered not an hour ago. You'll come to understand that centuries of alabaster powder now freight our gasping veins, that each drop of sweat on our limbs is like the mournful blast of a locomotive's horn attempting to warn stragglers away from the tracks.

This is all my way of saying it will soon be time for you to go.

The streets are waiting for that red dress you'll wear like skin, your shadow trailed by mine as I slide along the walls of abandoned buildings, the brass knuckles in my pocket. You now hear music? Would you like me to say the tunes seem to portray fairies, their ethereal voices, their languid tresses, that the tunes are like something that pours, spilling nectar from vases? I know I twist this language into taffy; it's sweet when you sink your teeth into it, but it doesn't make sense.

That's what you want. That's what I want you to want—as long as you know they're illusions.

But I can be accommodating as well. It doesn't all have to go my way, though it might seem like that at first. For example, because I know it will appeal to your adolescent sensibilities, I'll deny the music we hear is simply a common boombox outside, kicking with heavy boots of bass, forcing my heart ajar, that door in my chest long closed and held fast by its corroded deadbolt. I'll deny it and say that it's you, opening my heart and pouring your music into me.

ooooo

What does a fourteen-year-old know of love? I won't patronize you, Chantelle. You are a pretty girl with an angelic face the color of the dark-hued spaces between stars, but your teeth are picket fences planted in the otherwise verdant dell behind your lips, where the spaces of your mouth smell like rain, a green meringue of meadows. Your father—you called him Daddy, didn't you—said that he would put you in the capable hands of an orthodontist, if only you would leave your bedroom door ajar and camouflage his moans with the sounds he instructed you to produce in imitation of a young girl waltzing with nightmares after midnight. If your mother heard from her bed of echoes at the bottom of the empty vodka bottle where she slept, she would stir briefly as though to cast off her woolen blanket of booze, then return after a begrudging moment of besotted half-wakefulness to sleep, having convinced herself that what she heard was the sound of a daughter waltzing with nightmares after midnight, a girl too old to require the comfort of a mother's arms.

Do you see that piggy bank there on the dresser, the one I've stuffed with soiled bills? You see the words written in magic marker on its pink flanks? What does it say? It says, For Chantelle's Braces. Love equals accommodation equals braces.

ooooo

You remember the sword of an autumn river, the Ohio river, sheathed by a scabbard of glittering banks. Remember, I've said you must choose your illusions carefully. It might very well be that the glitter was simply the kiss of sunlight on discarded, uninhabited condoms. Down the raw scar of the road was a pier. Standing on that pier, regarding travelers flowing by in liquid vehicles, you saw their faces peering at you from behind rolled up windows, like faces peering out from the frames of portraits that hang slightly askew on the wall. The compulsion to straighten the frames of portraits with a fingertip's tap are always akin to the cruelest of temptations. Such faces, when glimpsed in their trailing scarves of speed, always seem unique and exciting.

But coming and going, the fatuous rapture of departures and destinations, is all the same thing: that kaleidoscope of shifting circumstances through which eyes ricochet from tragedy to tragedy in tragic technicolor.

Perhaps you saw my face, Chantelle, I would like to think so. Maybe I had just fled Sheboygan, Wisconsin, where the checks I recklessly wrote without money in the bank bought me the things I thought I needed. Or maybe I had just launched myself, a restless rock, from the slingshot of Orlando, Florida, pursued by the three Russians in a black BMW who were intent on collecting money I had borrowed and neglected to repay. They were moths mourning the vitality of my flame, pursuing the residual sparks of my dishonor as I sped through the striptease of winds before me. There are words in other languages that mean nigger, and I believe they must have shouted that word, building it up into a stack of blunt square alphabet blocks that rolled off their clacking mother tongue. But they did not realize, as we do, that America is the luminous nigger of the world, a place that built itself from nothing, from scraps of invisibility, and that to find me would be as difficult as finding and clutching invisible things.

So there you stood; I believe I saw you as I went zooming by, and just as I may have seen a girl struggling against the diminution of her daily losses, you may have glimpsed my eyes, which would have haunted you with my own vulpine premonitions. I imagine the rest: That you were driven to enact parables, that you scooped a handful of sepia water you held in interlaced fingers, racing back to your house and opening the trapdoor of your hands above a bucket; that you carried the bucket to your father, told him you had captured the wild heart of the river. He laughed at you, Chantelle, and told you that since the water in the bucket no longer flowed, you had forfeited the right to call it a river. He was a brutal one with a fondness for pressing the tip of the pin to the rainbow bubbles of childhood, but not altogether wrong in certain of his observations.

ooooo

You are my Salome of profits, of small future freedoms and luxuries: The caviar of dope we'll both feed on with our exquisite hypodermic implements; the limousine of bliss we'll ride in over the freeways of our pharmaceutical blood.

There's no reason for you to see those dances you'll lie down for on sweat-braided linens as anything more than a means to that end. I may even buy you veils, an array of silken garments, a silver tray on which to display the useless heads that will roll from men's shoulders after I've hacked them off with my rusty blade. There's no reason to pity the men who will come to you in humble concupiscence, those supplicants of the god of lust and loneliness.

Their wives will miss them for a time, until the insurance checks arrive . . . now what is it, Chantelle?

You say you don't feel well, you are retreating to the bathroom. Is this another form of playing hooky? I know that you despised the ninth grade, that jungle of mediocrity you were banished to each day, the girls who roamed the barren veldts of public-school education and watched you with roaring eyes, those lionesses of adolescence who lankily stalked you through the hormone-reeking halls, tossing their shrill and jealous manes. It was not your fault their boyfriends, mere dogs bounding through the fields of their tumid fantasies, sniffed at your skirts—did you wear skirts, or refuse them for fashionably mangled Calvin Klein jeans?—inhaling the listless odor of the progenitor's seed. You could not stop your father and so you betrayed him (that was the cyanide logic you swallowed at any rate), leaving through the back door of the gymnasium in the middle of homecoming dances with this or that gangly youth, someone else's date, ordering them to pull down their pants behind the bushes in the parking lot, then fondling the penis, which held you in its jerky aim, an executioner's rifle. But one day those girls caught up with you, Chantelle, made you drink down the quarts of outrage you had distilled in them, and in some corner of a building hidden from the hazy eyes of teachers, did things to you with a broom handle turned phallic, an assault which symbolized for them what they imagined you wanted. The blood blazed down your smoky thighs and when your mouth yawned open like a sewer lid to flood their ankles in pestilential pools of laughter, they feared you, angling away from you in a coterie of flight.

But you were too smart for school anyway, Chantelle, what could they teach you from books that you had not already read in the unexpurgated pages of everyday life? You have no reason to play hooky now. Now, you are the teacher and your pupils want only to learn the ways of a stern and pitiless heart such as yours.

ooooo

You must be feeling better, Chantelle, you are out of the bathroom, your complexion as flawless as the dark velvety button embedded in dandelion's fringe, your face just as round and budding with youth, but you are beginning to sound like a CD scarred into repetition by a clumsy scalpel of laser. Out there is a tree; you insist it displays chandeliers of branches, you keep claiming you would be content to watch them for all eternity, even though with each passing moment you find it increasingly difficult to refute my insistence that eternity only exists in the veins that tunnel through our bodies and carry us off to that timeless rose-tinted underground we would reside in forever if we could. One of us must go and do what needs to be done. If you loose me upon the world, I can't promise you the turns and twists of my odyssey will ensure my swift and speedy return.

Let me tell you something.

When I was in prison, the guards tried to mock me with the odor of freedom that starched their uniforms, but my catalog of remembered iniquities overpowered that mockery and made me patient as Job. No prisoner was more willing to serve his sentence than I was, for I had so much to savor, so many vivid condiments to sprinkle on the leathery roast of tedium they hoped I would chew and then choke on. Other prisoners saw themselves at the end of their incarceration borne aloft on parade floats, waving to bystanders who would no longer see them as convicts, for they would emerge scrubbed clean by the hard bristles of rehabilitation. But I went nowhere, did not imagine the benevolence that would greet me when I was set free; I wallowed like a sow in the sludge of blood I had spilled.

Yes, there were white men I slaughtered because their eyes, like irons manufactured by Black & Decker, steamed me to a creased crisp, forcing me to move as though I occupied a faded zoot suit lifted moth-eaten from some battered trunk. There was something outdated and absurd about the image of menace they dressed me in. It was as if I had no right, in these days accelerated and sanitized by computers, to feel the old dirty rage whose seeds they had planted in me centuries ago.

And yes, I killed black men too (only those to whom it would never occur to acknowledge me with a perfunctorily mumbled "brother" and that quick guillotine-blade of a nod when they passed me on streets, though I elect to be brother to no man) because of how easily they had been led, like foolish mules, to drink from the well of self-hatred, and now pecked at the keys of computers, machines that forget history the faster they are made to function. Downloaded from negritude, they think, into digital emancipation. One particularly gratifying memory strikes me now with most excellent force.

There was a black professor of semantics whose splendidly appointed Soho apartment I once broke into, and I never intended to find him there that night, a night that had let down its sable Soho hair to be combed smooth with white rain, though that detail now smacks of theatrical additament; it's quite possible I made it up, because I do so love rain, its mellow or raucous polyphonies; I never told you that, did I?

That I would have invented rain if I could?

By the time he sensed my presence in the room, it was too late. The professor, sitting at his desk, his eyes enslaved by the dungeon-dull glow of the monitor he stared into, finally turned and saw me standing there. He knew me with nameless intimacy, he knew he had struggled against strangling odds all his life not to become me. And then, do you know what he said?

Now this is a delectation, an éclair of irony, delicious to bite into.

He said, Please, brother . . . and raised his hand, a feeble gesture, in a salute that stayed frozen above his eyebrows, as though to coax me into visored focus. Put the light on me, I said, pointing to a frightened Ikea desk lamp with one of those snaking necks of ridged aluminum that are wrenched this way and that by seekers of illumination. He obeyed, and I rewarded him with a long weighted look before I knocked it from his hand, which moved like jagged encephalographic spikes.

Then I struck across the blunt bridge of his nose with that baseball bat you see propped there in the corner of our room.

I tell you this because I want you to know that I'm capable of protecting you, always. But I think you know that already.

What do you mean, why would they let a man like me who had killed go free from prison? They had no choice, Chantelle. I walked out because I grew weary of remembering and longed for new diseased adventures. I walked out wearing the clothes of the expert consultant who had come that day to recommend hermetic enhancements for their unassailable and vicious security systems.

But I know all your questions are just tactics. You want stories because they delay the inevitable; we all want that, and for that reason I'll refuse to be angered. Given time and the proper atmospherics . . . the dimness of this room, the REM-state shadows thrown by those somnambulant branches, the muted and buttery voices of the tenants above and below us smeared by the sponge of these walls into something that rejects the harshness of reality . . . given this watery montage of seductions, you're hoping I'll do what I haven't done before, that I will fall into your dark and virile arms, as though I were a member of royalty, a prince or king, who is seized in an uprising and led into the alarming purlieus outside the perimeters of the castle, then thrown into the arms of a swarming peasantry.

My Chantelle, you girlish heart opens its pink pages and invites the exotic calligraphy of silvery signatures.

I know that you live in a world of romantic fabrications, because when you drifted down like an ebony rose from the Greyhound bus where you had sat rooted to the seat for long hours, you carried nothing but a dog-eared volume of high-school poetryl; it was Wordsworth, I remember. Yes, I could close my eyes and evaporate into your dream of entwining limbs and allow my lips to frame a smeared dazed portrait of your kiss, but would I be any different from your father or the men who would stretch their bodies before you like puddles absorbing the litter of lost pavements?

Those brief aneurysms of pleasure you seek with me are nothing more than the vaporous gestures of the flesh.

Give me your arm, Chantelle, let me fortify the remote promise that my touch suggests with more immediate pleasures injected through the tip of this needle.

Do you feel it now?

It seems that you're whispering to me, Chantelle, that the words I hear you saying are, finally, joy.

ooooo

I listened to you recite the lush free verse of your past as we sat at the counter at Denny's and you devoured the Grand Slam breakfast with the medieval disdain for etiquette that celebrates gluttony, like those bloated kings in movies who tear into gargantuan turkey legs and toss the remains to dogs surging under the table.

So tell me if I have it right: Long before you began to dream of running away, you were already bruised by abandonment, a peach left to wither on the windowsill of your mother's melancholy moods.

She took long strolls from her bedroom to the living room and then to the kitchen, circling back then to the bedroom, while a vague parasol of isolation floated over and above her, immovable, casting off the light that seemed to fall unobstructed on other women, women whose husbands were not stricken with the sense of their of own inadequacy or failure. You grew accustomed to being ignored, and anyway there was always some never-flaccid schoolboy you could float away with on a misty zeppelin of marijuana and sangria . . . but one day you found a photo album encased in its sarcophagus of dust on a shelf in the garage, saw your mother at the age of fourteen, her face as vulnerable and smooth as an apple sliced in half, sweet and heart-shaped and brown as though from oxidation, as yet untouched by the abrasive tongue of the future, which would soon lap away at her innocence until her features melted into an acrid cider secreted by the shriveled core of manifold disappointments.

How horrible it was for you to see what your mother had not yet become, to know that things would go so wrong for her!

And who can blame a daughter for trying to hold up a shield to deflect the hurl of days and nights that were certain to arrive in her own life like a head-on collision, headlights glaring and horn shrieking on some vehicle of random lamentation, while at the same time striving to absorb some of the sorrow for foregone possibilities that assaulted the mother; for you were convinced that you could slice through the charred flank of loneliness laid out on the platter set before that older version of yourself, drink down the stale rumpled gravy that ran over the edge of your mother's sad plate.

Yes, you tried to help her, Chantelle, even when she fell in love with another man, a fellow who called himself a "tax specialist" and worked at Sears in a corner of that moribund store set aside as an outpost for H&R Block.

On a Monday that limply shrugged its shoulders in its threadbare garment of rain, dreary in that saturating way that only a rainy Midwestern city can be, she stopped to pick up the W2 that the man had prepared for your family, and on Wednesday evening they stood together in the parking lot as though leaning against the railing on a balcony of wistful moments, their eyes sweeping the horizon like windshield wipers as they awaited obscure signs and portents.

Sometimes a stranger is the archway to a vast coliseum of rapacity and need, and when we enter their lives, we do so as gladiators ready to take what we require and give what is demanded of us in dances of mortal combat, brandishing tears and laughter as though they were daggers, unsheathing the stories of our lives in slashes, parries and thrusts that will ultimately result in bloodlettings or the pleasurable exchange of bodily fluids.

They agreed to travel to the sinful purlieus beyond the commercial district where motels like so many gigantic tombstones surrounded an Amtrak station. Later, your mother revealed her secret to you and I know her pupils must have shone with diamond points of zirconian happiness that desperately mimicked authentic light, just as I know that you felt obligated to help her establish the logistics of her fretful assignations. For we all want happiness even though we come to realize that lasting happiness is an impossibility; we want it for ourselves and for others, we want it beyond reason and above all things.

Thus were you inducted by your mother and assumed your rank as general leading an army of her lies to do battle in the war of clandestine happiness she waged. You lied to your father each time you left the house in the evening with your mother, telling him that you were both taking hatha yoga classes at the YWCA downtown. Sitting in the car parked in back of the motel, you waited while your mother went to the room the tax man rented, shifting your eyes from the lines of the poem you were reading, Wordworth's "Ode on Intimations of Immortality," up to the window where you saw their shadows drifting together in a choreography of dire entanglement and embrace.

It was fascinating, wasn't it, Chantelle, to watch those shadows perform a slow-motion aikedo of clutch, release and eager realignment, gliding across the coyly lowered shade?

And at a certain point the shade lifted and your mother, clad only in her bra, threw open the window and leaned drunkenly on the sill, calling you, calling your name, beckoning you with an exuberant gesture of her arm, and you rose, answering that call, your body an elevator rising through the shaft of your mother's voice as it lifted you on cables of intoxicated laughter, until there you stood. There you stood, in the room, your mother now naked, lewd pearls dangled from her neck, a gift from the naked man standing behind her, his arms encircling the latex sag of her waist. You did what you were told, lifting the videocamera from the bed, fitting the cold cup of the viewfinder against your eye, taping them in their dissolve of intertwined flesh, zooming in to capture the startled and ferocious look on her face as she rode a sleigh of coarse moans and ululate sighs up and over the slippery slopes of her orgasm, his orgasm, hers again.

For this was to be her library, she explained, a record of stolen moments that would fill the empty screen of her life and offer her consolation for the escape she did not pursue, the flight she would otherwise have embarked on that would have severed the bonds to that house, that husband, and you.

ooooo

It was inevitable that one night while your mother was reliving the bedroom scenes you had taped, your father, unheard, would enter the sewing room in the rear of the house at an hour when he should have been sleeping, your mother's earplugs of vodka muffling his approach. And everything else that followed now seems the gaping of inevitable surreality, like hands long epoxied together in prayer stickily unclasping: your father calling you to the sewing room, arranging the chairs in a semi-circle before the television to promote optimum visibility, your father disappearing to the kitchen and returning with a large bowl brimming with misshapen skulls of popcorn, the air a garden of buttery scent that encouraged seeds of saliva to bear their anticipatory fruit, against your will, in what would have otherwise been your fear-parched mouth.

There were tall mugs of Cokes with mushrooming foam that released an applause of fizz that he thoughtfully set on TV trays for father and daughter, more vodka and pulp-free orange juice for Mom.

No one said a word, Chantelle, what was there to say?

Denials of your involvement would have been useless, the volume was turned up on the television, and your name could be heard as the couple exhorted you in the execution of bold, experimental angles. The three of you watched the grappling bodies, you were a member of an audience that seemed lazily suspended in hammocks of silence, until the last image succumbed to snow and snarl, the sleet of cathode oblivion, the terminal weather of exhausted technology.

ooooo

Were you angry, Chantelle? When your thoughts extended their flailing arms and embraced wild notions of fires that would be impervious to the blandishments of rushing waters, who did you see imprisoned in cellblocks of flame?

Each time your father brought his male coworkers home, and took them to the sewing room, served them ham and cheese sandwiches with ice-glazed pitchers of beer, then dimmed the lights in the room as though it were a theater, playing the tape of your mother and the tax man from Sears to the audience your father had assembled, the men watching at first as though bludgeoned by an appalled mallet of silence, then lifting their voices in a chorus of revelry encouraged by the cuckolded husband . . . each time, your heart expanded with the volatile helium of anomy. And that the men he ushered into that room were white was your father's inspired stroke of punitive genius.

When you saw the faces of those white men roll through a roulette of expressions, first shock, then deep undisguised fascination, you realized that they did not see what you had seen as they watched your mother thrash about on the bed and floor, a woman made grotesque with grieving, with sweet nepenthean cocktails. What they saw was a black whore who, with the exultation of one smothering finally flinging aside impediments to breathing, had freed an insatiable animal nature tenuously tamed by civilization, a creature amoral, carnal, palpitating with the percussion of internal jungle drums, devoid of higher faculties. For their eyes seemed to proclaim, I knew it, I was not wrong in suspecting as much.

Oh, Chantelle, that look on your face disappoints me; it's a mask of placation whose sole purpose is to grant a madman his delusions and thus avoid a scene. You think I'm injecting my own serum of bile into this cancerous body of facts? Did just one of them leave that room, that house, or even place his hand on your father's shoulder, ask him to describe the pain he had gripped in his hand like a stickshift, to explain why he brutally rammed it forward so that he sped down that desolate avenue of ugly revelation? I didn't think so, Chantelle, and I wish I could say I'm sorry.

But you must use the eyes God gave you to see the rich proliferation of ugly truths He has created for you. Just know that if I were God, I would have created a race capable of navigation without sight to inhabit this inexcusable planet. I can only do the next best thing, weave the black lace with which this world may be efficaciously shrouded.

Are you weeping?

I never intended to made you sad . . . ah, but now you're beginning to understand—you're holding your arm out to me. I'm here, Chantelle, and I will always have what you need if you'll just honor me with your trust, step forward with me onto this stage without benefit of a script, bow deeply, allow the curtain of your eyelids to descend upon the proscenium of sight, while the hands of the opiate applaud us, a mellow encore ringing in our ears.

ooooo

I had no idea, no idea it was so late.

The sun has relinquished its hold on its burden of mauve and saffron, slipped off its pedestal like a woman in narcosis who forgets the vertebrae's purpose and slides from her settee to the wild dark floor.

In your present state of wide-eyed sleeping you are laughing and mumbling, and now I know why you've been staring at the tree stretching its branches across our window.

It's not unlike the tree that grew outside your bedroom window in Bedford, that's what I'm hearing with difficulty as your clumsy mouth chews pebbles of speech, the tree your father planted from a single acorn the size of a large brown man's knuckle.

He told you it would grow tall and strong, a marvelous analog for your own budding heart. You were five years old, but still, still you remember. Years later you listened to those branches when your father entered your room that first night when the last member of his audience had reluctantly left, and he fell across the bed you sprawled in, exhausted by wickedness, and you felt the hot apology of his tears brand your cheeks, and you didn't know whether to hold him or vomit, and then, and then, and then, and then, and then he sank into you as though you were quicksand, and what did you do, what were you thinking, speak louder Chantelle, what were you feeling, they were nonfeelings, weren't they, what was the name of the fleshy spike between your thighs, what dream did you construct that refused to offer you refuge, what did you do with your hands, what was your name, when he called you Sylvia as he tumbled into the cave that you had become, Sylvia your mother's name, what echoes did you hear, what were those stalactites dripping in your eyes, what recourse did you have, what scraps of unauthored texts floated through your mind, what did you feel you owed him, and then that night a week later when he promised you the braces you knew he would never pay for, what did you grip with your hands, why did you not close your eyes, why did you not swallow your tongue, why did you not pull your hair out by its roots, what did you do, don't whisper, Chantelle, you must learn to shout, what did you do, where did you hide the sheets, there was only that tree, you anointed it with gasoline in the middle of the night, there were only those flames, skipping down the branches, playing hopscotch on the shingles of the roof, what was that thing that sounded like a siren in the distance, how had you become a victim, why did you not ask yourself *why* rather than *how* you had become a victim, why did you not laugh when you saw the house burning as you ran down the street with only a book in your hand, why that book and not another, why Wordsworth, why inutile poetry, why Hollywood, such a fucking cornucopia of questions, I had them too, I had them once, I was once a child, things happened to me, I too had trees, I too had books, like you perhaps I read so many books and found so few answers, a man such as I, black from birth and blacker still when the husk of childhood was peeled away by those pale eyes we know so well, such a man does not bother to read, that's how they looked at me, as though I would never think during all those years behind bars to pick up a book and read, and now speaking thus, of these assumptions by which men and women claim to identify each other, it occurs to me I haven't even told you my name, you don't know my name but I know yours, it's Chantelle or Mercedes or even Mary, it's amazing how long I've been able to glide with feline resource and cunning about the alleys and dumpsters of this world with not a single soul knowing my name, and now it's too late for that, Chantelle, you appear to be asleep on the floor, how long have you been sleeping, I hope that's what it is, are you dreaming of the money we lost tonight, if you are, don't dream that I'm angry, because tomorrow will be here soon, like the next breath waiting to be drawn, when you're awake I'll burn that tree, I promise we'll watch until it anchors itself in ashes, and eventually, the next day or the day after, there will be time enough for more words like these, more stories to tell, time enough for me to remember anew to withhold from you my name.

Kewl Kryptonian

It seems that Superman has fallen on hard times. His former fastidious appearance—the sleek tubular gloss of the blue and red uniform, the optical insurgency of pumpkin yellow as cubic backdrop for the bold insignia, the calf-high boots benignly suggestive of Schutzstaffel footwear—had once spawned imitative modes of dress among an adoring populace, once inspired fashion designers to christen the '80s as "the decade of imperial primary colors." Now, twenty years later, his uniform bears unmistakable signs of neglect. His once-beloved cape, impervious to puncture or penetration, flaunts an indiscretion of suspicious stains, vaguely masturbatory splotches, insomniac Magic Marker scribblings: a soiled tablecloth covering the furniture of deflated expectations.

The blue body stocking has lost its elastic cling; the external red trunks, once outlining the promising bulge of indefatigable genitalia, is a sagging diaper that seems weighted with excreta. This is the least of it.

His hair, previously molded by Brillantine into a wet-blackboard pompadour of ebony highlights, treble clef of a solitary lock scrolling down his forehead, seems a nest for the birds of his twig-frail thoughts, while his left eye strobes a stubborn tic.

On Lois Lane's advice, Superman is receiving treatment from an eminent psychotherapist who has written a book *Nurturing the Inner Superhero* that has risen to the top of the *New York Times* Bestseller List and hosts a popular weekly radio talk show called "Doctor Dave."

Doctor Dave has prescribed Superman Wellbutrin for depression.

Superman gazes wistfully, with lackluster eyes, out the window of the doctor's thirtieth-floor office suite into skies that had once been his trampoline, his boundless blue playground.

"How's the Wellbutrin working?"

Superman points silently to an unsightly rash that stretches in a sickle-shaped sweep from the edge of his bushy right eyebrow to the dimpled cleft of his prominent pale chin.

Doctor Dave frowns in concern. "You're exhibiting symptoms of systemic oversaturation. Ten thousand milligrams of the drug taken twice a day is apparently too much. Dosage levels are difficult to calibrate due to your many metabolic anomalies. Why do you think you're depressed?" the doctor asks.

"People," Superman answers, idly scratching the rash, "don't seem to appreciate me anymore. Something has happened."

"It must be difficult for someone with your abilities to find meaningful challenges. Why not fly to the nether regions of the universe? There must be wonderful things there. I've often wondered," the doctor muses, "what's on the other side of the universe."

"Nothing," Superman yawns finally. "More and more and more universe."

ooooo

The *Daily Planet*, once a beacon setting standards of journalistic integrity, has long since been shredded by hostile corporate takeovers into an insipid salad of supermarket tabloid publications. Over the years, Jimmy Olsen has clawed his way up and through the editorial echelons, leaving his cub reporter status far behind; as a majority stockholder he now controls the myriad tentacles of the operation as President and Chief Executive Officer.

Whatever earnestness he once possessed has been supplanted by shrewdness, cynicism. His face, though still boyish, now suggests something vaguely sinister.

It is this shrewdness that alerts him to Clark Kent's habit of disappearing during times when other reporters are on the telephone, frantically gathering information in the face of some crisis in progress.

It was that shrewdness that led him to follow Clark one afternoon as he ducked into the men's room on the fifth floor of the Daily Planet roped off for renovations. Accustomed to the pristine executive lavatory next to his palatial office, the newspaper magnate winced at the close bladdery stench that greeted him when he opened the door to the bathroom Clark furtively slipped into. He was shocked to see the reporter donning his uniform, windmilling arms a watercolor smear as the reporter transformed himself into the Man of Steel. Jimmy Olsen—assigned the moniker "J.O." by a retinue of sycophants—had produced his Diamond Crypto Smartphone with the built-in camera, tiny shutter like fingers snapping at a discothèque.

"I should have known. Your mysterious disappearances, your exclusive photos of Superman. Though I never suspected as much, it now makes perfect sense: Your guise of Clark Kent the nerd covers up for Superman's deep-seated sense of powerlessness." He slipped the diamond-studded cellphone into the breast pocket of his Kiton K-50 suit jacket and from the same pocket removed a Cuban Cohiba Behike cigar. "The psychologically maladapted personality submerged by the authoritarian persona. Like the middle-aged man who feels the need to disguise his impotency by purchasing a red sportscar."

"I am not a police officer," Superman said, "and what I have to hide is nothing more or less than what any mortal man or woman has to hide."

"It could be," Jimmy Olsen said, "that it is not Superman who nurtures his secret identity as Clark Kent, but the opposite."

ooooo

Scientists had detected a shifting of the earth by infinitesimal degrees off its axis; catastrophe was imminent. Superman was flexing before the bathroom mirror, as though to summon through bravado gestures a sense of confidence he no longer felt. "I have a world to save," the superhero announced.

"What presumption," J.O. remarked. "People do not need to be saved. What they need is to be taught to contend with the chaos of life."

ooooo

After the photos exposing Superman's secret identity were published, the world evinced disappointment with the ruse; they felt duped, betrayed, victimized by paranoia played out on a grand scale. What possible purpose had a secret identity served?

The *Daily Planet* conducted man on the street interviews. One such interviewee happened to be a professor of philosophy at New York University. The reporter kept pace with him as he was walking toward the triumphal Roman entrance of the American Museum of Natural History on Central Park West, thrusting a microphone into his face.

"Professor, does the whole secret identity thing bother you?"

"Not really," the professor replied haughtily. "We all, in a sense, harbor secret identities. After all, our personalities don't exist in the way that a chair or a car exists—our personalities are fluid constructs. But here's what does bother me. Why tights? Why a cape? A grown man so attired could only fail to feel ridiculous if his array of faculties were not completely intact."

ooooo

Superman swoops down from the sky, using his cavernous lung capacity to blow out the shawl of flames draping a burning apartment building.

Public sentiment slides precipitously downhill and pools in a mudslide of vilification at Superman's feet. "Down from the sky, it's a bird, it's a plane—naw, it's Superpig, come to bust some heads!" shouts a young man wearing a purple NYU sweatshirt.

When the fire is extinguished and Superman has rescued from certain death the three people who had been trapped on the fifth floor of the building, he approaches the youth wearing the sweatshirt. The crowd, thronging the sidewalk, parts as he approaches the young man.

"Why do you say these things about me?" Superman observes the expression of terror wave its banner over the youth's face. "Please, speak freely. No repercussions. I'm just curious."

The young man is emboldened by Superman's passivity. "Dude, what's up with the tights and shit? You need to let me hook you up with my tailor. That shit you got on is played out as Run DMC. Another thing. All this trash-talk about right and wrong, all these bogus absolutes. Who are you to impose your standards on us?"

The crowd ominously mumbles its assent.

ooooo

Superman's popularity continues to deteriorate. Those with political or ecological agendas find in his sky-streaking torpedo trajectories subliminal advertisement for nuclear warheads or claim the supersonic booms left in the wake of faster-than-sound speeds are further shredding the ozone layer.

Superman observes with dismay that the majority of the detractors are African American, Hispanic, Middle Eastern, but suppresses within himself the formulation of disturbing conclusions. Nevertheless, impelled by the moral imperatives of an earlier age, the Man of Steel continues to lift limp rag doll survivors from the wreckage of derailed Amtraks, collapsed skyscrapers, remnants of jumbo jets found twisted in accordions of impact, bearing the victims skyward and away to the overutilized emergency rooms of besieged county hospitals.

Class action suits are initiated by a legal coalition insisting that such interventions are a violation of civil liberties, callous infringements on the individual's right to die. As a result of costly litigation, Superman declares bankruptcy.

ooooo

Although his alter ego Clark Kent rents a claustrophobic roach-ridden studio apartment, Superman sequesters himself during this difficult time in the shimmering crystalline cocoon of his Fortress of Solitude, a sprawling secret citadel shining with the intensity of a diamond in the pure acrylic-white wasteland of the Antarctica.

He wanders as though lost through the Fortress with its many chambers, desperately in search of a diversion.

In his Chamber of Technology he sits down at a computer and, after surfing the Web with no destination in mind, finds himself for the first time in a chat room. After observing the real-time conversation taking place between someone calling herself Bambi and two other participants, Rocketman and Hotstump, Superman decides to join the online dialogue.

Bambi: Smack it up, flip it, rub it down, oh n-o-o-o-o-o-o!

Rocketman: Unh! Unh! Unh!

Hotstump: Yo, smack that shit up.

Man of Steel: Hello?

Bambi: Man of Steel . . . daaamn. Somebody's got skills.

Man of Steel: I feel so alone.

Bambi: Stretch it out, stretch it out, stretch it w-a-a-a-a-a-y out!

Rocketman: Unh! Unh!

Hotstump: Yo, stretch that shit all the way out.

Man of Steel: I don't understand any of you. Please talk to me.

Bambi: 2 inches or a yard, rock hard or if it's saggin, I ain't 2 proud to beg.

Man of Steel: Bambi, are you in some kind of trouble?

Bambi: I'm not in trouble but trouble is in me, steel man, even tho I'm just 14.

Man of Steel: Tell me where you are. I can help you.

Bambi: Tell U where I'll be. U know the Motel 6 over on West 27th? I'll be in front this afternoon at 5.

Man of Steel: Just hold on, Bambi. I'll be there.

Rocketman: Unh!!!

Superman disconnects. He has time to kill before he rescues the girl, Bambi, and spends the next several hours accessing, through the use of memory crystals, interactive holographic recordings of his father, Jor-El, the pre-eminent Kryptonian scientist, and his mother, Lara.

"My dear son Kal-El, our planet, Krypton, will soon explode," Jor-El's spectral image intones, white-haired, patriarchal, regal. "I've tried to warn the ruling Council of Elders, to no avail. And so I am sending you, my infant son, to the planet Earth in an escape rocket. On Earth you will have super powers, but you will never fit in, no matter how hard you try."

Saddened by his inability to remember his parents, by the bitter poignancy of father's prediction, Superman opens the door to the Fortress, filling the hollowness inside him created by the sadness with a titanium resolve to help the girl. Stepping outside into the laser-white snow, dwarfed by towering walls of ice, Superman finds himself surrounded by the cylinder of a spotlight crashing down from a helicopter above. In a single bound he catapults up and hovers next to the pilot's door.

The window opens and the pilot looks down at the Fortress of Solitude. "Superman . . . so Batman was telling the truth. The Antarctica!"

Only Superman's closest allies and friends know the location of the Fortress: Lois Lane, Batman, a few others.

"Batman told you where the Fortress was?"

The pilot rubs his thumb vigorously against the tip of his index and middle fingers. "For cash. A lot of it." He leans over and reveals in a confidential tone: "The government paid him well for the info. I guess times are tight for everybody, even superheroes." The pilot hands Superman an envelope. "I hate to be the bearer of bad news . . . but since you declared bankruptcy, you've fallen behind with your taxes and, well, looks like Uncle Sam is going to seize the Fortress of Solitude and auction it off."

In his daze and devastation, Superman forgets about the girl and returns to the Fortress, shuffling aimlessly through the crystalline hallways and chambers. Time with dreamlike fluidity passes. When he hears a banging at the Fortress's door, tall and broad as a mastodon, he wonders what day it is.

Another helicopter hovers in the desolate polar sky. The NYPD police officer standing before Superman has been lowered from a harness.

"Sorry, Supe, but I've got to serve you this warrant." He hands Superman an envelope. "We've been running a sting on Internet predators. There is no Bambi. You're under arrest. Would you mind?" he asks, holding up a pair of handcuffs.

"The law has to be upheld," Superman philosophizes, allowing himself to be restrained, "even when it fails to reflect the truth. How did you find me?"

"Batman. Money gets the better of friendship every time."

ooooo

Superman is eventually exonerated and the charge of online enticement is dropped, but the damage has been done. When he shows up at the Daily Planet as Clark Kent and sits at his desk to begin the day's work, Jimmy Olsen bursts out of his office.

"What's the point of the secret identity thing?" J.O. asks peevishly. "Everybody knows Clark Kent is Superman."

"I thought the uniform would be disruptive to others in the office," Superman reasons.

"You're fired. This paper doesn't employ child molesters."

"But I was exonerated," Superman protests.

"Doesn't matter. Perception is reality. Image rules all. Please, just clear your desk of personal belongings and get the hell out."

ooooo

From behind the counter Superman watches the man slip a packet of Hostess Ding Dongs down the front of his pants.

"Sir," Superman calls out. "Just a minute."

Superman has a day job now, clerking the midnight to morning shift at a 7-Eleven in a gang-plagued neighborhood gray as an octogenarian.

The man approaches the counter in a stiff splay-legged gait meant to prevent the Ding Dongs from stuttering down his pant leg to the floor. Extravagant innocence cloaks his face as he leans against the counter. "Yes?"

"Here." Superman holds out a Hustler magazine. The thief reaches for it warily. "Go on. It's yours, free of charge."

The man snatches the magazine and walks as though on peg legs to the door. He does not say *thank you*!

A moment later the manager of the 7-Eleven rushes out from the stock room. In his face rage wrestles with incredulity. "I watched him steal Ding Dongs, and then I watched you give him a Hustler. Why didn't you stop him?"

How can Superman tell the manager that he customarily turns a blind eye to customers who stuff Ding Dongs and malt liquor into waistbands and jacket pockets? They are the poor, the weary, the hungry, the disenfranchised, with whom, he realizes, he has nothing in common and therefore has no right to pass judgement or to make citizens arrests as a deputized agent of the state.

Superman shrugs helplessly.

"The door," the manager says, pointing. "Walk through it."

ooooo

Lois Lane walks through the door of Superman's section-eight, third-floor apartment on 56th and Hudson with a gumball-sour twist of the lips and withholds the support and encouragement she freely lavished during happier days. "Super duper pooper man," she greets him.

That is not all she withholds. In bed her taunts are fists of thistles and thorns. "Man of Steel? I think not."

Superman is unable to get it up; Viagra, granting recourse to synthetic virility, would seem an admission of failure more debasing than the inability to attain an erection.

Lois has resorted to pleasuring herself in his presence with vibrating marital aids while simultaneously watching television with sound muted. During rare moments when her ice of hostility and resentment momentarily cracks, she analyzes his dilemma, proposes PR remedies.

"You are experiencing a form of celebrity backlash. You need to change your image."

"What do the people want from me?" he asks.

"The public is fickle," she continues, "but in this case, you have justified it. First of all, your name is Kal-El. Use it. It has a neoteric ethnic ring. Now that there's a long overdue awareness in the media endorsing multiculturalism . . ."

Superman interrupts to pose a question. "Is the media to be trusted?"

Lois Lane extravagantly demonstrates forbearance, refrains from rolling her eyes. "No, of course not, but you can use it to your advantage. Please don't encourage these digressions, you know how I hate to digress. I was where? Your problem is, you're the great white hope of an untenable status quo, privileged and pampered, ultraconservative and dogmatic in your notions of an absolute right and wrong. Champion of freedom and the American way? Freedom to buy, to consume and discard, freedom to seek endless diversions and entertainments, sure, sure. Why have you not melted all the guns on the face of the earth with your super-hot X-ray vision? Why have you not melted, for example, all symbols of Swastikas?"

"If I do away with one symbol, I would have to do away with them all," Superman replies.

But Lois Lane, on an avalanching roll, does not hear him. "What good is the power to literally move mountains "—she inflects the word *lit-trilly*, an affectation invoking traces of the wealthy Cape Cod upbringing she has striven to replace as an adult with less damning egalitarian accents—"if you can't stamp out racism? What good is power if you can't change what's in the heart of a man or a woman? You could have been somebody, you could have been the ultimate outsider. Instead, you're just another cocky white boy who, number one, believes he is the arbiter of righteousness and who, number two, took the path of least resistance."

Superman plucks from her fingers the joint Lois Lane is puffing and replaces it before she can detect its absence; he inhales deeply, demonstrating to himself the willingness to change. In his bloodstream THC molecules are interpreted and intercepted as an immuno-intrusive presence by white, white, white corpuscles and neutralized before liberating psychotropic effects can be felt. Of course he had known the marijuana would not have an effect and is aware his demonstration was self-deception. Yet self-deception, he reasons, is acceptable in the absence of viable alternatives. Yet . . .

Lois Lane sighs and reaches for the marital aid on the bedside table. Tonight he will be unable to bear the high-pitched drone it will make when she turns it on (two octaves above middle C), then the lower-pitched muffled hum as it is launched wombward.

"I think I'll sky it for a bit," Superman tells her. "Clear my head."

"Close the window when you go, it's a bit nippy. And could you please bring me back a pint of Dryer's No-Fat Praline Yogurt, stupor man?"

This resurgence of belligerence hastens his exit. Superman keeps flying, keeps flying until he plunges, like a tiny wriggling spermatozoa breeching an immensity of ovum, into the fathomless molten core of the sun. Lois Lane may well be right, he decides, about the potential benefits of an image makeover; thus for an hour or so he allows himself to become driftwood tossed by tides in a turbulent nuclear sea.

Streaking homeward, he keeps his eyes closed tight, navigating by memory, engaging super-hearing to detect sound waves bouncing off particles small as dust motes, until he perches on the windowsill outside his apartment, an overgrown pigeon in an ill-fitting costume. Opening his eyes, he stretches out his hands, gazing at them and at the reflection of his face in the dingy window: not even the hint of a tan, skin still white as Liquid Paper.

ooooo

Once again a shifting of the earth by infinitesimal degrees off its axis is detected; catastrophe is imminent.

An intergovernmental panel of world scientists on axial displacement have gathered at the UNESCO headquarters in Paris to assess the looming predicament.

Sitting at a huge oval conference room table, a Nobel Prize-winning quantum physicist wearing an obscenely snug Hawaiian shirt addresses the group. "As we know, the Man of Tomorrow has always prevented this catastrophe. Even so, there are always unexplainable events and phenomena that happen in the wake of the averted disaster."

"The degree of randomness underlying events becomes more readily apparent," an astro-mathematician elaborates, nodding sagely. "Definitions that had seemed fixed and solid lose their reliability, consensual reality fragments into jigsaw puzzle pieces too heavily dependent on interpretation."

The other scientists begin to enumerate examples.

"Children in spelling bees declare that the word 'werewolf' contains an 'h' and the judges argue among themselves over the validity of phonetic variants."

"The precise locations of well-known landmarks become the subject of violent debate."

"Customers return corned beef sandwiches to delicatessens, insisting that they've been given pastrami."

"Even so, we need Superman."

ooooo

Fuck it, Superman decides.

High-level government authorities and the scientific intelligentsia are desperately trying to contact the Man of Steel. So what? He turns off his pager, unplugs the telephone that is his hotline to the White House. He ignores newspaper headlines that both appeal to the sense of duty that has forsaken him and attempt to shame him into action: "Superman in Selfish Seclusion While World Tilts Toward Abyss."

His efforts to freeze fluidity have always arisen from obscure inner mandates; at the very least, they constituted the brunt of his job description as savior of mankind, but as Lois Lane has so often insisted, perhaps there are valuable lessons to be learned in loosening up, going with the flow.

In addition to suffering from a paralyzing occupational burnout that precludes his response to entreaties for his help, he has other, more pressing, concerns.

He meets with his arch-enemy, Lex Luther, for coffee at Starbuck's at the criminal genius's request.

"What gives?" Lex Luther asks. "I have to resort to pharmaceutical stimulants to provide the natural adrenaline rush that was the byproduct of our monumental engagements. I need you back in action."

"The people," Superman sniffs, "no longer appreciate my efforts on their behalf."

Lex Luther nods. "A nasty business, that," he agrees.

"The people I've taken oaths to protect, I no longer know who they are," Superman concludes. "Have I made irrevocable errors in judgement?"

Lex Luther smiles ruefully. "Demographics have betrayed you. You no longer represent the prevailing constituency in this metropolis. You are the Lone White Ranger in a world where people are no longer content to play the role of Tonto."

Superman buries his lantern-shaped head in monolithic hands. "What, then?"

"You fear change. 'In the destructive element, immerse.' Drastic steps are necessary, a gesture of faith on your part is necessary. Let me help you," Lex Luther offers.

Superman reaches across the table top and embraces his arch-nemesis, eyes gushing bayous of tears. Aggrieved employees wearing galoshes appear with mops and industrial-sized buckets.

"There, there," Lex Luther says, "let it go, big guy, just let it go."

ooooo

In an attempt to demonstrate his willingness to reach out to the public and to connect with the common man, Superman appears on the phenomenally successful O____ W____ talk show, hoping to brighten his tarnished image. The overhead lights on the set are an oven, baking perspiration into his makeup; in the monitor he sees his face as garishly clown-like. O____W____'s face, he notices as he squirms on the sofa, is flawless, plush, the makeup smooth as caramel icing.

The interview proceeds pleasantly enough, but at a certain point he detects a shift in O____ W_____'s tone; her questions become slyly challenging, increasingly direct, and finally openly confrontational.

"Man of Steel, I have a sort of disturbing check list here that I'd like to read. Statistics indicate that a large percent of the suspects you detain and question in his pursuit of misdemeanor perpetrators results in high numbers of false arrests among African American or Hispanic males between the ages of sixteen and twenty-four. Choke-hold mishaps for minorities are alarmingly disproportionate. Sightings recorded by ACLU surveillance teams of Superman patrolling ghetto airspace dwarf his token visibility in upscale communities. Would you care to respond?"

Superman walks off the set.

ooooo

There is much to be accomplished and they set about it quickly. Lex Luther establishes The Institute of Racial Empathy, funded by generous foundation grants from corporate leviathans. The media promotes the institute, stating that it will function as the "Gateway To A New Understanding Between Business And The Minority Community."

Top-ranking representatives, impeccably groomed, executive faces shepherded by fanatical devotion into smiles deemed appropriate by Microsoft and Snapple, are taught down-and-dirty Ebonics, the significance of Kwanzaa, "cultural chameleonics 101."

Superman is, of course, a star pupil. At the end of the first week of emotionally draining seminars, while attendees in the audience lean forward in their seats to identify lapses of colloquial or idiomatic authenticity, Superman struts across the stage in an old-fashioned pimp-roll contemporized by hip-hop aesthetics to coordinate new shoulder-sway with old lower-limb drag. Reaching for Lex Luther's outstretched hand to engage it in a cat's-cradle of complex greeting that is substitute for the conventional handshake, he slurs, with admirable mimesis, "L.L., my niggah," to spontaneous outbreaks of applause.

ooooo

Lex Luther employs his criminal genius to create a pill that breeches the bastions of the superhero's esoteric body chemistry. "A tab a day keeps the honky at bay," Lex Luther explains.

Superman savors the pill's transubstantiative power as it dissolves on his tongue. His complexion deepens, eclipsing his paleness beneath a deep mahogany sheen.

ooooo

Lois Lane is demonstrably pleased; she coos, calling him to bed, spurring him on with yawning porno-diva thighs.

"Have at it, superstud, show me no mercy, bitch slap me if you like your rocks off rough." Her musky heat melts through his inhibitions, unhinges his hips with innovative erotic choreographies of clockwise and counterclockwise plunge and thrust. "The blacker the berry, the sweeter the juice," Lois Lane exclaims, simple orgasms multiplying into complex calculus.

ooooo

Superman's new uniform is underwritten by Snoop Dog's Rich & Infamous clothing line. Though the color scheme remains the same, new stylistic motifs sing of youthful street-corner a cappellas. The cape now trails smartly from an oversized blue-hooded sweatshirt draping his shaved skull; accessories exploit chains, platinum rings, a "grill"—gold plating for his two front teeth—chunky Rolex, a cane that combines flash and function, releasing sexy pulses of creamy crime-busting laser ejaculations with the push of a button.

The overall effect is one of nonchalant flamboyance, Mac-Daddy chic. Hip-hop producer Dr. Dre is commissioned to write a catchy anthemic jingle highlighting Superman's unique ethnicity called "Kewl Kryptonian," which rockets to the top of pop and R&B charts. The lyrics, rapped by Superman himself in a surprisingly sensuous Barry White baritone, build to affirmation on a series of silky negations:

I ain't Cally
I ain't Bostonian
I'm a new kinda suppa niggah
Cold kewl Kryptonian

Composer John Williams is not pleased, implies in a press release that the tracks abound in orchestral deficiencies, that they disguise the lack of mythic melodic motifs beneath a barrage of savage rhythms.

Soaring platinum sales restore Superman to solvency. He considers donating a portion of the proceeds to the United Negro College Fund.

ooooo

The world is still atilt on its errant axis. Walkers lean slightly forward from the waist, negotiate flat pavement as though laboring up inconvenient inclines. A mere tap from his fingertip would restore Earth to orbital viability, yet Superman does nothing, bidding his time, testing the waters.

He waits, perhaps not without a certain vindictive satisfaction, for the results of recent Gallup polls to bestow statistical validation, waits for the weathervane of public opinion to whirl in his direction.

On the cover of *GQ Magazine* the Man of Steel is shown sitting in a wicker chair with a great rounded back, beret aslant on his head, face militantly devoid of expression, pose and posture redolent of Huey P. Newton's, long slain cofounder of the decades-defunct Black Panther Party. The caption bears the quote, "I be chillin."

High government officials of the officially nonexistent U.S. shadow government summon Superman to a secret summit meeting in Geneva, demand to know what it all means. "I be chillin," Superman answers noncommittally. Then adds, "It's a Kryptonian thing, you wouldn't understand."

ooooo

By all accounts Superman should be exuberantly riding the crest of his newly established vogue with the ethnic demographic, exploiting his hard-won popularity among the young and hip who, paradoxically, from the margins of a culture that resists their absorption into the mainstream, set standards for the nation's trends by establishing subversive anti-trends. He is not unaware that this is supreme irony in a nation whose history is in large measure the history of co-opted anti-trends. Drifting down from the sky he alights with the insouciance of a feather into mobs of African American teenagers seeking his autograph.

"Fuck that bourgeois shit," Superman announces, pushing away pencil and pen for the greater sincerity of a heartfelt embrace, "I'm everyday people."

When questioned by the media for his refusal to avert the impending global catastrophe, Superman has this to say: "No mo handouts, no mo super-affirmative action, no mo Kryptonian welfare. 'Bout time the people of the Earth learn some self-reliance, pull up on they bootstraps, do for theyselves."

ooooo

Superman's inability to view his situation through a lens of triumph, his depression, his flattened affect, is a source of concern for both he and his psychiatrist. Yet the fact of Lois Lane's sudden departure, doctor and patient agreed, was not a major contributing factor. Her admission of deep disappointment in her own inability to withstand the internal pressures of sustaining the burden of an "interracial" relationship during a time and age when such factors should have been considered anile had driven her away when the novelty of exotic sexuality lost its power to superficially titillate.

"I did not know I was so shallow," Lois Lane had told him.

"Perhaps you are not only shallow but a ho as well," Superman suggested.

"Goodbye Superman, goodbye Clark Kent, goodbye Ka-El," Lois Lane said.

Superman explains to the doctor that her bowed head and posture of defeat as she gathered personal effects from the apartment and walked through the door will forever fill the portrait frame of his recollection of those final moments.

"You are fixating," the doctor says.

Superman answers, "I am fixating and I have observations to make."

"Vent them," the doctor advises.

"Well, then. Nothing has been clarified by my transformation; in fact, contradictions and unanswerable questions flourish. Is this all there is to belonging, to ethnicity, to race: habits, customs, words, rituals, behaviors? All of these merely reflect the provisional nature of the self," Superman observes sadly.

"You are either very close to insight," the doctor says, "or very, very far from it."

"There is no point," Superman explains, "at which the gene yields satisfactorily to the language which defines cultural reality: octoroon, quadroon, mulatto, indeed black and white . . . believe me, I have used my super-vision to scrutinize the gene closely."

"Identity," the doctor sighs, "the mystery of it."

"I disagree, it is precisely unmysterious," Superman retorts. "I've been hoodwinked. I've been had. I've been took. I've been led astray, run amok. I've been bamboozled."

The doctor frowns. "You are paraphrasing."

Superman laughs bitterly, the first laugh of bitterness ever to escape his lips, typically a stern line of demarcation rarely crossed by spontaneous smirk or smile. It is, this bitterness, like sterilized air, not sour, not sweet. "Is not the world paraphrasing itself?: Scientists, once again, detecting a shifting of the earth by infinitesimal degrees off its axis; catastrophe, imminent?" Then he goes on to ask, "Should I save the Earth?"

The doctor replies, "You are close to a breakthrough. I encourage you to do the right thing."

ooooo

Saving the world is one thing, the looming specter of foundational transformations, another. Superman gloomily considers his options and settles on a solution rarely invoked, a solution that is, for him, an ethical taboo. He will fly around the globe faster and faster, cross the line that separates being a concerned participant in the affairs of humankind into monumental historical intrusion, lasso the world in dizzy ropes of speed to reverse the flow of time. He will wind chronology back to a day and place before this day, this place. For at a certain point some people had evidently wanted more, had suddenly found themselves pursuing fluid symbols, cryptic ambiguities, the tragic grandeur of insupportable myths.

Now these same people, watching Superman's orbiting blur, tear comic book pages in half, in quarters, in eights, watch them flutter away violently in crematoriums of wind.

Superman, ever stolid, does not say "ouch."

The English Teacher's Pupil

Cory needs the pills. His face is painted in sweat; thick brush strokes of anxiety leave runnels over his cheeks like a Picasso of tears. He needs them to steady the hand that grips the riding crop he has removed from his back pocket. He needs the pills to silence the roaring red ambulance of blood screeching through his veins.

It is 3:00 a.m. and Cory's hysteria of craving has brought him here, to the twenty-four-hour Sav-On Drugs on East and 73rd where he used to work and where now, in a fever of movement like pinball off paddles, he ricochets through the narrow aisles.

As he wavers toward Leonards' office in the rear of the store next to the glass-partitioned pharmacy, Cory's desire kindles a fantasy that does not seem morbid anymore—that he is dying a lingering incremental death in a cancer ward, his body engulfed by a pain so cavernous that they allow him to self-administer the pain medication. Around the clock, he presses a button that feeds a solution into his dream-freighted bloodstream from an IV attached to a morphine drip-bag.

Cory is praying that the predominately black low-income patrons who swarm each day into this store have today set before Leonards, the obese night-shift manager, the landmines and roadblocks of a thousand exasperations and vivid ignominies; that he has already suffered through the kind of day that has thickened his hatred of these shoppers to a yeasty bile in his throat, reddened his contempt to a scalding intensity that blurs his vision, planted his conviction of their buffoonery and inferiority in some deep root of nausea that branches through Leonards' stomach.

There is a ring attached to the belt of Leonards' gray polyester pants that is overgrown with a wild thicket of keys. These are the keys to all the locked drawers and doors and counters and bathrooms and offices in the store. These are the keys to the pharmacy, now closed.

ooooo

Worthless, less than worthless, weak, like your mother. Cory has not spoken to his father for months, but even as he rushes to Leonards' office, he hears the voice, echoing through his brain like static. It speaks to him with the same stern dismay his father used on so many occasions when he was growing up and could not meet the old man's expectations. Cory had attempted to burst into adulthood wearing about his narrow shoulders the same Superman's cape of accomplishments his father had worn as he rocketed through turbulent skies of racism by the sheer force of his embittered industriousness to become the first black mayor in a small Midwestern town in northern Michigan.

But Cory's high school years had been a canvas daubed with pigments squeezed from bright little tubes labeled chess club, drama club, photography club, computer club, student council, and the colors they left were abortive splotches, ugly smears that painted a muddy portrait of failure. When his mother had fled, Cory had stopped trying, though his father's presence forced him to maintain the pretense.

One afternoon, Cory came home after school and heard the familiar volcano of rage erupt from his father's throat as he cursed his mother for failing to hang the towels on the bathroom rack with the fetishistic symmetry he always insisted on, and he watched his father drag the flailing woman through the house and into the garage, where he commanded her to remove her clothing. When she hesitated, he impatiently ripped her clothes off and removed the riding crop that he kept inside a shiny toolbox, helping his wife, with a peculiar ginger solicitousness, to lower herself to her hands and knees. Then the strap sang its soprano of leather and chewed into her shivering back and buttocks until the old man was bathed in sweat.

She finally fled the joyless Protestant ethic that was annexed to the physical violence and ultimately more damaging. But his father viewed her departure dismissively and was able to justify everything to Cory.

"I owe my success to the Mississippi crackers of my birthplace who tried to grind me into the dust," he often said, after his wife had left. "The ethic of my success was born out of violence. I was mistaken to expect that a common bitch might come to appreciate that." He seemed to savor the irony as though it were a hard candy tucked tartly under his tongue.

Cory went through his mother's closet—she had fled in a precipitous hysteria that preempted packing even a single item of clothing while her husband was out of town attending a political convention—and found hidden bottles of pills scattered behind Macy's shoeboxes, a miniature pharmaceutical city in disarray as if evacuated during an apocalypse. He took the little white pills labeled *for pain* and liked the numbing effect. His emotions were planed by the pills into smooth varnished boards. That was the beginning, and he would take them for years. His mother saw to that.

She had been badly injured once when Cory's father had kicked her and she had tumbled down the stairs to the basement, dislocating disks in her lower back. And though she had fled to a nearby city in Michigan, she came back at fugitive intervals to keep her doctor's appointments and obtain refills for her prescriptions, which she turned over to Cory.

"I know it's wrong," she would tell him on the phone in a floating, faraway voice. "But I needed them to function, to stay as long as I did with your father. If you take them, it'll make things easier. It's all I can think to do for you."

"Let me come and live with you," Cory pleaded. "I wouldn't be any trouble."

"I don't work anymore, Cory," she explained airily. "I'm on permanent disability. I couldn't look after you."

"I could work. I could look after you," he said. "Let me come and take care of you."

"I can't, Cory. I can't see people, I can't talk to them. I'm afraid to leave the apartment. I'm afraid of everything. Maybe by the time you're in college . . ."

"Please, Mama." He whispered into the phone so that his father, who spent all his free time in his garage workshop making crude wood carvings of African slaves whose wrists and ankles were festooned in chains, would not hear.

"I'm sorry." She was always the first one to end those surreptitiously whispered conversations, the terminal punctuation of her teardrops dribbling into the silence of disconnection.

Around that time, an English teacher in the twelfth grade whose F would have prevented Cory's high school graduation, resulting in the whip, or worse—Papa's punishing shame and the son's face drenched in an August of hot saliva from the sun of wrath Papa's mouth would surely widen into—this teacher, the only black faculty member at Sycamore High, Cory attempted to nudge to mercy with a seduction of tears, and when that failed, he had acted on rumors of the teacher's homosexuality and dropped to gelatin knees after school in the teacher's office and unzipped his slacks and taken the putty of groin into his mouth where it erupted in a pungent lava of musk.

ooooo

As he now makes his way to the back of the store, in his mouth the taste of his detoxifying system rises to coat his throat, alkaline sponge of opiates absorbing all saliva from his tongue, his shoelace of veins tied into knots. Cory is an ejecta of desperation weaving toward Leonards' office. His brain is aflame with scenarios of what he would do to get what he so deeply needs, even if it means pretending, as he has done many times before, that Leonards is his high school English teacher.

ooooo

The English teacher had told Cory many things over the course of the month that was like a season of dream and hallucination, when the two would meet on the outskirts of town and wander deep into the moaning woods where they watched ballerinas of moonlight dance to December symphonies of wind, the flat lambent table of the lake extending to the far horizon, the distant city of Chicago sprinkling the salt of its illumination on the ruffled tablecloth of the waves.

"Why don't you teach black books?" Cory asked him once. They sat on the dark skull of a massive boulder surrounded by a skeletal cluster of smaller rocks while the frosty lake worked its fingers into all the cracks and crevices. They listened to the bottle-hollow wind, to the brittle leaves swishing above, to the water making flat dull slaps below their dangling legs. The English teacher wore a navy blue pea coat buttoned all the way up to his neck, while Cory wore only a black sweatshirt with the hood pulled up.

"Why should I?"

"Why shouldn't you?"

"I've been tempted to add James Baldwin to my reading list. *Giovanni's Room* would rip their eyes open, wouldn't it?" A brittleness and a bitterness drew its drawstring tight on his little pouch of laughter.

This book was not familiar to Cory. "Why?"

"Because he was like me. He wasn't afraid to see the beauty in men."

But Cory saw beauty in neither men nor women. "What about all the rest? I read *Native Son*. Isn't that a good book?"

"Oh, my beautiful brothers and sisters. My long-suffering, orphaned, stripped-of-history black sisters and brothers. Treated like beasts, spat upon, despised the world over—maybe even in outer space, for all I know. You would think they learned something from it, wouldn't you?"

Cory stopped swinging his legs.

"I'm hated, I'm spat upon, despised by my own people. A pariah. If you continue on this path, you'll be a pariah—I warn you. I'm a pariah twice over." A thin dribble resembling laughter seemed to spill down his chin. "I don't owe anything to black people. I don't owe anything to anybody. I'm free," he said, and he laid a gloved hand absently on Cory's leg. "But I blame my father for not beating my own worst tendencies out of me. I blame myself for you, too. Maybe I even blame you, for making me be me."

And a short time later, in the small town in northern Michigan hemmed in by woodlands that perhaps Hemingway had trudged through, stomping over the soft green banks that held the rivers he thought he had established kinship with, but only knowing them by trampling them underfoot as he lumbered deep into the wilderness and drunkenly fished the cold waters (the English teacher disliked Hemingway), he punished himself for his breach of ethics by finding in the woods a tree such as Hemingway might have called a good old strong tall tree that had grown from the earth that Faulkner (whom he disliked a little less) might have called the unvanquished and immemorial depths of the fecund and inscrutable earth and from that tree, the English teacher hung himself.

ooooo

Cory feels no affinity because he is black for the crackheads who wandered through the shatter of ghetto streets and jangled the tambourine of their impoverished laughter, ringing the air with their rap-song patter, thieving and moving about with shrewd haste, pick-pocketing the wallets and handbags of their own futures. Cory had admitted this much and more shortly after Mr. Leonards had hired him as an associate in the Sav-On manager-in-training program.

By the time Cory had made this particular confession, he'd had many strange conversations with Leonards, who had dubiously peered at Cory's application form during the interview and expressed reservation at hiring someone who appeared to be overqualified.

"I wonder why you aren't trying to work somewhere where you could be pulling down some real bucks?"

"I don't think I know everything there is to know. I think what's important is to start at a place that allows you to learn all you can. Then, what you end up with is what you've earned," Cory answered with appropriate gravity.

Leonards leaned back slowly in his chair, his mountainous stomach cresting into view. "What would you do," he proposed thoughtfully, "if someone were to call you a nigger?"

"Who would be calling me that?" Cory asked without blinking.

"Let's say, a white customer, though we don't get many of those in here. Let's say, a white customer who was irate and went too far, took it out on you. Unfairly."

"The customer," Cory said, shrugged, smiling, "is always right."

"I'm not saying that happens, mind you."

"I understand. It's my ability to handle interpersonal situations that's in question," Cory said.

"Mind you, I'm not saying that happens. Because Sav-On, as a corporate leader, doesn't condone that sort of thing."

"I follow you."

"Not in this store. Though I can't stop anybody from saying anything if they're dead set on saying it. It's a free country." He winked conspiratorially, Cory nodded collusively. "Well, let's give it a shot," Leonards concluded with an expansive gesture. "You might be just what I'm looking for."

Indeed, he was watching Cory closely with his iceberg-blue eyes. Something in this veiled expression was very familiar to Cory. "I think you'll find me to be a very patient mentor."

ooooo

"I'm much better," his mother had told him, and he heard her exhaling firmly into the telephone. "I have to stop hiding and get on with my life. It's been years. You've graduated from college and you'll do well now." After a pause the voice ventured ahead bravely. "I've been through a rehab program. It's nothing to be ashamed of these days."

"Congratulations," Cory said. He had just moved from his father's house into a flat above a roach-infested laundromat. At night, he listened to the industrial-sized drum of washers and dryers rotating bulkily, his mind spinning in an infinite falling loop until he was bleached into clean, sanitized sleep.

"Don't say it like that, Cory."

"Like what? All I said was congratulations."

"I don't have to worry about you now that you're out of that house. You'll be fine. You don't need the pills anymore."

Cory's heart tilted, the beats rolling out in smeared triplets of sudden adrenaline arrhythmically released. "You know it's not that easy. Remember, you left me." The accusation was pointed, but it was not weighted with emphasis. "All I had was what you left me. Now, you want to take that away too."

"All right." Her sigh tapering to a tremble. "All right."

But when the time came for Cory to pick up his refill, the pharmacist pushed the insurance card back across the counter, shaking his head. "He didn't authorize the refill," he said. "Tell your mother she'll have to call the doctor."

Cory looked over the pharmacist's shoulder and saw the bottle from which, on previous visits, the little white pills had been effortlessly meted out. That the pills were so close and yet inaccessible made him feel as though he had been struck between the eyes with a platinum bullet. The nausea of thwarted desire whirlpooling through his limbs, he tried to dig his fingers into the counter's edge.

Through the thickening fog of the misery secreted by every cell in his body, it dimly occurred to him for the first time that the pills should be black, not white; black pills to pay symbolic homage to someone like the English teacher who had seen things set before him only to be withdrawn out of reach, placed on a shelf, behind a gulf that could not be crossed, a zone of absence that a person could only dangle over.

ooooo

"Why do they all have to shave their heads like that?" Leonards had asked after Cory's second week at Sav-On, sitting behind his desk and tossing the ring of keys up and down. "I almost liked it better when they wore those big afros years ago—though it was hard to take seriously. I mean, it looked like that character Eddie Murphy used to play on Saturday Night Live."

"Buckwheat," Cory offered.

"That's it, Buckwheat!"

Cory sat across the small desk from Leonards, punching numbers into an adding machine next to a framed 8 x 10 photo of Leonards' expressionless wife and two expressionless girls wearing the over-starched uniforms of the Catholic school they attended, then writing the totals neatly into columns on a ledger.

"Now, your own hair seems very neat. It's very respectable looking, collegiate. If they all wore their hair like yours, I think they'd get farther in life, don't you?"

"I guess kids have their own styles."

"Kids, hell. They can't be that much younger than you. You're what, twenty-five?"

"Twenty-six in December."

Leonards rose with difficulty, puffing a little, his stomach lapping over his belt like a wave heaving itself upon the shore. With a heavy oscillating shuffle, the outer edges of his loafers buckling under his enormous weight, he approached Cory and stood next to him, looking down at the ledger book. "They all look like thugs, and then they wonder why they don't get hired for jobs. You hear them talking gibberish and know they can't even put a proper sentence together."

"They're just kids," Cory said.

"Adults, too. Muthafucka this and muthafucka that. Why, they can't even say that filthy word properly. Playing their jungle music and dancing their lives away. What about contributing to the larger society? Say what you like about Jews, you have to admit, they gave the world Freud, Einstein, they contributed, in spite of their greed. We're supposed to believe that throwing a ball through a hoop is a contribution?"

Cory was silent.

"Not all of them, mind you," Leonards went on with a note of appeasement. "Look at you. A conservative-looking young man, well groomed, polite . . . May I?" he asked, extending his hand.

Cory kept writing as he felt Leonards' hand lightly, experimentally, touch his hair.

ooooo

After that, nothing more had happened. Leonards' hand had seemed to lay coiled in waiting, a snake frozen in a stillness calculated to render itself invisible to prey. The passing weeks had been like a kettle on a stove containing the stew of Leonards' soliloquies, at times simmering, at times boiling vigorously above the variable flame of the manager's perplexity or outrage, while Cory tallied receipts or took inventory or stocked shelves and Leonards sat or hovered nearby in garrulous obesity.

Most of the time Cory was as silent as an exemplary library patron, speaking only when prompted to respond. His was an easy buoyant silence furtively extracted, in circumspect quantities, from large plastic bottles brimming with Vicodin, Demoral, Percodan, Dilaudid.

ooooo

One evening, Cory was on his knees in the darkness when Leonards came up behind him. "This is very serious. You do know that," he said softly. "It's not just a matter of stealing merchandise. This is a violation of certain very serious federal codes."

Cory's hand cupped three Percodan and he was raising them to his lips when Leonards, who had gone to the bathroom and usually spent fifteen minutes at a time there, appeared suddenly to discover Cory on his knees behind the pharmacy counter, screwing the lid back on one of the bottles.

"Cory," he said, looking down. "You disappoint me."

Chewing the pills, swallowing the sour dry pulp, he remained on his knees, head bowed.

Leonards shifted his bulk closer. ". . . A violation of certain very serious federal codes," he repeated.

Cory did not fear being arrested or prosecuted for violating federal narcotics laws—not because he thought that Leonards wouldn't press charges, but because the reality of this possibility was eclipsed by the more visceral and immediate prospect of a life lived in full exposure, without narcotic armor.

"How did you get in here? If you'd picked the lock, the alarm would have been triggered."

He told the truth only because he was suspended in the purgatory of languor that preceded the effects of the Percodan; without the rush released by the drug, his imagination did not have the fuel to manufacture lies quickly and efficiently. "You couldn't find your keys that night because I took them. I had a duplicate key made the next day and then told you I found them behind the cosmetics register."

"The night I called my wife and she brought my extra set from home."

Cory nodded, still looking down. He felt Leonards looming over him in the darkness like a parade float. A wall of sweat was pushing itself forward behind Cory's flushed face, but the silence was long enough so that he began to detect the sensation of liquefied pepper spreading in the pit of his stomach, the giddy tingling like a suction of well-being at the base of his skull, and he knew suddenly that everything would be all right, everything would be fine.

"Well. I know that nobody is perfect, Cory. Mind you, I have my own demons and battles. Maybe you deserve a second chance. Maybe something could be worked out."

Cory looked up only when he heard the key ring secured to the belt rattling, the belt buckle tinkling beneath fumbling fingers, the zipper slowly descending.

ooooo

Artillery of nerve-endings firing beneath skin's surface, intestines shrilling an aria of imminent diarrhea, he bumps into a rack filled with Hallmark cards, the display carousal rotating wildly, Cory rotating wildly on his own carousal; he is a Hallmark card with legs, a Hallmark card celebrating 3:00 a.m. holidays of Oxycontin, morphine tablets, sledgehammer pills the equivalent of pharmaceutical-grade heroin.

He waited too long this time, miscalculated, stash minus tolerance equals deficit, thinking he had set aside enough to gain a few days of freedom from the taste of Leonards' rancid orations, the taste of his genitals like something scraped from a tin can, some sort of glandular Spam. Cory now had proof that when men, like the English teacher and Leonards and his father, hold back their fears and desires for so long, these fester like sewage in the body's plumbing, spew out in stale words or a reeking rubbish of sperm; the proof was branded in his taste buds indelibly, the Listerine he used compulsively could not swish it away. Maybe Cory had known he would not have enough in his stash; maybe he hoped he could be equal to the grinding machine of the withdrawal. But when it began this morning, he knew immediately he was wrong, and repented. After all, he was still his father's boy, weak, cravenly, forever failing; and he was his mother's son, too, with flight encoded like wings in his genes; he was the English teacher's pupil, dangling in the noose of an apprenticeship he did not understand.

Tonight, leaving his apartment above the laundromat in an insanity of haste, he only had time to grab the riding crop he had stolen from the toolbox when he left his father's house, and even now, in the store, he is unable to reach Leonards, his unlikely savior, fast enough.

ooooo

Four weeks ago, Leonards had explained that he could not, in all good conscience, allow Cory to continue with his employment at Sav-On. But the demons that Leonards had alluded to rose from the bed where they had been sleeping and held their arms open in fiery welcome, grinning hideously at Cory twice a week when he arrived at 3:00 a.m. and sat with Leonards in his small office during the Sav-On manager's thirty-minute "lunch break." Their relationship went on much as it had before—the stream of Leonards' interior monologue issuing on an implacable tide of perplexity and disgust that washed over endless speculations regarding "the black race"—but now the sessions ended with Cory performing fellatio in exchange for pills that Leonards acquired, in circumspect quantities, from the pharmacy.

But Cory, with something invisible that on an insect would have been identified as antennae, combed the air and struck against strands vibrating from Leonards' eyes; it was something that might have been boredom, a creeping acclimation to the forbidden, an adjustment to tropic temperatures of lust, as though the sight of Cory's head buried and bobbing between Leonards' mephitic thighs, the lurid histrionic decibels of suctioned saliva, were becoming less vivid, muted, paling into the realm of the commonplace.

Alert to anything that ultimately threatened Leonards' supplying the pills, Cory raised the stakes. Realizing that a chasm yawned between Leonards' rage and the orgasm that was like a weary hitchhiker attempting to cross the vast highway of Leonards' flesh, he constructed a bridge, one fashioned with the sweat-soiled leather of the riding crop, to convey that weary traveler to the other side at more exciting velocities.

"What is this?" Leonards said warily, when handed the whip.

Cory unbuttoned his blue denim shirt, stepped out of his jeans, leaned across the desk, dramatically sweeping aside heaps of paperwork that then hung in the air like angry windowpanes.

"They come into the store, jabbering with their thick, ugly lips," Cory prompted. "Stealing, cursing, just like a herd of dumb, stupid, animals . . ."

"I've only tried to ask why," Cory heard Leonards saying softly, wonderingly. "I've tried to understand, but I can't. Tests don't lie, do they?"

"Loud, uncouth, better off swinging through trees . . ." Finally, Cory heard the soprano of the leather tongue licking through air, licking greedily down his back, feasting on his sweat-marinated skin.

"Trying to make us believe you should be proud you come from goddamn Africa," Leonards cried incredulously, lashing down in earnest. "But genetics don't lie, IQ tests don't lie . . . it's a test, for christ sake, how could it?" His voice began to break with a rhythm that punctuated his effort, every forth or fifth word accented by a sharp grunt. "Women with nappy hair, big fat asses, trying to make everybody think that's beauty, 'I be' this and 'I be' that . . . using the word nigger like it was a joke, just another word . . ."

"It's not a joke, it shouldn't be a joke," Cory let his voice pant out.

The whip fell in a final exhausted chorus of moist leather, as though the wielding arm were a wind-up mechanism whose momentum was now spent, and a belated shudder jerked through the flesh of Cory's back as though it were a panel settling into a frame from which it had been lifted by a violent gust of wind.

"Quickly, quickly," came the whispered demand, and when Cory turned around, he saw Leonards leaning back in the chair, a befuddled calculation of thick fingers feverishly working at the algebra of the belt buckle, his face dangerously flushed.

ooooo

It is 3:10. Cory's hand now grips the riding crop pulled from his back pocket as he reaches the door to Leonards' office, his other hand lifted to knock, sour, heated breath trembling through the Sahara of his chest, face laced tight in cords of urgency and sweat. The door opens and a man neatly dressed in white shirt and tie, an older white man wearing glasses that magnify his eyes, stands gazing tartly at Cory, as though he had been expecting him.

"Yes?" the man asks, crossing his arms.

"I . . . is . . ." Time, broken into a dance of moments without cohesion, waltzes away with the name. "I . . ."

"You're here for Mr. Leonards, is that right?"

"Yes, Mr. Leonards . . . is he . . ."

"Mr. Leonards no longer works here. Mr. Leonards was fired." He stares at the whip in Cory's hand, directs his words at it. "Mr. Leonards was a thief, and he no longer works here, at Sav-On." His eyes flick up, scraping the grit of Cory's face, like a damp match finally struck. "Now. Can I. Help you. With something."

Desperation pushes through the mockery, makes him speak when his thinking has stopped. "Did he leave something for me? A package, something I was supposed to pick it up?"

"You are Cory, is that right? I believe your last check was mailed to your home two weeks ago."

On his way out, Cory passes the cashier who had always grimly watched him go to Leonards, then shoulders through the automatic doors that do not open quickly enough to accommodate his headlong momentum. He finds himself out in the stadium-sized parking lot colorlessly lit by sodium lamps perched atop high thin stalks.

During all the times he had rushed through the parking lot, whether hastening to or from Leonards, his thoughts had centered on the pills with an intensity that overshadowed his surroundings and made them invisible to him. Now, as though a blindfold has been suddenly snatched away, Cory is baffled by what he sees, shocked that so many people should be standing around aimlessly at 3:10 a.m. in a Sav-On parking lot on a week night. Men and women with hardened faces mill about in clusters, teenagers lean against cars smoking marijuana or Newports, young children chase each other, shrieking and throwing hangers, rocks, or sticks. Some of the loiterers are zombie-like with alcohol, stir slowly into slurred motion; others have accelerated beyond any possibility of sleep, eyes radiant with raw-edged chemicals.

Approaching an old woman in a shapeless dress pushing a shopping cart heaped with junk, he holds out the riding crop imploringly, but she curses and backs away. Moving from cluster to cluster . . . offering the whip . . . pulling up his shirt . . . *jabbering ugly lips . . . stupid animals . . . I be* . . . he attempts to incite them with some of the same words and phrases Leonards had used, but they merely watch him with jaded expressions, as if those words no longer had the power.

Stumbling over to a group of three men arguing among themselves, trying to force the whip into their hands, explaining that his back is on fire, that they can use the whip to put the fire out. One of the men, wearing a stocking cap and dark glasses, pushes him away, calling him crazy, Cory falling heavily.

Lying on his back, rolling about as if to extinguish flames, his eyes aching for sleep or tears and filling instead with the sight of onlookers pouring the flesh of their faces down through funnels of apathy. Staring. Their eyes like books with blank pages, their hands buried deep in empty pockets.

That Will Be Then and This Is Now

Dreams are boring, Daryl, and you know it. How many times have you smiled absently at your girlfriend as she narrates whatever details from the previous night's dream she's able to summon into memory and coherence, the two of you eating breakfast here on the patio, the cheap all-weather furniture purchased on sale from Builder's Emporium wobbling in precarious counterpoint to her every lively gesture? Her habit, maddening, is to sit with her spoon frozen in the air above her favorite white ceramic cereal bowl, the one with the cheesy feline motif, the spoon dipping every so often as though to plunge wholeheartedly into the arid brown tweed of the bran flakes, only to be arrested in its descent, then used to underscore some particularly exciting or puzzling or repulsive aspect of the dream. Once again, you smile, Daryl, since you pride yourself on the sensitivity and receptiveness you display in all matters concerning communication and listening, especially with the opposite sex, and you hope the queer scintilla of vacancy in your eyes isn't apparent. It's not, evidently, because she goes on and on, encouraged by the fixity of your sightless gaze, by the well-timed nodding of your head which punctuates from time to time her fragmented storyline. You appear to be so fascinated by what she's saying that you even forget to pick up your coffee mug. In fact, you won't pick up the coffee mug until she has offered up the anarchy of her dream in its entirety for your interpretive scrutiny. You fake it, improvising expertly, grabbing onto the dream's more obvious elements and tossing Jungian and Freudian theoretical fundaments together in a fairly convincing pasticcio. You don't necessarily like this tendency you have toward facile deception, this unblinking delivery of half-lies, but you seem to be really good at it.

Yet there's a principal involved here. Since you are bored by your girlfriend's recitation, you don't think it would be fair to tell her about the dream you had sometime after 4:00 a.m., after rising from the tabby cat of oblivion your consciousness had curled into, stumbling to the bathroom to empty your bladder, then returning to bed and sleep. (When the hypodermic of sleep injects you into the vein of nothingness, your sleep is typically dreamless, a mysterious vacancy into which you disappear, and you're often terrified when you wake up and think about it, so the cute tabby cat image you dress the oblivion in removes some of the terror. The hypodermic needle image appeals to you, based on your wayward past of extensive drug experimentation.) What happens then is that instead of being more or less seamlessly transported into sleep, you're aware of a deluge of hypnogogic images like road signs streaking backward, as seen from the window of a speeding car. Suddenly, you're in the dream. Everything is hyperreal: the colors, the scale, the sense of depth and dimension in the scene. The atmosphere is one of arrested turbulence, flux barely contained, as though bolts have been employed by the hidden mechanisms of the dream to hold everything in place and prevent it from dissolving back into the chaos from which it was constructed.

You're back in Wisconsin where you grew up as a child, in the backyard of your next-door neighbors, the Rushens. In "real" life, the backyard seemed to be little more than a depository for junk, boxes, old furniture, broken appliances, rotting garbage and car parts. The house was a ramshackle double-storied affair the neighborhood kids loved in the summer, because the parents of the Rushen children worked nights and there was no parental intrusion into the exuberant pandemonium that flourished there daily. But, in the dream, the backyard is spotless, filled with perfectly parallel rows of slender trees. You know these trees—they're white ashes. The leaves shimmer and enliven the air with a plasmic chrome-tinted radiance and there's an aura of palpable purity so intensely beautiful that it brings tears to your eyes. You stand there in awe, Daryl, gazing open-mouthed at these trees that are spangled and webbed with a silvery beauty, and you spread your arms wide as though to embrace it all and the tears turn to a sadness deeper than any you have even known, because it occurs to you that all this luminous beauty is a fragile illusion—an illusion not because you realize you're dreaming (you don't), but because you realize that it will all disappear for you one day when you die, it will all be taken from you. All of it will simply vanish as though it never existed, and the ephemerality of everything strikes you as being cruel and unfair and tragic beyond words, and the horror of it, Daryl, is your sense that there's no escaping or altering the outcome. The horror of it is that this is the very structure of the universe and that the structure is wrong but can't be altered or amended. The formidable force of your combined will and intention and desire and focus won't change the way things are. There's no door you can go through to get to another place where the rules of the game are different. It's the same feeling you had when you were once on a plane flying to Mexico City (in "real" life). Everything was fine until some weird faucet of awareness was suddenly turned on and you realized you were miles above the ground and sitting, absurdly, in a narrow tube soaring through air. That if something were to happen, there was no place to go, no place to walk away to, no way to remove yourself to a safe and solitary observation post somewhere. It's the same in the dream, that nightmare feeling of claustrophobia, of being trapped in a vast horrible closed system with no escape hatches, no exits, no way to finesse your way out of the way things are.

When you can no longer stand this painful and intense welter of emotions you are jolted from the dream. Your face is wet with tears. You can hear your girlfriend singing a very old song in the shower, "When you're alone and da da da da da da da you can always go . . . DOWNTOWN," and you roughly wipe the tears from your face. Daryl, why don't you want her to see the traces of tears? Why would you be embarrassed? After all, you consider yourself to be a man of thoroughly modern sensibility, a turn-of-the-century millennial Renaissance man of sorts, an enlightened young black man politically and socially and technologically aware, a man not afraid to reveal his deepest and innermost thoughts. But aside from all that, your feeling is one of tremendous, ecstatic relief. Everything is as it should be, Daryl, and it was only a dream!

When your girlfriend comes out of the shower, a purple bath towel wrapped turban-style around her lovely wet hair, the swell of her bosom crushed modestly in a broad armillary of white terrycloth, you virtually leap from the bed to embrace her. She's clearly puzzled by this uncharacteristic display of energy and enthusiasm, expecting instead your usual early-morning, slow-motion trajectory from bed to bathroom to closet. Even your girlfriend's cat slinking in a fluid figure eight about your ankles fails to irritate you this morning. Yes, it was just a ridiculous dream, and you feel liberated, exhilarated to have gotten, as it were, a second chance.

And that's finally why you decide not to tell her about the dream this morning, Daryl, why you're content to sit here and listen as your girlfriend finally wraps up her unusually lengthy monologue: dreams are ridiculous and boring.

This is what you don't know yet, Daryl: three months from now, you and your girlfriend will be invited to your sister's house. Your impression will be that your sister received a promotion at the advertising agency where she works as a junior copywriter and that you are all to lift your glasses in a Saturday evening toast to her good fortune. But when your sister opens the front door to let you in and you step across the threshold, you'll be confronted by a mosaic of festivity in primary colors: balloons, crepe banners, streamers, a roomful of people wearing party hats. You'll watch them blow noisemakers, applaud, hop up and down. "Happy birthday, Daryl!" they'll cry out in thunderous unison. You'll be genuinely surprised, then touched by the thoughtfulness of your family and so many well-wishing friends, and then, following so closely on the heels of your gratitude and happiness that the discrete links of the segue will escape your awareness, you'll momentarily be immersed in the texture, the ambiance, the atmosphere, the currents of emotion that ran through the dream you had that time. Right there in the middle of the party, you'll have an epiphany of sorts, accompanied by a feeling of dread. You'll remember how you woke that morning with a deep exhalation of enormous relief. How you were flooded with joy to realize that the whole awful business was just a dream. Then, holding a paper plate with a piece of birthday cake on it, it will hit you hard, and you'll think, stunned—hey, wait a minute, the universe really *is* a closed system, there's no way to change anything, there's no way to escape the finality of the ephemeral, the structure of reality can't be altered. You'll realize it wasn't a dream after all. Your loved ones on that night will raise their glasses high to toast your good health, your prosperity, your longevity. You'll wonder how and why it was possible for you to wake up that morning with a feeling of jubilation at having narrowly escaped doom. Wiping crumbs of cake from the corners of your mouth with one of those sandpaper-coarse party napkins, you'll look around at the beautiful faces of your family and friends surrounding you and know that they are white ash trees.

After the party that night, you'll climb into bed early, wanting to be left alone. Your girlfriend will think you're depressed because you're another year older and won't ask you if you'd like to make love. You won't really be depressed. You'll just be wondering how it's possible or why it should even be desirable for anyone who knows, really knows what you know, to go on doing anything. To continue brushing their teeth, buying clothes at The Gap, debugging computers, popping movies in the DVD player, hanging out. You'll have the feeling that you won't ever be able to shake what came to you in the dream, that you'll live with it for the rest of your life. You'll dwell on the prospect of spending your entire life in a desperate attempt to seize the beauty of the moment. This thought will exhaust you further. But you'll continue to think long into the night, Daryl, because you won't know what else to do. At some point, you'll remember that the morning after you had the dream, you weren't really listening to what your girlfriend was saying during breakfast, and this will sadden you deeply.

But, luckily, that will be then and this is now. Your girlfriend is late. She gives you a hug and a kiss and then leaves for work. You'll clear the breakfast dishes off the table this evening, because you've got to get moving, too, and you don't have time to do it now. You have someplace important to be, in a part of town that never seems familiar, no matter how many times you've been. A man you've always been a little afraid of is expecting you, Daryl, and won't tolerate your being late.

The Girl with Two Left Breasts

AA'ers, start the clock. That little clock there on the card table in the back with the urn of melted-tar coffee and stale donuts and the donation basket and the chip basket filled with cheap-ass plastic coins that are meant to be the souvenirs of this, our celebration of however many days of sobriety we've managed to claw out of the calendar. I don't know about yours, but my calendar bears claw marks that, if you hung it on the wall, you'd think resembled exposed biological ganglia. Now here's what I want. I want my full fifteen minutes up here and not a minute less. I won't be cheated this time. Tony, Big T, I don't mean to cast into doubt your clock-watching ability, but last time I spoke here at the podium, justice was not served by whatever lapse you fell into when you allowed the clock to rudely ring at twelve minutes. You fell into a lapse on your way to the full unconsciousness of a jelly-smeared sugar coma, would be my guess. Maybe a little less attention this time paid to the jelly donuts and a little more attention paid to the clock. Not too much to ask. What? Well, damn, I'm sorry. How could I forget my favorite part of the evening which is the privileged moment of introducing myself to my fellow bottle-emptying Ak-a-holics?

Hi, my name is—some of you have objected when I use my full name, Raymond Datcher—and I am not a pill popper or gas sniffer or hypodermic injector, I am not a hyphenate addict-alcoholic like some of us feel obligated to use that qualification; no thanks, I am just your authentic last-centimeter-from-the-bottle-vacuuming Ak-aholic, thank you.

And for that rousing welcome, thank you. "Hi, Raymond!"—I just always look forward to that.

Nothing against my cross-addicted brothers and sisters; I was only trying to stress but that this is not an NA meeting, it is an AA meeting. Last month I listened to that little girl up here talk about how she would pipe up in her tiny apartment and I couldn't begin to relate to what the hell she thought she was talking about. I could relate to the lonely apartment aspect of it somewhat, but, then, that was it. As I recall, she kept referring to something she called "putting out neck fires," as I recall. Her lighting up the pipe and reaching back almost absent-mindedly all the time under her hair because she was convinced she felt something there, but nothing would be there; it was, apparently, just her hair's heat, but slapping at the neck anyway, over and over every time she would hit the pipe, until she was convinced the neck had somehow combusted and caught on fire and she was putting it out, compulsively slapping at the neck over and over again, even though she realized there was no way the neck could just spontaneously combust like that. But then ten minutes later, starting the same sorry ritual again anyway.

Big T, fair's fair, so shave a few minutes off that damn clock until we have all settled down. I think the time for the ritual of settling down is past, Double A'ers. The hallway leading to the church's kitchen should be a clear passageway with no bodies straggling in and out of it; I'm sure the fire marshal would agree with me, a man I had the opportunity to meet in my own incendiary time of need some years back. You're all familiar with the story of my trailer burning like the ignited raw plastique of hell itself. This constant straggling obstruction of the hall leading to the kitchen is an example of the kind of purposeless back and forth meandering that spotlights one of our, excuse me, *my* worst character flaws, in my opinion, of not being able to just sit still and take whatever needs to be taken one moment at a time like an earnest sobriety-seeking man or woman. The bathrooms aren't back there, you go back out the front and around the side yard past the rusted lawn mower in the side yard where you'll see a door that says B—A—T –H—room. The kitchen, which is now dark, I would say very much indicates that there is nothing to be found there except a battened-down kitchen. Irma, I think her name is, I can see that she's straggled back there and she's a first-night newcomer so that's her excuse, but when I see Maurice straggling back there behind her, well, I can't help this festering of suspicions, now can I? Hey, Maurice? Ak-a-holics Anonymous is based on the twelve steps, how about you try that thirteen-stepping after you get a nice one-year chip and a relationship is more than just something to just bounce hangover throw-up off of? My man Maurice!

No cross talk, my for-the-time-being-juiceless comrades. Isn't that what you're always so quick to tell me? How's about let's apply the time-honored goose-gander principle, here.

If I have a burning desire to share at the end of fifteen minutes, I just might go a bit over. I realize that when we have a full house, time is of the essence and everybody should have the opportunity to share, and so limiting the sharing to fifteen minutes is essential. But I have invoked the Burning Desire clause, which allows the speaker to go over to finish, if it's important. I'm just letting you know preparatory to the desire, I can already feel positioning itself for full burn.

So settle down now and just listen, now. Because that's all you have to do. You have already suited up and you have shown up, that's ninety percent of it, and now it's just the listening for the other ten percent. Expectations are modest and can be easily met in this room, Twin-A'ers. Unlike in other rooms in other places. Like the rooms you work in, or the rooms in your home. The rooms in your head. Many of us have rooms that still hold, against all odds, jobs and families. Confidently I say it's a miracle when you consider what goes on in some of those rooms while you're still in the grips of the disease and the disease is walking all over you and all you can do is lay beneath it like a sidewalk that just got its ass kicked.

Think of coming home to one such room to a spouse one evening, after you've put up with your boss's stale-data breath, who likes to get dead up in your face to tell you that the report you've run has a column of information in it that's suspect, and on the way home driving, you hear a thump and suspect you just hit a cat running across the road, and your feet are hurting as you come in and see your spouse sitting on the couch with that glazed look on his face, three days after he promised you wouldn't ever come in and see him with that glazed look again, on his face. You can't confront him yet because he's chewing Juicy Fruit gum angelically and pretending to read the paper, and what you need is definitive proof of glaze. Without wanting to seem to search the place, you do just that, you begin searching. Thank god you don't have a backyard or a garage. Not anymore you don't. The backyard and garage was the place five or six houses ago, and the current place represents the culmination of a decline, though not the absolute lowest point, obviously, because it's still a roof over your head.

My friends, AA'ers, you and I both know volumes could and should be written on the bizarre psychology behind the places wily Ak-a-holics come to designate as cunning hiding places. You, as the searching spouse, are aware of all these demented tricks of hiding bottles in places that are so obvious that you, as spouse, would hopefully ignore them in favor of searching for other more esoteric hiding places.

The more esoteric places would include, for example, inside the toilet tank, which place you discovered because the toilet kept running all night and you kept shaking the handle to make it stop, but it did not stop, and, finally, in frustration you raised the heavy lid off the tank to see a fifth of Popov vodka tangled up in the apparatus of the floating bulb and the chain, making the water continuously hiss and run as though all it needed was the shake of the handle. Lo and behold, Duel A'ers, the spouse finds the Popov there. Or, more esoterically, inside the television. The screws on the back of the television having been unscrewed so that the back can be pulled straight off, and inside the television is a pint. Random sparks jetting from the rear of the home entertainment center in the middle of *Sex in the City* was the tip-off in this case, where it turns out the pint, wet with spillage, came in contact with a certain wad of no-nonsense wires. A fifth or a quart wouldn't fit, otherwise you would have found a fifth, or a quart. The obvious places for hiding the bottle are audacious and cunning, and your glazed spouse hopes that you'll be blinded by the familiarity of such places.

Like right there in the kitchen in the spice rack over the stove, between the oregano and the paprika, for example. Lo and behold. But tonight you seek, almost biblically, and you cannot find. Hmmm. It's possible your spouse may have simply consumed the bottle, went outside, and tossed it in some bushes somewhere, but this is problematic for your spouse, who, after a while, will mightily desire another drink, so the bush toss tactic is unlikely. How many times in one night can a person slip outside to check on a bush to see if everything is as it should be with the bush?

One night you discovered your spouse, outside, at midnight, deep in the bushes, with the poor prop of a pruning shears in his hand; so the bush is off limits, to him, remembering that failed attempt. But tonight you watch him with biblical hawk-like eyes, but see nothing. Tonight he goes to the bathroom and leaves the door open. He does this and that, all of it in plain sight. But at the end of the night, he's more glazed than ever.

After the fourth night of coming in to find the spouse more and more openly glazed and, in fact, almost so defiantly glazed that he is now asleep on the couch and drooling, you are touched by divine intuition which leads you to ponder the sight of a straw next to the fish tank. The fish tank hasn't had fish in it for months. The fish died and floated to the top of the tank and you're the one who scooped them out, one by one as they died, and flushed them down the toilet. Because there's a straw there, and your mind jumps up a notch. And yes, so you go over there to the bookcase; you haven't really been watching him over there the past few nights because he just kept coming back with a book; you go over where the tank is and as you're bending to pick up the straw, you get a whiff. A good strong one. That's one unmistakable whiff. You feel lo and beholdness itself lurking, waiting to burst into full revelation. You follow the whiff and it leads you to the tank. And you're truly amazed. Spouse, you are just absolutely amazed, to the extent that you want to congratulate him for his wiliness and cunning, but he's passed out on the sofa and wouldn't appreciate this heartfelt acknowledgement.

What the spouse has done is filled the fish tank up with vodka. You'd both kept the water in there because any day now he was supposed to bring back another black molly to put in it so it could eventually float up to the top and be dispatched without ceremony to the toilet's sluggish vortex. The fish tank still has coral in it, and sand, and a plastic mermaid with a bad paint job that makes it seem that the mermaid's eyes are a little cockeyed, and the filter is running, and the little clam shell ornament that the filter hose is attached to is bobbing open and shut with the rising bubbles. It's all per normal except that the whole damn thing is a substitution of water with five gallons of Popov vodka. You've never in your life seen anything like it. In many ways, it's amazing.

And then, as sometimes happens with stone Ak-a-holics, your spouse rises in a dead blackout and doesn't see you're standing right there and staggers over and picks up the straw, right in front of you, sucking vodka from the fish tank so greedily that the straw collapses and he begins lapping at the tank's booze with his face lowered into the tank. A few grits of coral have somehow been sucked up through the straw and are now caught in his throat and the choking begins. The choking grows to become a matter for your serious concern, and you think about applying the Heimlich, yes, but you associate the Heimlich with dislodging more substantial clots of edibles and wonder if a few feeble coral grits could even be forcibly ejected from the throat. Breaking out the heavy artillery of the Heimlich with its possibility of a broken rib or two seems overkill for one or two grits, and in the middle of your debating, luckily, the coughing and choking subside.

After that, he pisses on the floor next to the fish tank. It's the suggestion of fish = water = water = toilet = urination, in his mind, that leads him to think that he's in the bathroom, looming over the toilet's sluggish vortex. These are the kinds of things that take place in the rooms that have the misfortune of being places the Ak-a-holic occupies.

These have been my rooms.

Deuce of A, tonight I went to Kenbrook Liquor because I was in a state, and I am still in that state, and I did something I haven't done for four months. I slapped my hard-earned money on the counter and told Mr. Kenbrook himself that I wanted a pint of vodka. Old man Kenbrook himself. Popov's, please. Mr. Kenbrook, I now know, is a man who will do anything for money. Because I know for a fact that my wife has personally spoken with Mr. Kenbrook, telling him that her husband, Raymond Datcher, is a Ak-a-holic and that under no circumstances should he, Mr. Kenbrook, sell any liquor to Raymond Datcher or to anyone even remotely resembling Raymond Datcher. And I believe Mr. Kenbrook agreed. It's hard not to agree when you're facing a woman who asks you that, and you see that, as an added inducement, she's holding something in her hand that looks like a hockey stick and is staring at your head like it's a potential puck. But I put my money down and Mr. Kenbrook looked over his shoulder at the door, like he expected the Missus to come bursting in, and when he was satisfied she wasn't, he winked and served me the pint of vodka.

Which pint is now in its bag snugly in my back pocket. Wait. All right. Let me present this pint as exhibit A, as in, yes, Ak-a-holic. Some of you right now have that wrestle-the-poor-bastard-to-the-ground look, especially you, Maurice, but remember, in my younger days I had welter-weight champion aspirations, and I'm bristling with resentments. Resentment is my middle name. I live to resent. Cogito ergo I resent. If I'd had, as a welter weight on the circuit many years ago, the seething resentment I carry around with me now, I would have been able to use it to successfully bash through the requisite number of skulls to become the welter weight champion of the U S of A, which is to say, The World. I'm fifty-seven now, but head bashing is like riding a bicycle; you never forget how to do it. When I went into the ring, I was sober as a stone, but by the time three rounds had transpired, I was a juiced-up specimen of fuming Ak-a-holic fury. Between rounds, sitting on the stool, my corner man would hand me my water bottle, which was filled with raw pugilistic vodka. I would take a mouthful, throw my head back, swish, and pretend to spit, all the time swallowing. If you've never tried it, it's difficult to pretend to spit, it does takes some practice, but you eventually get the hang of it.

At the sound of the bell I would charge into ring to meet my opponent with something that to those watching must have resembled a kind of gladiatorial spasticity. My footwork, never fancy to begin with, became absolutely balletic, AA-ers. Many a time my opponent would simply stand there, mouth agape, transfixed as he watched my feet describe a frenzied tic-tac-toe of flurry and feint, and with his guard down, I would pirouette—which isn't a movement you see too much in the world of professional boxing—I would pirouette in and dispose of the astonished fellow with a thunderous and satisfying crack to the jaw, which would then hang on its hinge loosely and sometimes even garishly. Sometimes. At other times my footwork, taking on a cartoonish life of its own, became so complex and speed-ridden and blurred that I would be overcome with a debilitating nausea from the sloshing booze and almost freeze from the waist up, while my feet still swirled under me. The freezing from the waist up was so as to still and contain the nausea, and my opponent, if he wasn't utterly hypnotized, would take advantage of the stationary target I presented to him from the waist up and smash me in the side of the head and I would go down.

This began to happen more and more. Given that the opponents I faced had done their homework and came to expect the footwork aspect of my game, they were no longer hypnotized by it and in time I lost the advantage of my surprising footwork, and I received more and more blows to the side of my head and that, as they say, was that. I became one of those guys who tells his son to hit him as hard as he can in the stomach and the son never really wants to do it, but he finally does it, after many drunken exhortations on the father's part, he does it with his childish eyes gigantic with persecution and grief, a single half-hearted, limp-wristed blow more like a tap, and then immediately retreats to his room with his head hanging low, and who can blame him, who can blame the boy's attitude toward the whole sorry ritual of fucking misguided masculine compensation?

I'm hoping, times-two-A'ers, that by the time I'm through, I will willingly and willfully deposit this bottle in that trash bin by the door. We tell each other our stories, well, why not add a little suspense this time? Will he dispose of the bottle? I make no promises. This is the sort of suspense I think a writer might appreciate, which is another thing I wanted to be, and that now, outside of the ears of my wife, your ears only have heard, are now hearing. Yet another thing I thought it would be a good thing to be, especially because writers had in the past been notorious boozers and drug takers, and, let's be honest, that held just a tremendous resonance and appeal, for me. It seemed a very attractive occupational incentive at the time, one I'd only have to halfway prepare for, the writing half, because I had mastered the other half, or quarter, the boozing quarter, since I had neither interest or experience in the drug-taking quarter—though for the sake of the writing, I might have gone ahead and explored that quarter. There, but for the grace of the raging neck-fire god, Raymond Datcher might well have gone.

So what I did, I bought myself some good Bond paper with sufficient rag content—this was back in the days when people used typewriters—and I set about the task of writing a novel I called *The Girl with Two Left Breasts.* Catchy, id'nit? A true life saga based on the experiences of yours truly, based on a booze-fueled infatuation I had before I met my wife with a girl who had serious issues of a mammary nature. Morbid issues, I think it's fair to say. For reasons I never quite understood, she was convinced that both her breasts, which I have to admit did both incline a little to the left, she thought that through some genetic mishap, maybe, that she had one genuine left breast and a second genetically mutated breast that was also a left one in the right one's place.

Oh, now it's finally quiet in here? It's more quiet in this room now than it's been all night. What does that tell you? Like that ad I used to see years ago in the newspaper, want ads that said SEX in big bold letters and then continued with NOW THAT I'VE GOT YOUR ATTENTION and went on, disappointingly, to talk about a goddamn used car stereo or whatever some desperate bastard was trying to unload.

Well NOW THAT I'VE GOT YOUR ATTENTION I'll go on to say that the obvious thing would have been for me to deny that this girl had two left breasts, but I didn't want her to think that I was just humoring her, you know, that I didn't take her obsession seriously. I wanted to demonstrate empathy. I wanted her to know that even if she did have two left breasts, she was still worthy of love. I wanted this to create a bond between us and for her to feel the same way about me, that even though I was a piss-on-the-floor alco—Ak-a-holic, that I wanted and deserved to be loved unconditionally. That maybe, even given her imagined deformity, she would feel grateful that anyone could love her and cling to me in gratitude while accepting my drinking. I know we've all seen that movie, what was it, *Leaving Las Vegas*, where the drunk tells the angelic prostitute that she must never try to get him to stop drinking, and she agrees. In the beginning, at least. And who here in his secret heart of hearts hasn't wished for the same, a blind eye turned away from our deepest most passionate though self-destructive act?

So there we were, living on the houseboat—did I mention that she lived on an old peeling plaintive houseboat moored to a broken down Mississippi River dock, in some little Mississippi hamlet, that she had inherited from her grandfather?—she, speculating endlessly on the causes and deeper meaning of being stricken with a sinistrally-afflicted bosom, and me drinking Wild Turkey every second the clock tick tocked. Which, I know because I can see, has registered my full fifteen minutes, and I'm well aware that the clock's alarm hasn't gone off, Big T, I thank you for your consideration. We're now officially in overtime, the Burning Desire To Share segment of my time at the podium.

She also forbade me to touch Doris and Daisy out of a fear that, whatever it was that had engendered the affliction, would somehow be stirred from dormancy, is the only way I can really explain it. The source of the leftwardness might somehow be aroused and other wayward anatomical manifestations might take place. Moles might appear, or some such, sprouting to the left. "Doris" and "Daisy" were names she had given the breasts, so as to personalize them and render them less abstract, more knowable, less prone to inspire the blind fear and terror she felt when she contemplated the mysterious source of the leftwardness.

I couldn't touch the breasts, Doris and Daisy, like I said, I was forbidden. And so like anything that was forbidden to me, I longed to plunge forward into it. I stole opportunities to brush against Doris and Daisy, but secretly, slyly, on the down-low. For example, I would fling my arm out to swat at some imaginary fly—Mississippi seemed to have more than its fair share of them, real ones, in the months I lived there—and oh-so-carelessly brush the bosom with my fingertips. Gradually, I became inflamed, and tried to find more and more excuses to accidentally touch the bosom. I came back once from the library with a book on sign language, telling her that I had a cousin who was deaf, and I practiced making the signs while she stood near, signing with a fake gusto and passion that allowed me the excuse I needed to cast my hands out and collide with the bosom as I finger-flicked long multisyllabic words. Any excuse, any reason. And the thing is, it was completely non-sexual, this sense of being inflamed was. The whole thing, twain A, became a sort of ritual with me, a compulsion equal to the compulsion of drinking, if you can imagine that. Frankly, it was horrible and I was drenched in the horror of the weirdness of it. And so was she, so was she. I would pretend not to touch while touching and she would pretend not to feel while feeling, but the weight of the pretense was too much for her.

One night I came staggering into the raggedy wretched houseboat—from where, I don't know, I'd probably been outside wandering with these pigs that didn't seem to belong to anybody, through the decaying woods that skirted the river—and there she was, sitting cross-legged on the floor, with a bloody kitchen knife in her hand. The houseboat was rocking sluggishly in some feeble backwash of muddy little waves driven by a miserable wind that might as well have been hot exhaust spat out of a tailpipe. Doris, or maybe it was Daisy, was cupped in one hand, the dripping blade was perched above it in the other.

There's no need to go on with what I saw. I'm not feeling a burning desire to share that particular detail, at this time. But I'd certainly driven her to this, with my shenanigans, to the point where she was always focused on the bosom she was trying so desperately to deny, when she wasn't going on and on about it. Relatives appeared, in the night, and she was whisked away, to an institution of some kind, I later found out. The relatives allowed me to linger in my grief on the houseboat for a time, then I was evicted. How long had I been there? All together, with and without the girl, maybe six months.

I stood on the bank and watched them unload garbage bags full of empty pint and quart bottles, hundreds in bags that were wheeled down the dock in wheelbarrows. Then, they herded the pigs I'd been wandering with in the woods onto the boat, why I don't know. The pigs finally had the home they deserved. The whole long time of my uninterrupted blackout became the basis for *The Girl with Two Left Breasts*—hundreds of pages chronicling my time with the girl, with Doris and Daisy, and the flies, and the pigs. Rejected by dozens of publishers. Though one publisher did take the time to personalize the rejection note and told me that the title was a keeper and that I should think about rewriting it as a screenplay. I bought a cat I named Lefty solely for the purpose of having the cat go into a litter box I had also bought so that I could line it with the rejection slips instead of litter, and then I took the rejection slips, reeking of cat shit and piss, and put them in envelopes and sent them back to the publishers. All 135 of them. Including the editor who'd thought the title held some promise. I'd have rather sent them envelopes filled with pig shit, but the pigs were no longer readily available.

Shortly after is when I met my wife. Which is why I'm here tonight with a bottle in my back pocket. Not because of the story you've all heard before, the Alzheimer's. I won't stand here and say I went to Kenbrook's because of that, because you'd all see though it. If ever there was a reason that might sound like a justification to drink, watching her lose herself a day at a time to that disease would be it. But we all know how easy it is to find a reason to drink. Lose your job? Drown the sorrow in booze. Just found out you got a promotion? Celebrate with booze. No, this frame of mind wasn't caused by the usual watching her wander around in a pretense of remembering things she can't remember anymore, and getting mad if I don't go along with the pretense and questioned her about some discrepancy or other. It took me a long time to understand why she'd fly into a fury if I corrected her and told her that no, her mother was not coming to visit, unless she was coming in the coffin she'd been buried in, transported by sorely confused pallbearers. The doctor, or maybe it was my son, told me that the whole behavior of denying not being able to remember things was typical behavior for Alzheimer patients at a certain stage in the disease, but I still had a hard time not saying that her mother wasn't coming over for dinner, hefted on the shoulders of pallbearers, in her coffin.

No, it's because last night I was listening to her singing, and the sound of it slammed me back to a specific incident where because of my state of drunken belligerence, I ruined an opportunity she'd had to become a singer with a record company that at the time, it was then one of the biggest labels, RCA. And the man who had the power to make her famous, the bastard's name was Joe Glazier, I'll just say that he's on the long list of individuals who deserve amends from me because of what I did. My wife being another, of course. In fact, I so chose last night to make amends with her regarding the terrible thing I did, after I'd been sitting listening to her sing. She sings the way I drink, putting everything she has into it, in a style that, when you listen to it, your first impulse is to say she sounds a little like Etta James and a little like Ella Fitzgerald and a bit like some others, but then you realize that although these others have all influenced her, she has something that's hers exclusively, and that's the mark of a true artist, id'nit? Her mother sang and so she sang, from the time she was a little girl, and when I met her, she was practicing everyday, recording her practice sessions on a Bell & Howell tape recorder. She'd take a line to be sung, and begin tearing it apart, looking for a way back in, a way to phrase it; she told me she would practice singing one line a hundred different ways, even in her sleep, until she found it.

The thing is, when she won this national contest that was sponsored by RCA and she came in second place on the strength of a piano-vocal demo she'd made, I knew she was going places. I'm telling you, my ex-libating friends, that I should have been happy, and in a sense I was, but I was paranoid more than anything else. An attractive woman in an attractive sort of gownish piece of apparel standing on stage with the spotlight shining on the split in the gown, revealing the long expanse of cinnamon-tinted calf and thigh, is how it was summed up for me. The microphone, I'd be thinking as I drank, was a hell of a device, a device invented by someone who clearly couldn't keep his phallo-centric obsessions from intruding upon the very design of the device he'd invented, the microphone held up to those lipsticked lips O-ing and ah-ing as she crooned, with the band behind her, the drummer pounding all over his little drum kit as he took in the view of the singer's ass swaying to the rhythms he pounded out, and more, the men involved in every step of promoting her career hitting on her at every opportunity. And there I'd stand, off to the side, smiling like I wasn't noticing what was going on before my very eyes. Like I needed another layer of denial in my life. The proof that I wasn't imaging the probable titillation and allure of her standing there on the stage in the thigh-revealing gown was that I myself, thinking of it, would become unmistakably aroused. Do I have to spell it out, A-raised-to-the-second power? The details of the arousal, the intricacies of what we refer to here in our genial little club as the worst example of 'stinking thinking'? I read an article in *Newsweek* talking about the benefits of masturbation. It's in the open and it's okay, now. The past is past, gone are the days when the act was demonized, when engaging in it was thought to result in blindness and handlessness or whatever. Now in every other movie, if you subscribe to TMC, you see women masturbating gracefully on beds, or in bathtubs, or in cars or elevators, in classrooms and in closets. Men, not so much. Maybe because for men the act does not translate so appealingly and lacks the gentle aesthetic quality seen in women asprawl on beds? Because since when is the motion of a demented piston in any way appealing?

What I'm saying is, I won't bother to paint a picture of Raymond Datcher heavily drunked up in his own bathroom, on fire with images of his own wife, the titillating image she'd without a doubt present to strangers, men—and many women, yes, that too—Raymond Datcher drunked up in his bathroom engaging in an act that for men just doesn't come across with the graceful sighing sprawling flair that women convey, although I'm sure that there must be plenty of women who go at it with a man's stripped-of-all-aesthetically redeeming single-mindedness and aggression. I'm sure there are some women here tonight who could attest to that.

I see Dora nodding, there, by the coffee urn. Honest to a fault, eh, Dora?

Well, why not? It's okay these days, it's even commendable. Secrets are safe in this room, or at least that's the party line. Hell, I'm sure even the neck-fire girl had other fires she vigorously tried to extinguish, when she wasn't busy with the neck.

But the point I'm trying to make is that, all the how healthy it is aside, in *Newsweek* and everywhere else, it didn't feel healthy to Raymond Datcher, it felt pathetic. If you're reduced to engaging in the act, you at least want some faceless breast-implanted pornographic image in your mind to do the deed by, not your own wife. But that proved something to me, or so I thought: if I was driven to such an act by an image so powerful that it pushed aside more visceral ones, revealing my own imaginative poverty, centering on my own wife rather than some garter-belt wearing bimbo then how much more broadly and all-encompassingly would other men be driven to it, seeing her?

So on Monday, February 23, nineteen-hundred-and-fifty-something, I think, we traveled to Chicago, Elizabeth and I, for a meeting with this hot-shot executive-type Glazier fellow, to discuss the possibility of a recording contract. The first-prize winner had been awarded one, a white girl from Idaho who couldn't hold a candle to Elizabeth and who sounded like one of the Andrew Sisters without the rest of the Andrew Sisters; I mean she sang in a voice that was built for providing only background bolster, a straight-arrow sort of voice that sounded its best buried in four- or five-part harmony. I'd preyed on Elizabeth's fears of being taken advantage of, drawing a picture of a world full of white men just waiting for a beautiful black woman to prey on as they, quote, helped her, unquote, climb the ladder of success. So I was accompanying her in the capacity as husband and manager-slash-agent, so she wouldn't be taken advantage of.

You're seeing where this is headed, bifold A, I know you are. AA'ers, we're nothing if not experts in tragic endings.

His office was at the top floor, many stories up, in a building full of shiny glass. His office was so big it was just fucking ridiculous. And the man himself, as we sat on a little couch adjacent to his big desk, looked like he had walked off a used-car lot and into the office. I saw that he was wearing a toupee. As expensive as they are, you can always tell—eh, Charlie? Oh, come on now, Charlie, lighten up. Don't hate the player, hate the game. You borrowed my copy of the Big Book, remember, and never returned it, and I've never asked for it back, remember? So just sit back down. Laughter's the best medicine, and there's no sharing that's been done here tonight that's more pathetic than my own. That's better. I'm wrapping it up now, three-minus-one A. I'm deep in the flames of the burning desire.

So in Mr. Glazier's office, he's going through the motions, asking what her career aspirations are, drawing pictures of the career that's waiting for her, what he has in mind, and how does she feel about it, about traveling everywhere, and etcetera. I'm the one who's doing the talking, I mean the answering. And he doesn't like it one bit, this whole husband-manager-agent thing. Of course, before we went in the office, I made a quick run to the bathroom and emptied my flask. I drank that flask down like a living advertisement for empty flasks, and in the mirror I cocked my hat on my head, snapped the lapels on the double-breasted Italian job I was wearing. Raymond Datcher could cut a dapper image, in those days. Look at me now. But no, look at me then. We had a war of colognes going on in the room, mine versus his. Mine won. We had a war of the mustaches going on, too. Mine was thinner, more debonair. The hat that was cocked over my eye stayed that way, I didn't bother to take it off. Glazier seemed to sense something. He produced a bottle of bourbon and poured himself one, and poured one for me. He didn't offer any to Elizabeth; he offered her a tiny polite flute of champagne, which she declined in a lady-like way.

He watched me drink mine down, and by this time, what with the bourbon piggybacking the vodka, I was good and drunked up. My laughter at his jokes began to sound like snarls. I felt Elizabeth kicking my ankle, little secret warning kicks. Music was playing, Elizabeth's demo, and we all sat nodding our heads. He began talking contracts and had one ready to go. He didn't expect us to do any signing, he said. We'd want to let our attorney go through it first, of course, he said. As I skimmed it, I said, damn right our attorney's going to have a look at this. I can look at this and see right now that our attorney is going to have a field day with this clause, and this clause, and this one. I took out a pen and put stars next to the clauses the attorney we didn't have would have a field day with, and by the time I was through, the contract looked like a sky on a cloudless night, full of constellations.

Glazier saw what he'd have to deal with, dealing with me, this husband-slash-agent-slash-manager who'd always belligerently be in the way, and he got a look in his eyes that was shrewd and that said no way am I dealing with this guy. But he played the game through, nodding as if I hadn't blown it. I knew that when we walked out of that office, we'd never hear from him. And then the coup de grace, my binary-A-ed brothers and sisters, the coup de grace. He was determined to keep everything civilized to the very end, he was determined to see us smiling out the door. The coup de grace: as we stood,

I saw him glance at Elizabeth's hips as she stood and made a little adjustment to the dress she'd worn, tugging it down in that discreet way that, when it's done out of genuine modesty and not coyness, is almost touching. His glance happened in the blink of an eye, but I think he wanted me to see it, a sort of adding insult to unspoken injury.

He extended his hand across the desk for me to shake and instead of shaking it, I reached out to grab him by the lapel, but I missed the lapel and my hand slid along his neck and I ended up grabbing his hair, and the toupee came off in my hand. Redder a man has never flushed, deuce of A. Now, you all know me. If I know you personally, I'm saying I don't care, you can be anything—white, yellow, green, I've got no problem with you on that account. In the abstract, with Caucasians as a group, I'm the first to admit that I have some problems that I need to work on, maybe. Raymond Datcher is not a racist but I have to say that this flushing red business that such a rosy picture has been painted of in Victorian novels and the like is not all that it's portrayed as cracking up to be. It's not attractive to see a grown man or woman change into a vegetable right before your eyes, a beet or a tomato, I'm just sorry, but no. It's just not a color that looks good on skin, no matter how much it might be romanticized to be. I may be black as midnight but it keeps my emotions where they belong—it's skin, not a billboard for beets. I hope there's no hard feelings, here. I'm just saying.

So here is Glazier now, red as a baboon's wiped-raw arse. Sputtering and trying to grab the toupee, which at this point I'm waving around a bit like a flag, out of his reach, teasing him forward so that he falls, sprawls out across his desk as he's grabbing at it. And Elizabeth, aghast, her hands raised up to her mouth. And as I'm walking backward, pulling Elizabeth in one hand and dangling the toupee in the other, Glazier is stumbling after us, still snatching for the toupee. Well, this is not enough for me. I want the bastard to remember this. So I shove the toupee down the back of my pin-stripped pants and wipe my warm rump with it and throw it in his face. The man is so devastated he doesn't know what he's doing, at this point. Wouldn't you be? He catches the toupee and puts it on his head, even though I've just done what I've done to it, and yells to get out, get out, get the fuck out and go back to bumfuck, Wisconsin! Oh, don't you worry, I'm going, I say to him when I reach the door, I say, by the way, nice toupee there, Joe, Mr. Glazier. I'm tempted to get one just like it, I say, but I'm afraid I wouldn't look as good as you do in it, Joey.

Some of you are laughing and some of you aren't, I see. It wasn't my intention to bring racial polarization to the room. But I had to share that with you.

Because the worst part has yet to come. So you guys who aren't laughing will have the last laugh anyway. The worst part was last night, when I could hear Elizabeth singing in the living room when I was sitting on the bed in the bedroom untying my shoes. You see, we never talked about what happened, not once in all these years. But I know she hated me for it. Like Mr. Glazier, she never came out and said anything, but she blamed me and had a right to. I ruined what she could have become. Greatness was in her, and I fixed that, didn't I? And so last night I decided to make amends. Twenty-five years after the fact, twenty-five years too late to change a damn thing. All the damage was done and had sunk down to the bedrock and none of it could be undone. But I walked out into the living room and I went through the whole thing and I found myself on my knees. I begged for her forgiveness. I told her how I let my being jealous of the attention she'd get ruin things for her. And here's the thing, now. She looked at me like I was insane. She looked at me like she didn't know what the hell I was doing. "Raymond, what in the world are you talking about? Get up, right now. Are you drunk? Foolish question." Then it came to me: she didn't remember any of this. The Alzheimer's had taken it from her. She had no recollection of it any longer. All she had was this feeling toward me of resentment and bitterness and rage and she had no idea why or where it came from or what had caused it. She didn't have to live with it any longer. Only I did. It was over for her, but it's not for me. I can't even make amends, it's too late. And so I'll go to my grave with it.

So I suppose what I'm saying is, if you have amends to make, make them. Just make them, though God only knows what for.

Deuce of A, it would be a shame to subject you to this and then to have you know that I'm going home with this bottle, so here it is. Maurice, just toss it for me, would you? What can I say. Make your amends.

Time for me to say the words. Sometimes I like this part almost as much as I like the greeting. Maybe not tonight, though, AA'ers. But hey, there's always and always and always tomorrow. Here it is: Thanks for letting me share.

Printed in the USA
CPSIA information can be obtained
at www.ICGtesting.com
JSHW022320140824
68134JS00019B/1206